THE HALLOWED GRAIL

Will Adams

Opalmaze

Copyright © 2025 Will Adams

All rights reserved

The characters and events portrayed in this book are fictitious. Any similarity to real persons, living or dead, is coincidental and not intended by the author.

No part of this book may be reproduced, or stored in a retrieval system, or transmitted in any form or by any means, electronic, mechanical, photocopying, recording, or otherwise, without express written permission of the publisher.

ISBN-13: 9798304699471

Cover design by: Victoria Barbera

To James and Ellie, without whose generous hospitality over many, many years, I'd likely never even have known of Badbury.

With thanks and all best wishes

His body was discovered at Glastonbury in our own times, in a hollowed oak deep beneath the earth, hidden between two ancient stone pyramids and sealed with miraculous tokens. They carried him into the church with full honours, and there transferred him into a marble tomb. A lead cross was fastened to the underside of the stone, not above it as we usually see. I myself have traced the letters engraved upon it— not facing outwards but rather turned inwards to the stone. It read: "Here lies our glorious King Arthur, with Guinevere his second wife, on the Isle of Avalon."

GERALD OF WALES C1146 – C1223

PROLOGUE

Avebury, Wiltshire

483 CE

T he man on the dappled brown mare had plaited long hair and tattoos all over his arms and chest and neck, along with frightening quantities of dried blood. Not that the blood was his own, judged Tully, for he jumped down with impressive ease for a man of his size and age, showing no hint of fresh injury or wound. Only scars. Lots and lots of scars. He threw his reins to one of his footsoldiers then strode across to the side of the track, where the man who'd caught Tully was holding him prisoner by his ear. 'What's that you've got there?' he asked.

'Not entirely sure,' said this other man, short and thin and so stealthy of movement that he'd somehow had his knife to Tully's throat before Tully had even heard him coming, despite him having hidden himself in among these giant stones – a precaution he'd only taken because everyone in the village had been so on edge these past two days, what with all the talk of a great battle between the king and the usurper, and no-one yet knowing which side had won. 'It squeals like a pig, though, when you pinch its ear like this.'

'Ow,' said Tully.

'Good stuff,' said the big man. 'I'm starving. Shove a stick up its arse and we'll cook it over the fire.'

'I'm not a pig,' said Tully, blinking away his tears.

'It talks. It's a blooming miracle.' He crouched down low on his haunches until he was on Tully's level. He had an unmistakable air of authority about him, yet his eyes lacked the cruelty that Tully had seen before in such men, so that – despite all his scars and blood and tattoos – he knew instinctively that he wasn't the kind to hurt children. Not if he had a choice. 'You got a name, boy?' he asked. 'And don't even think of lying.'

'Tully,' said Tully.

'And you live round here, do you, young Tully?'

Behind his back, the double line of soldiers tramped wearily onwards, either side of a train of wooden carts. It distressed Tully to see all the wounded men lying upon them, and to hear the anguish in their groans. Worse was to follow, however, for the next few carts were stacked high with dead, their lifeless limbs jerking and jolting over the winter potholes. Yet the greatest shock by far was reserved for the next cart, though it only had the one body in it – a body that should have been covered head to toe by a rich red robe, except that all the bumping around had thrown it off enough for Tully to glimpse the face beneath. The sight made him so dizzy that for a moment he thought he'd faint, for he recognised him instantly from the day he'd ridden bareheaded through their village on a great white stallion, his armour gleaming and his famous sword hanging from his belt, all while attended by an honour guard of a dozen men almost as big as himself. He'd looked extraordinary that day. Untouchable. Immortal. 'See,' his father had told him proudly, while scruffing up his hair. '*That's* who I'll be fighting for.' But now he just lay there in the back of a wooden cart, half covered by a dusty, bloodstained robe, with a gaping great wound in his chest.

'He's dead,' muttered Tully, stunned, as the cart trundled by. 'The king is dead.'

The big man looked around. 'For the love of god,' he scowled.

'Keep him covered up. That's your one bloody job.' He turned back to Tully. 'I asked you a question, boy. Are you from around here?'

It took an effort of will for Tully to tear away his gaze. 'Yes,' he said.

'You have family? A father?'

Tully nodded. 'He was one of you,' he said. 'He was the *best* of you. The king told him so himself.'

'Did he, now? Maybe I knew him, then. What was his name?'

'They called him Tully too,' said Tully.

The big man stood up, looked around. 'Anyone know a Tully?' he shouted out. 'Lived around here somewhere.'

One of the footsoldiers came limping over. His arm was in a sling, and he looked wearier than any man should rightly look. 'There was a Tully in Gawain's crew that I think came from around here,' he said. 'A right mad bastard. Always first to put his hand up. Could tell a cracking story too. We lost him a year or so back, outside Bourges.' Despite his weariness, he looked at Tully with kindness in his eyes. 'That would make your mum Aggie, right?'

The moment was so bittersweet that it took everything Tully had not to cry. He had to nod instead.

The big man crouched back down. 'Okay, then,' he said, giving Tully's shoulder a friendly squeeze. 'I want you to listen carefully to me, Tully son of Tully. You didn't see any of this here today. No retreating soldiers, no carts, no bodies, especially not *his*. If even a whisper gets out, it'll be a disaster for us all. I mean that. Those murderous Saxon bastards will be straight over, to steal all your land for themselves. But it's not them you should fear the most. It's me. Because I know your name now, and your mum's, and where you live. You hear me?'

'Yes, sir,' said Tully, for though he didn't for one moment believe the threat, he'd taken to the man, and didn't want to disrespect him in front of his men.

The shorter, slyer man was still squatting down behind Tully, holding him by his ear. 'Word's going to get out anyway,' he said. 'You know it is. Too many people saw him going down, on that bastard traitor's side as well as ours.' He spat sideways then wiped his forearm across his mouth. 'All we can hope for now is to shape the story.'

'Shape it how?'

'Well, for a start, we could have the boy go home and tell everyone how he saw him sitting up in the back of one of our carts. Wounded and bandaged, yeah, but in good spirits, chatting merrily away, making plans for his return.'

'You think they'd believe him?'

'Maybe, if we gave him a token to show them.' The king's cart had pulled into the side so that his body could be properly covered. The man jumped up onto the back of it and pulled aside his robe once more, then stripped a ring from his finger that he tossed to Tully to catch. But Tully had always been hopeless with his hands, and inevitably he dropped it into the churned up mud.

The big man reached down to pick it up. He wiped it clean on his tunic and gazed inscrutably at it for a moment or two, then held it out for Tully to take, though without letting go of it just yet. 'Did you get all that, son?'

'Yes, sir,' said Tully.

'You better have, because if word of this gets out, the whole world will be at our throats. All our throats, I mean. Not just mine and my men's. Yours and your mum's too, and all your friends. You get what I'm saying?'

'Yes, sir.'

'Go on, then. Tell me what you've seen today. And make me believe it.'

Tully nodded vigorously. He lacked his father's courage, no one would dispute that, but he had at least inherited his gift for telling tall tales. 'I saw the king passing by,' he said, closing his eyes, because picturing stories in his mind helped to make them real. 'He was sitting up in the back of a cart, joking with his men. He saw me standing by the side of the track and waved me over. There was a bit of blood on his tunic, so I asked him if he was badly hurt. He laughed and tossed me this ring and said he was going to have to rest up for a bit; but that I wasn't to worry, he'd be fighting fit again very soon, in plenty of time to...' He broke off, struggling to remember how the man had phrased it. But he'd lost the trail somewhere, and had to find his own way to the finish. '...in plenty of time to help us in the hour of our need.'

'The hour of our need,' grinned the big man, giving Tully the ring along with a friendly pat on the arm. 'Yes. That's the stuff to give them.'

ONE

CHEPSTOW, WALES

It was a gorgeous Friday afternoon in Chepstow, and cheerful too, what with the sun out and everyone leaving work early to celebrate the spring bank holiday. Boisterous crowds of locals and visitors thronged the streets and castle grounds, enjoying the medieval pageantry of the entertainments put on to celebrate the 750th anniversary of the building of the town's famous Port Wall. Minstrels in colourful clothes strummed lyres and sang their fah-la-la lyrics as they wandered to and fro. Drums were banged and trumpets blown. Stallholders yelled out for custom, offering bites of mouthwatering foods or trying to interest passers-by in their lovingly-crafted dolls and jewellery. Friends hailed friends they hadn't seen all winter. Families flapped out rugs to picnic on the grass. Children shrieked in delight as they played catch and tag and Frisbee. And a hopeful father ran back and forth in a fruitless effort to launch his kite, despite the stillness of the day and the mortified look of his young son.

Anna Warne was getting none of that, however. She was sitting inside instead, at a table by the front window of Chepstow's oldest bookshop, gazing enviously at all these happy folk. How she wished she was out there with them, rather than stuck in here for the afternoon, trying vainly to sell copies of her new book on William Marshal, history's greatest knight. She'd had some faint hope that it would be popular here, if nowhere else, for he'd been the town's most celebrated lord, having rebuilt its castle back in the late twelfth century before going on to serve as England's regent. But nearly eight hundred years had passed since then, and the town's good citizenry seemed to have developed a healthy lack of interest in the man – at least when it came to a straight fight between him and the May sunshine. And those few who did come in managed somehow to look anywhere but at where she was sitting with her stack of hardbacks and her pen at the ready, as though that whole section of the shop was swathed in some kind of invisibility cloak. Two hours she'd been here already, and only three copies sold – and one of those to the bookshop's owner, embarrassed for her, and taking pity. And so she thought dark thoughts of her editor, who'd suggested this trip to give her sales a boost, and vowed to have words with her next time she found herself in London. But she knew in her heart that the fault was truly hers, for writing a book that was too academic to be popular, and too popular to be academic.

The bell above the door gave another of its melodic chimes. She'd come to dislike it in an almost Pavlovian way already, signalling as it did yet another disappointment. A great bull of a man strode in, tall and broad and meaty, in his mid to late fifties and with his scalp shaven close, presumably to hide the baldness she could make out in the shadow left behind. Of Indian or at least subcontinental heritage, though dressed very much like an English man of business, with polished black brogues, a powder blue silk shirt and a pearl grey suit that looked incongruously formal for a bank holiday weekend, all covered by a gorgeous Astrakhan overcoat that was surely far too heavy for so pleasant a day. His face was flushed and shiny with perspiration, and he was breathing hard, as though he'd been walking fast. Yet, now that he was here, he didn't seem in any particular hurry. He looked around the shelves with an expression of mild contempt, as though he hadn't read a book since leaving school, and was proud of it too. Then, to Anna's surprise, he noticed her sitting in her lonely corner and came marching on over. He picked up one of her hardbacks, turned it around and held it out at arm's length to check her face against the photograph on its back cover, like he was working at passport control. 'You wrote this?' he asked, with more than a hint of suspicion, clearly thinking her altogether too young and too slight to have produced so substantial a book.

'No,' she told him. 'I just had the jackets printed up so that I could sit here all afternoon answering daft questions.'

He gave a grunt of what might equally have been umbrage or amusement. 'Name's Ravindra,' he told her, in a disconcertingly broad East Midlands accent. 'Ravindra Pandey. Can we talk?'

'We already are.'

'Not here. In private. I'm parked nearby.'

'Are you for real?' asked Anna, who'd learned in the most brutal way possible never to trust strange men who wanted to get her into their car. 'I'm signing books.'

The man looked disdainfully around the near-empty shop. 'I'm sure they can spare you for ten minutes.'

To her relief, the doorbell chimed again before she had to answer, and two more people came in – a handsome woman in her late thirties, slender and of medium height, expensively dressed in a leopard-print haircalf jacket, tan wool trench trousers and suede ankle boots. She had striking bright green eyes and a pair of designer sunglasses that she'd pushed up like an Alice band over her crinkly, shoulder-length russet hair. She was closely followed by a diffident-looking man of fifty or so, short, hunched and a little overweight, with thinning salt-and-pepper hair and a pair of tortoiseshell glasses on a string around his neck. He was wearing trainers, baggy blue jeans that slouched down over his hips despite his leather belt, a plain green T-shirt and a thin blue waterproof jacket, all well worn and rather shabby, and made to look even more so by the elegance of his companion. 'Sorry,' said Anna to Ravindra, glad of the excuse. 'Looks like the afternoon rush has arrived.'

'Don't mind them,' replied Ravindra. 'They're with me.'

She gave him a sceptical look, for they didn't seem to have much in common. But indeed they came straight over. 'You walk so fast, Ravi,' complained the woman.

'I didn't come all this way for the sightseeing,' he told her. He took a step back and crouched to check the cardboard boxes beneath the table. 'How many copies?'

'I don't know,' said Anna. Except she did. Her editor had, rather optimistically, shipped six boxes down here, both for this afternoon's signing and then for her evening talk. At eight copies apiece, minus the three she'd sold, it made the maths painfully easy. 'Forty-five.'

'And how much are they a pop?'

'Nineteen ninety-nine.'

'Nineteen ninety-nine? Bloody hell.' But he took out his wallet anyway, strode up to the counter. 'Pack them up, then, love,' he said, over his shoulder. 'I'm having the lot.'

TWO

Quentin Parkes had just turned fifty-three years old, yet he'd still not fully conquered the childhood shyness that had made him stand in dark corners at teenage parties, praying that his clothes would blend in with the wallpaper, or at least that his fellow guests would mistake him for a standard lamp or coat-rack. Diffidence was the last trait you needed as a university lecturer, of course, but thankfully he'd discovered in himself an ability to perform, to adopt a brash persona even as he'd walked into the lecture hall. Yet sustaining that illusion was so draining that once he'd strutted and fretted his hour upon the stage, he'd always deflated back into his true self, as uncomfortable as any self-respecting Englishman with people making scenes anywhere, but most particularly in bookshops. And so it was with envy as much as with embarrassment that he watched Ravindra dominate the place like a circus barker, making sure everyone there knew he was buying Anna Warne's complete stock of books, save for the few she insisted on keeping back for her talk that night. He wasn't sure what he coveted most – his air of command, his indifference to opinion, or his absurd wealth.

'Are you at least going to help us carry them to my car?' Ravindra asked Anna, once the transaction was done. And what could she say to that? She shook her head in bemusement but picked up one of the boxes, as did Melissa, leaving the others for Quentin and Ravindra. The bookshop's owner gave them a delighted smile as he held open the door for them. They filed along the pavement to the zebra crossing then across the road to the car park, where they packed the boxes away into the capacious boot of Ravindra's beautifully waxed royal blue Rolls Royce Phantom.

'Well?' Anna asked Ravindra, rubbing her hands on her trousers. 'You know how to grab an author's attention, I'll give you that. What do you want with it?'

'It's not me that wants it,' he said, nodding at Quentin. 'This is all that one's idea.'

Quentin found himself hesitating. Anna was younger than he'd expected; younger and smaller and scruffier, attractive enough of feature yet dressed in shapeless drab clothes and with messy short brown hair, making her look more like one of his old archaeology students than an authority in her field, so that suddenly he felt foolish for ever having suggested they come. But then he reminded himself that, however mousy and innocuous she might look, she'd dispatched first a Russian mobster and then a murderous rapist on her way to finding King John's lost crown jewels, before seeing off another equally vicious killer during the Beowulf affair. So maybe there was more to her than first appeared. Maybe she was the right person for this after all.

There were too many people milling around for comfort, however, especially as they were still close enough to home that he might be recognised. 'You don't know me,' he told her, in a low voice. 'But it's possible that you might know *of* me. My name's Quentin Parkes. I gave a pair of guest lectures at Nottingham University some years ago, though I think probably before your time there. I also once wrote a book you might have—'

'Material Culture in Sub-Roman Britain?' she said eagerly. 'That was you?'

'You know it?' he said, unable to hide his gratification, not just at her words but at her look of admiration.

'Of course,' she said. 'It's a wonderful piece of work. Though...'

'Yes,' he said ruefully, finishing the thought she'd been too polite to. 'It has been rather overtaken.'

She touched his arm. 'I didn't mean it as a criticism. It's just that so much has been discovered in the last, what? Fifteen years?'

'Twenty, now,' he said, with a shake of his head. It was hard for him to believe how much time had passed. He'd intended – he'd *expected* – to achieve so much. 'Of course the world has moved on. It's a good thing.' Then he added, with a smile: 'Though I admit it can sting a little.'

'It's great to meet you,' said Anna, shaking his hand warmly in both hers. 'Though I have to ask: what has your book to do with me? With all this?'

'Nothing,' he told her. 'At least... I mostly said that by way of introduction. To reassure you that we're not about to abduct you or hurt you or anything crazy like that. We're here for a good reason. A *historical* reason. An *archaeological* reason. Only it's one that we can't afford to get out, at least not yet.' He nodded at the car behind her. 'So would you please trust us enough to join us inside there, so that we can be as sure as possible that we won't be overheard?'

She gazed at him a moment or two, then at Melissa, and finally at Ravindra, his arms folded impatiently, not bothering to hide his irritation with all this dancing around the point. Then she looked at the various people collecting belongings from their boots or packing up after their picnic lunches, and at the pair of burly stewards in bright yellow bibs who were standing by the exit. Yet clearly she still wasn't satisfied, for she took out her phone and snapped their faces in turn, then went around to the back of the Rolls to add its licence plate before letting them know that she was uploading the photographs to the cloud.

'Good lass,' said Ravindra approvingly. 'I only hope my own granddaughters grow up as sensible.'

'Ten minutes,' said Anna. 'Then I need to get back.'

They climbed inside, with Anna and Melissa in the rear,

Ravindra at the wheel and Quentin in the passenger seat, so that he had to turn uncomfortably around to let Anna look him in the eye. 'So,' he said. 'I'm Quentin Parkes, as you already know. That's Melissa beside you. Melissa Ward. And this is Ravindra Pandey up here with me.'

'And you're all archaeologists?'

Ravindra gave a scornful laugh. 'You think I could afford a ride like this by digging up old pots? No, love. I own a company called Aston Farms. Melissa here is one of my oldest employees.'

'One of his longest serving employees,' corrected Melissa, with a reproving look. 'Not oldest.'

'Sorry, yes,' said Ravindra, unabashed. 'Longest serving and most trusted. We have a bunch of different interests, but our main business is poultry. We're the second largest producers in the country. On our way to becoming the largest.'

'Poultry?' said Anna, baffled.

'Chickens, mostly,' said Ravindra. 'But turkeys and ducks too. Even a few geese and guinea-fowl. We supply all the main supermarkets and restaurant chains. If you like the odd plate of buffalo wings, or you've ever had a Christmas dinner, or you're partial to a Sunday roast, then like as not you'll have eaten one of ours.'

'Okay,' said Anna.

'We're not just a *big* company,' said Melissa, taking over. 'We're a *growing* company. Ravindra is too modest to say it, but he's turned the handful of free range chickens he started out with into the largest privately-owned poultry supplier in the country. And we're not done yet. Supermarkets know they can trust us. They keep pushing us for more. So we're always on the lookout for new locations for our farms. They're not easy to find. At least, the farms are easy enough. It's the planning permission that's the curse. People have the wrong idea about what we do. They fear our barns are going to be noisy and smelly and cruel, and that they'll be a magnet for the animal rights brigade, even though we take the welfare of our birds very seriously. Not that those people really care about...' She paused and smiled and gave herself a moment, lest she head off on a tangent. 'Anyway, we're always looking for new sites, like I say. We acquired another one a few years back. It looked ideal. Zoned for agriculture, yet the soil not great for arable or livestock, so available at a reasonable price, despite people like Quentin here trying to outbid us.'

'I put a kind of consortium together,' admitted Quentin. 'But it was hopeless. If we could have done something with the land, then maybe. But, like Melissa says, the soil simply isn't good enough. Ravindra's opening bid was already twice our upper limit.'

'We don't care about soil quality,' said Ravindra bluntly. 'What we want is space. Enough that we can site our barns a fair distance from the nearest neighbours, to get past the planning committee, yet close enough to the motorway and our main processing plant. Permission was still a slog. It always is. The locals fight us tooth and nail, despite the jobs we'll bring, which the area is crying out for. They claimed that the local infrastructure couldn't support us, that we'd destroy a site of outstanding natural beauty and ruin a popular walk. All the usual stuff. It's touching how people who'd shriek and run a mile if they ever saw a bat suddenly develop such concern for their roosts. But we're patient, we have good lawyers and architects, and we cleared each of these hurdles in turn. And finally we prevailed.'

'Are we getting any closer to the point?' asked Anna.

'I'm overseeing the redevelopment myself,' said Melissa. 'We knocked down the existing outbuildings about two months ago now, then we dug up the ground to lay new foundations for our own first barn. We'd barely started before we made a rather gruesome discovery. A human skull.'

'Christ,' said Anna.

'Quite. Obviously we stopped work at once. We called in the police. They found more human remains beneath. Long bones, teeth, hips, ankles. You name it. And more skulls, of course. It turned out that at least a dozen people had been buried there. Thankfully, it also turned out that we hadn't bought the place from a serial killer. The bodies had been there a long, long time. The soil is very clayey, you see, and its right next door to a hill, too, meaning that all the rain – of which there is a lot, believe me – drains into it. You'll know better than me, I suppose, but apparently wet clay is good at preserving organic remains.'

'Yes,' said Anna.

'Anyway, the coroner told us we needed to contact the county's Finds Liaison Officer, a woman called Ursula Platt. She was away, but she put us in touch with an archaeologist called David Connelly from the local museum. She also suggested that I invite Quentin here to come take a look, because he lived nearby, and they'd worked together before, and he knew the local history better than anyone. I wasn't exactly delighted by this, as you can imagine. He'd fought us pretty hard over the farm. But, to be fair, he'd fought us precisely because he believed it to be an important heritage site, and so deserving of preservation. Anyway, I called him and he came straight over.'

'We found at least a dozen bodies, as Melissa says,' said Quentin, taking the baton. 'Likely a great many more. It can be hard to tell, as I'm sure you know. Several of the skulls and long bones had violent fractures that showed no sign of healing, suggesting they'd died very quickly from their injuries. We also found scraps of rusted chain-mail, the hilts and blades of some broken swords, a few fighting knives and a dozen or so spear points.'

'A body pit,' said Anna. 'Have you managed to date it?'

'Very broadly, yes. We were lucky enough to find a silver coin in there. A Honorius *siliqua*, in case you're curious, giving us a *terminus post quem* of—'

'In English,' said Ravindra irritably.

'Forgive me,' said Quentin. 'An earliest possible date of around four hundred CE, which was when the coin was minted. But it was pierced in the middle, so it seems likely to have been worn as a medallion, which was very much a post-Roman fashion. And the weaponry looks post-Roman too. Though, honestly, we know so little of the era, who can truly say?'

'So you're thinking, what?' asked Anna, intrigued. 'First half of the fifth century?'

'Fifth century, yes. But we're not so sure about the first half. Not yet.' Quentin hesitated, then added: 'The body pit obviously suggests a very serious skirmish or even a battle of some kind. The location would indicate that it was most likely between the Britons and the Saxons. So it probably wasn't *that* early, because, as far as we know, the Saxons took a fair few decades to get that far west.'

'How far west are we talking?'

'Forgive us,' said Melissa, before Quentin could answer. 'We need to keep that confidential for the moment. Though of course if you agree to help…'

'Help how? You still haven't told me.'

'Don't worry,' said Ravindra dryly. 'Another day or two, I'm sure they'll get there.'

'You want to take over, do you?' asked Melissa.

'I want you to get to the point. As Ms Warne clearly does too.'

'Fine.' She turned back to Anna. 'But first you should know that Ravi is a stickler for social responsibility. In spirit as well as in letter. It's one of the reasons I'm proud to work for him.'

'We're unpopular enough as it is,' said Ravindra, looking mollified. 'No need to make it worse.'

'Exactly,' said Melissa. 'So of course we'd already done a thorough archaeological survey as part of the planning process. Quentin here made sure of that. We took high resolution aerial photographs of the farm and the surrounding area, and we had a team survey the fields in question with metal detectors.'

'VHF metal detectors,' grumbled Quentin. 'Not even pulse induction. I offered them my own. Thanks but no thanks. And they wonder why they didn't find anything.'

'Do we really need to go over all that again?' sighed Melissa. She turned back to Anna. 'Anyway, after we found the body-pit, Quentin suggested we bring in a completely different machine. I forget what it was called, but it looked a bit like a large lawnmower.'

'A ground penetrating radar,' said Quentin. 'There's a company nearby that mostly runs surveys for industrial companies and utilities. But they do some archaeology on the side, at a substantial discount. Kind of *pro bono*. Mr Pandey hired them to survey the farm for us. The whole of it, to be fair, not just where he wants his barns.'

'And?'

'GPR data is a nightmare to interpret, as I'm sure you know. Mapping out pipes and sumps is one thing. Even tracing old ruins or roads. But making sense of an ancient battlefield...' He shook his head. 'Their analysts are good, but it was taking up far too much of their time, so they sent us the raw data instead, and we've been plotting it out ourselves, one field at a time. And we've been finding all sorts. In places where we think the fiercest fighting was, there are bits and pieces scattered everywhere, but mostly a good metre deep, which is how come the detectors came up so dry.'

'Have you dug test trenches?' asked Anna.

'Of course. We've already made some fascinating finds. Enough scraps of weaponry and armour to rewrite our notions of post-Roman warfare. Though it's still far too early to say exactly how. We've also found what appears to be a Roman villa. Or at least, the foundations of a large building with columns, walls, and part of a mosaic that'll blow your socks off when you see it, I promise. If you agree to help us, that is.'

'The villa is well away from where we want to site our barns, thankfully,' said Melissa. 'But not all the finds are. And obviously word is already getting out. Our local objectors, who'd just about made peace with us, have been given new hope. They're demanding that the whole property be taken from us and given to the National Trust or whoever.'

'I don't mind Quentin here riding that particular horse,' said Ravindra. 'He's been on it from the start. But none of those others care two pins for heritage. All they care about is stopping us. Screw them. We were granted permission for our barns fair and square, and we intend to build them. But the situation has turned increasingly ugly. They spray-painted disgusting slogans all over the front of the farmhouse. They vandalised our construction equipment and dug pits to disrupt our excavations. They sent threatening messages to us at Aston Farms, and to our contractors too. They've yelled at and spat at Quentin and our other archaeologists.'

'They smeared shit all over my windscreen,' said Quentin, with a shudder of memory. It had been an icy cold morning too, so that it had frosted to the glass, making it a nightmare to scrape off.

'Some mornings, they'll get a crowd together at the end of the drive,' added Melissa. 'They'll yell at everyone who turns up, including our volunteers, even though some of them are still just kids. They wave placards with horrible pictures of battery hens on them, which aren't from our farms and have nothing to do with how we operate. They've scared half of our crew off, though thankfully we still have enough, like Quentin here, who are prepared to brave it.'

'It's our nation's history,' said Quentin simply. 'It's too important to play games with. That means working with Aston Farms, rather than against them. But that's too much for some of my old friends and neighbours. They call me traitor. They accuse me of animal cruelty. They shun me on the street and in the shops. Honestly, it's such a mess. I'd give it up if I could. Except I can't.' He gave a helpless shrug. 'I'm an archaeologist.'

'Have you notified the police?'

'Of course,' said Melissa. 'They send along a car for each new incident. They shake their heads and take notes and file reports. But they don't *do* anything. They tell us that reasonable protest is allowed. They tell us that it's too late to catch the people who did these horrible things. So there's been no real investigation at all, as far as I can tell. No-one's even been interviewed. And it's not that they're overstretched, though they are, and which I understand; it's that their sympathies are with the locals. A couple of them even live nearby.'

'Okay, fine,' said Anna. 'I still don't get what you need me for.'

Melissa nodded. 'Three nights ago now, I was at home with my two young girls. I was lying awake in the small hours, as I mostly do these days, worrying about what new horrors the morning would bring, when I heard this strange metallic slapping noise from downstairs. It carried on long enough that I went down to investigate. It turned out to be my letterbox opening and closing so that a foul-smelling liquid could be poured in, soaking the doormat and a lovely old rug I'd brought in Marrakesh, and forming a puddle on the tiles. And the moment I turned on the light and shouted, they struck a match and dropped it in.'

'Christ!' said Anna.

'Quite. The liquid turned out not to be flammable.' Her lips tightened at the memory; her throat and cheeks flushed a violent pink. 'It turned out to be piss. But they'd still waited for me to come downstairs and turn on the lights before dropping in their match, presumably to give me the scare of my life. It worked, I can tell you. I ran to the door to stamp it out. I got my feet soaked. I was half naked, and petrified, so I didn't dare look out. But I heard them scampering off. I called the police in again. They said all the right things, but I could see in their eyes that they thought it was just a nasty teenage prank. A horrible one, yes, but not a threat to life. I don't see it that way, though. The way I see it, someone was telling me that they know where I live, and no doubt where my two girls go to school. The way I see it, it was a threat against their lives. It's doing my head in. Every time my phone goes, I think it'll be their headmistress or the police.'

'I'm sorry. That's awful. I can't imagine.'

'Thank you.' She took a breath to calm herself. 'What we do isn't popular. I get that. Farming can be an ugly business, even when you do it right. We've had to deal with these sort of issues before, and we will again, and that's fine. I'm happy to take a certain amount, not least because I know Ravindra is a good man.' She threw him a glance of such warmth that he flushed a little, making Quentin wonder – not for the first time – just how strictly professional their relationship was. 'He doesn't allow our standards to drop. He doesn't stand for threats against his staff either. When I told him what had happened, he promised to sort it, whatever it took.'

'Mel's been with me almost from the start,' he said. 'She's like a daughter to me. Anyone coming after her and her kids might as well be coming after me and my own. I won't put up with it. I just won't. Whatever it takes, like she says. Which is why we're here today.'

Anna shook her head, more bemused than ever. 'I'm sorry you've been through this. Truly I am. But what can I do?'

'I've had my letterbox sealed up, and I've had better locks put on my windows, and all of that. I've given my girls panic alarms. We've beefed up security at the farm as well, though it's too big to make completely safe. We've put up some more fencing and a couple of cameras, and we've brought in an old friend of Quentin's as nightwatchman. But if people want to get at you badly enough, they will. So it's time to turn proactive. It's time for us to find out who's doing this. Find them and stop them before they can do us any real harm. Obviously we're not investigators ourselves, so Ravindra suggested bringing in a London firm he'd used before. This isn't exactly their thing, though I'm sure they're competent enough. But, as Quentin pointed out, it's unlikely to get us anywhere.'

'It's not that I think it's a bad idea,' explained Quentin. 'It sickens me, what they've done to Melissa. Especially as whoever's behind it is likely one of my neighbours, maybe even a friend. So we absolutely need to find out who's doing this, and put a stop to it. But, honestly, the community is too small and tight for such a blunt approach. If a team of London investigators suddenly descends upon us, knocking on doors and asking intrusive questions, it will only make people even more antagonistic. And no one will talk to them anyway. So ideally what we need is to carry out the investigation without provoking a backlash.'

'And you think I can help?' frowned Anna.

Quentin nodded. 'I saw on a message-board a couple of

weeks ago that you'd be here today. I was actually thinking of coming to your talk this evening anyway, before I got landed with all our survey data to interpret. And you must admit that you and your detective friend Mr Elias have quite a track record at this kind of thing.'

Anna couldn't help but laugh. 'After all this, it's Ben you want? Not me?'

'No,' said Quentin. 'We want you both. We *need* you both. It won't work without the two of you.'

'Why not? And what makes you think they'll open up to us any more than to Mr Pandey's London investigators?'

'Well, you're famous, for a start,' said Melissa.

'Famous!' scoffed Anna. 'I've been on TV a few times.'

'That makes you A-List, where I'm from, believe me,' said Quentin. 'More to the point, didn't I read that you're developing a series for the BBC? On lost British treasures?'

'We've had some discussions, that's all. Nothing's been signed. To be honest, it's hard to come up with enough treasures for a full series.'

'A few discussions is plenty for our needs, trust me. Don't you see? It gives you a way in that no-one else has. You can legitimately claim that you've heard whispers of an exciting discovery, and so have come to find out more. That way, the locals won't see you as the enemy, but rather as a wonderful potential ally in their fight to stop the barns. They'll welcome you with bunting and a parade. They'll tell you everything you need to know, without you even having to ask. You and Mr Elias both.'

'And what if I should come to think they're in the right?' returned Anna. 'What if I come to think the farm should be a heritage site?'

'Let me be clear about this,' said Ravindra. 'I paid good money for that land. I want it for my birds. I'm not going to give it up, just because it *might* be heritage. Maybe it's a site of moderate importance that we can coexist with. Maybe it's nothing much at all, and we can ignore it altogether. But maybe it really is special, like Quentin here has always claimed. In which case, fine. It *should* be in public hands. The thing is, though, I don't trust him or his museum friends to make that judgement. They have too high personal stakes in the outcome. Same for the locals. They'll say anything to make us stop. But I reckon I *can* trust you. If I pay you as a consultant, at least. I back my judgement when it comes to people, and I reckon you're too honourable to take a man's money and then cheat him. Isn't that so?'

'Yes,' admitted Anna, a touch surprised. 'You're probably right.'

'Good. Then this is what I propose: If, at the end of all this, you tell me it's a site of genuine national significance, I'll do as you recommend. I'll notify the British Museum or Historic England or whoever, and I'll enter good faith discussions about selling it or even donating it to the nation. Does that sound fair?'

'Of course,' said Anna. 'More than. But this is all so fantastical. I've no idea what you're talking about, or where this is, or whether Ben would agree to come, or how we'd even get started.'

'One of our neighbours at the farm runs a bed & breakfast,' said Melissa. 'She's worried for her livelihood if a bunch of poultry barns gets put up next door. She's exaggerating the problem in her own mind, I'm sure, but you can see her point. She's very pretty and very charming, which is why our friend Quentin here has a teeny little crush on her, but—'

'I do not,' protested Quentin hotly.

'Very well,' said Melissa, with a knowing smile. 'A major crush, then. But she's as tough as old boots beneath, and smart with it, so she's become one of our more formidable opponents. If you and your friend were to spend a couple of nights at her place, claiming you were there on behalf of the BBC to investigate some intriguing whispers you've heard about the discoveries next door, she's sure to try to recruit you in her fight against us. Play it right, she'll introduce you to all her friends. She'll have them tell you everything.'

'And if she doesn't have rooms for us?'

'She does,' said Quentin. 'We've already reserved them for you both. In the main house, tomorrow and the night after.'

Anna gave a dry laugh, simultaneously amused and appalled by all this plotting. 'I don't know,' she said. 'It all seems so underhand.'

'It *is* underhand,' agreed Melissa. 'But someone pissed through my letterbox the other night, while my girls were asleep upstairs. Then they waited until I was on my way down to drop in a match, to make me think we were all about to burn. I can't believe you're okay with that.'

'Of course I'm not.'

'Then do this for us,' she begged. 'Find out what's going on, whether it was meant as a serious threat or just an ugly prank. Until I know that my girls aren't really in danger, I'll never have a proper night's sleep again. That's all I really care about for myself, but our construction crew deserve to know that too. And Quentin here, and all our other archaeologists and volunteers. If it's just teenage larks, then great, we'll live with it. But if it's more than that, as some of the threats we've got suggest, then we need to find out who's behind it all, and stop them.'

'We'd pay you, of course,' said Ravindra. 'We'd pay you well. Two thousand a day each for you and your mate, plus expenses. A minimum of two days, but then for as much longer as it takes, or until we call it off. Plus what I said about donating the farm to the nation.'

'There's one more carrot too,' added Quentin. 'If the excavation turns into what I think, it could lead to a lost British treasure that… Well, I can't say what, exactly, but let's just say that the BBC would ask you to name your price.'

'You clearly don't know the BBC very well,' said Anna. But then she sighed. 'Fine. I'll put it to Ben. If he agrees, I'll be in, at least for a day or two. To see how it goes. But you'll have to tell me what this lost treasure is first, or he'll simply laugh.'

'Ah,' said Quentin. 'It's not that easy. I can show you what we've already found when you come to visit. Some of it is absolutely fascinating. As for the lost treasure itself, I can't tell you *what* it is yet, for the simple reason that it could be any number of things, any one of which would make for a blockbuster episode. But what I can tell you is *where*.'

'And?'

He allowed himself a mischievous small smile, curious of her reaction. 'It's just a mile or two outside a little Wiltshire village called Badbury,' he said.

THREE

Ben Elias allowed himself plenty of time to reach Swindon before Anna's train was due. His old Nissan Leaf was fine for getting him into Ingatestone for the shops and the railway station, but it wasn't suited to cross-country jaunts like this any more. For the hundredth time, therefore, he told himself that he needed to trade it in for something better; yet he'd grown oddly fond of it, and it felt disloyal. In consequence, however, not only did he have to stop to recharge it along the way, but it needed a further top-up after he'd arrived, so he found a supermarket on Coulston Street with a free bay to plug it into, then he went inside to reward himself for his early arrival with a plate of bacon, eggs, beans and fried tomatoes in their in-house café.

He wiped his plate clean with some buttered bread then checked Anna's progress on his phone. Her train was running ten minutes late. Not bad, for these days. He felt a sudden rush of excitement and pleasure at the prospect of seeing her again. They chatted or texted pretty much every day, but it had been months since they'd met in person. Not indeed, since their Beowulf adventure, which had ended in such a brutal assault upon Anna that she'd only just survived, with Elias himself hauling her out of her earthen grave in the nick of time.

She'd suffered multiple broken bones in that episode, along with severe internal injuries and the loss of enough blood that it had almost done for her. But he'd kept her alive just long enough for the air ambulance to arrive. They'd intubated her and given her plasma and flown her to Ipswich Hospital, where she'd been wheeled straight into theatre for emergency surgery followed by a stint in the ICU before being moved to a general ward for further observation and recovery.

Anna being Anna, however, restlessness had quickly taken hold. The final draft of her book on William Marshal had been due, yet she'd found it impossible to work on it in the hubbub of an overcrowded ward, especially with her writing arm in plaster, leaving her reliant on voice-to-text. She'd duly discharged herself early, against the advice of her medical team, and despite being nowhere near fit enough to manage alone in her York bedsit, what with the four flights of stairs up which she'd have had to carry her shopping.

Elias had taken leave from his job as a London-based security consultant in order to stay in Ipswich and visit her every day. He'd been on hand, therefore, to drive her from the hospital to the railway station. That, at least, was what he'd told her, to get her into his car. Over her half-hearted protests, he'd then driven her straight back to his Ingatestone cottage instead, where he'd installed her in his spare room, the one he'd had decorated and furnished for the twins, but with the bunks replaced by a proper bed and a desk for her to work at.

Over the next fortnight and a bit, he'd done the shopping for them both, and driven her to her follow-up appointments. He'd picked up her prescriptions and had nagged her into doing her rehab. She'd stayed a total of seventeen days in all. They'd been among the happiest of his life. He'd had to return to work after the first week, yet even that had become a pleasure, returning home on the train each evening to find that she'd cooked what could generously be described as dinner for them both. They'd then spent hours at his kitchen table, with him telling her about his day, while she'd talked him through her progress on her book, the problems she was having with it, the occasional breakthroughs she'd made; then sitting together on his couch, streaming a movie or simply chatting over a glass of wine.

Nothing physical had happened between them. He'd never even made anything close to a pass, though he'd thought about it all the time. They'd barely even touched. Not, at least, until the last day, when he'd driven her back up to York. He'd carried her bags and two week's worth of shopping up to her bedsit then had turned to bid her farewell. They'd taken each other in a hug that had gone on and on and on, one minute, two minutes, three, just holding each other tight and swaying gently, as if to hidden music. He should have said something then. He should have told her. But he'd lost his nerve instead. He'd let go of her and admonished her to look after herself, and to call him if she needed anything, anything at all. Then he'd gone back downstairs and out to his Leaf, cursing himself for his feebleness all the way home.

He checked the train times again. Ten minutes late had become twenty. He returned to his car to fetch his copy of her book, a tad guilty that he'd only managed the first five chapters so far – but work had been so full-on recently that he'd been too tired to read by the time he made it home. He bought himself a second coffee and sat down to it. Ten-thirty arrived. He went back out. The railway station was only a few minutes away. He parked in short term and went inside. Anna's train rolled slowly in. He waited by the newsagents for her to appear, and suddenly there she was, still limping slightly from her injuries, hauling an old tan suitcase with a broken wheel so that it hiccuped over the tiled floor. He hurried to greet her. She let go of her case and opened her arms wide, and he couldn't help himself, he took her in another hug and held her past anything that was polite before finally bringing himself back under control and letting go of her again, feeling embarrassed. But she only put a hand on his arm and smiled. 'It's good to see you too,' she said.

He took her case, made to lift it by its handle – only to find it so heavy that he set it back down again and flapped his hand. 'Bloody hell,' he said. 'Has there been a bullion heist I've not heard of?'

'It's books,' she told him. 'The ones I didn't sell.'

'I thought your chicken baron mate had bought them all.'

'I kept a box back for my talk last night.'

'Ah.' He gave a sympathetic grimace. 'How did it go?'

'It was good. It was good. I think they both enjoyed it.'

'Oh Christ. Tell me you're exaggerating.'

'A little. But not by as much as I'd like. Publishing is a tough business, it turns out.'

'At least you'll have one left to sign for me.'

'Are you telling me you haven't bought one for yourself yet?'

'Of course I have. Just not a signed one. I thought it was great, by the way. Though you're far too kind to me in it.'

'That was my editor. She insisted.'

He laughed and gazed fondly at her. Every time they met, it baffled him that he'd left it so long to see her again. But she lived in Yorkshire and he in Essex, they both worked long hours, and their lives had such little natural overlap that it was hard.

She put her hand on his wrist. 'I had a panic after we spoke last night,' she told him. 'This wasn't one of your weekends with the twins, was it?'

He shook his head. 'I never get the bank holidays. They're in Paris, I think, with their mum and her new man.' He turned and led the way out of the station, dragging her case behind him, still hiccuping away. 'So another fun jaunt you've got planned for us, eh? After that Beowulf business, I'd have thought you'd have had enough.'

'This won't be like that, I promise. The worst we're risking is a bit of piss through the letterbox.'

'Is that some kind of euphemism? Sounds unpleasant, either way.' He patted his side to indicate her ribs. 'How's it all healed?'

'It's fine,' she said, despite the way she was still slightly favouring her right leg, even without having her bag to haul. 'It's good.' They reached his Leaf. He heaved her suitcase into the boot. 'So where now?' he asked.

'Hillview Manor. It's a bed & breakfast a few miles south of here, just outside a village called Badbury.'

'Okay.' He found it on his phone, set it up to give him

directions then clipped it into its cradle. 'So are you going to tell me what this is all about?' he asked, checking over his shoulder before reversing out of his spot. 'You were so mysterious on the phone.'

'Yes. Sorry about that. Too many other people around. And it's legitimately kind of confidential.'

'That much I gathered. And?'

'So those two people I told you about – Melissa Ward and Quentin Parkes – will be showing us around the farm where this is all happening in about ninety minutes from now, so I'll leave that part of it till then. But you'll need some general historical background first, for it to make sense. How much do you know about post-Roman Britain?'

'Only what I got from that Beowulf business.'

'Okay. So this is a century or two before that, although it overlaps in places. Very briefly, then, back in the years BCE, England and Wales were really a disparate collection of small Celtic kingdoms. We had valuable stocks of tin, gold and silver, good fertile land and plenty of potential slaves, so the Romans fancied adding us to their empire. Julius Caesar tried first, in 55 BCE. He claimed victory but in truth he mostly got his arse handed to him. He came again, the next year, and did a bit better. But it was another hundred years or so before they made it stick, largely by setting the various tribes against each other.'

'Divide and rule. So that's where we got it from.'

'Yep. Learned it from the best. But England and Wales were as far as they got. Scotland and Ireland proved too much. That meant frontiers, however, and frontiers are trouble. They built Hadrian's wall to keep out the Picts, but they still had to station a disproportionately large part of their army here – many tens of thousands of men. Time passed. The British elite became increasingly Romanised, which meant becoming Christian too, after Constantine made it the state religion. Then the Huns invaded northern Europe from the east, driving Germanic tribes like the Goths and Franks and Alans across the Rhine into the Roman empire. Vast numbers were assimilated, joining the legions and taking over much of the fighting from the native Italians, which was popular, but also gaining in wealth and power, which was not. The old consensus started to fracture. A game of thrones began. Legions were summoned home by ambitious generals and nervous emperors as they vied for power, stripping Britain of its defences and leaving it as easy pickings for all those displaced Germanic tribes I just mentioned.'

'Which would be when the Angles settled in Suffolk and Norfolk?' suggested Elias.

'Exactly, yes. Though we're more interested in the Saxons right now, who took over much of the south and south east. It was fairly peaceful at first, as best we can tell. There's even reason to think that they were invited here and given large parts of Kent in exchange for their help fighting the Irish and the Picts. If so, it wasn't long before the Saxons realised they didn't need to be *granted* land. They could simply *seize* it instead. With me so far?'

They headed south out of Swindon along the Marlborough Road then joined a short queue at the M4 roundabout. 'With you,' said Elias.

'Good. A series of battles took place. The Britons got pushed further and further back, losing ground but gaining toughness and valuable fighting experience in exchange, until finally they managed to give the Saxons such a bloody nose that it put an end to their advance for at least a couple of decades. We know all this thanks to a monk called Gildas, who is pretty much the only surviving British source from the two hundred years after the Romans left. Sadly, he was also a bit of a prick, more interested in scolding his contemporaries for their godlessness than in giving us detail, so we don't know when this great encounter took place, other than it was in the year of his birth. Unfortunately, that could mean any time from around the second half of the 400s through to the early 500s. All he tells us is that it started as a siege that turned into a battle. The Battle of Badon Hill.'

'Badon Hill?' frowned Elias, as they passed a signpost to

Badbury. 'Any connection to this place?'

'Give the man a gold star,' said Anna. 'Yes, etymologists draw a direct line from Badon Hill to Badbury – though there are plenty of other candidates, to be fair, including Bath. But Badbury makes good historical sense, because this is pretty much exactly where we think the front line between the Britons and the Saxons would have been. And we have some archaeology to support it too.'

They turned east onto the Ridgeway, a narrow country lane bordered on both sides by high hedges and fields of ripening crops. 'See that?' she said, pointing out through the windscreen at the sharp rise in the ground ahead, made to look steeper and higher than it was by the flatness of the surrounding country, like a fruit-bowl upturned upon a table. 'It's called Liddington Hill now, but many people think it was the original Badon Hill. We know for sure there was a fort upon it at one point, though it fell into disuse.' Hill-forts had been common across Britain back in the Iron Age, a way to dominate and defend the surrounding land. But they'd proved no match for the Roman legions, whose siege engines and superior tactics had allowed them to scale their palisades or breach their gates with ease, turning them from strongholds into death-traps. The forts had been abandoned, therefore, at least until the Romans had left again, at which point a few had been rebuilt and brought back into service. 'They've made some interesting finds up there, and from the right period too – though not enough to draw any firm conclusions from. But then it hasn't been properly excavated, of course. The old story: too many sites; not enough money.'

They turned right off the Ridgeway down Liddington Way, a single track lane with passing places every hundred yards or so. It was in such poor condition that Elias took it slowly, the numerous potholes being made harder to see by the confusing shadows thrown by the trees on either side. But then it opened up around them, revealing fields sloping away to their right, currently being grazed by sheep, and a grand Tudor mansion to their left, though so well shielded by its front brick wall that all Elias could see of it was part of its tiled roof and a quartet of twisting brick chimneys. And not the friendliest of people, to judge by the great big NO TURNING sign on its front gate, or by the row of limestone boulders on the grass verge to stop people driving up onto it when they encountered other traffic. 'And that's where this body-pit is?' he asked.

'Pretty much. Except not on the hill itself. In one of these fields along here. Or so I understand. That's where they think the battle might have been.'

'So they've found an old battleground,' said Elias, as they left the high brick wall of the Tudor house behind and passed instead a converted barn before finally arriving at a drive with a badly weathered sign welcoming them to Hillview Manor, their home for the next two days. 'Is it really worth all this cloak and dagger?'

'The cloak and dagger isn't for the battle itself. It's for the man who led the Britons in it.'

'Come on, Anna,' sighed Elias, as he indicated and then turned up the drive. 'Do I really have to beg?'

She smiled across at him. 'His name was Arthur,' she told him. '*King* Arthur.'

FOUR

Hillview Manor proved to be a charming old farmhouse set in a grassy dell at the foot of Liddington Hill. It had a large cobbled courtyard, one half of which was wet and gleaming, while the other half still sported its winter coat of mud, moss and grass, like the before-and-after shots in a power sprayer advert. The main house was to their right, a half-timbered affair of whitewashed lath and plaster. Its pitched tile roof was covered in moss and lichen, and it had a glass conservatory, south facing to catch the sunlight, while its rear was covered by ropes of ivy so thick and old that they'd burrowed beneath the paintwork.

The creosoted barn to their left had clearly once belonged to the Manor back when it had been a working farm, only to have been separated off by a tall wooden slat fence when being converted into a private home. A row of other outbuildings – stables, perhaps – had also been converted, this time into three self-contained holiday apartments, each with its own front door, painted respectively blue, green and red, and each with a little paved area out front with chairs and a table for eating breakfast at, or simply for enjoying the sunshine, all of which were separated from each other by high trellises of climbing plants. But no one was using them right now.

Parking bays had been painted onto the cobbles at some point, but the whitewash was so badly faded that they'd been completely ignored by the several vehicles present: a pair of

Range Rovers, one silver and brand new, the other old, battered and navy blue; a dark red Ford Fiesta; a white minivan; and a racing green Jaguar XJ-S of that awkward age, too old to be stylish, but not yet old enough to be a classic.

Anna got out to stretch her legs. The Manor's back door banged open and a woman in her mid forties came hurrying out, trying to work her feet into a pair of muddy black gumboots. If this was their hostess, Anna could see instantly why Quentin might have fallen for her – not just because she was pretty, but also because of how cheerful, charming and fun she looked, with her trim figure, her welcoming smile, her lively bright blue eyes, and her fair yet freckled complexion. She was wearing little makeup or jewellery: only a dab of lipstick, a gold wedding ring and a silver chain around her neck whose pendant was hidden away inside a blue-and-gold rugby shirt that was at least a couple of sizes too big for her, so that it fell like a miniskirt down over her thighs, which were encased in faded black jeans tight enough to show off the leanness of her legs.

She paused before she reached them to finish pulling on her gumboots, hopping first on one foot and then the other. But finally she managed it, and greeted her success with a smile of such self-deprecating good humour that Anna warmed to her even more. 'It *is* you two,' she said, wiping her hand dry on her shirt before offering it to them each to shake. 'I thought it had to be, what with your names; but you never know, do you, not for sure?'

'I suppose not,' said Anna.

'I'm Samantha, by the way. Samantha Forrest. Though my friends call me Sam, so you must too, or I'll be terribly insulted.' A light breeze was coming from over her left shoulder, blowing strands of her frizzy straw-coloured hair forwards over her face, so that she was constantly brushing it back behind her ear. 'Welcome to my home. Oh, and do please forgive the mess out here. I started on the spray cleaning, as you can see, in honour of your arrival, only something else came up. That's the trouble with running a place like this virtually by yourself – something else is always coming up. Then I heard on the radio that we're in for a terrible big storm tonight, and it hardly seemed worth the effort, not just for a few hours. I'll finish it off tomorrow, if I get a moment. And everything inside is spotless, I assure you – except for where my dogs go, of course.' She bit her teeth anxiously together. 'You do like dogs, I hope?'

'Doesn't everyone?' asked Anna.

'You'd be surprised.' She dropped her voice a notch, threw a dark look at the green-painted door. 'Between you and me, I never altogether trust people who don't. I mean, my two are the friendliest you could ever hope to meet. Not that you'll even have to meet them, if you don't want to. They have their own spaces indoors and out. And they know better than to annoy my guests.'

'I'm sure it'll be fine,' said Anna.

'Good. I'll show you around, then.' She offered to take one of the bags, but Elias assured her he had them, only to frown a little with regret when he picked up Anna's suitcase and remembered how heavy it was. Sam led them to the back door, clearly the preferred way in and out, close to the courtyard and the cars as it was. It took them directly into a small sitting room with several rattan armchairs around a coffee table on which lay a selection of tattered old magazines. A parish newsletter was lying on the mat. Samantha picked it up and threw it down on the coffee table as she kicked off her boots to reveal the thick grey woollen socks beneath. She led them up a steep back staircase to the pair of rooms at the top, one on either side of the passage. They were spacious and freshly painted in white and pastel blue, and each of them had a desk, a fridge, a wall-mounted TV, a pair of comfortable leather armchairs and a solid king-sized bed with fitted sheets, winter duvets and lots of pillows. The first looked out over the conservatory and a narrow strip of front lawn to the hedge and the lane, while the second looked onto a large back lawn studded with various pieces of garden furniture, a badminton net and a gated children's area with a swing and a slide and an inflatable paddling pool. Two horses – one chestnut and the other piebald – were grazing in a large, white-fenced paddock beyond, in which a number of practice showjump fences had been set up as a course. Beyond that, Liddington Hill itself rose steeply to a wooden viewing point on its peak, from which a pair of hikers were gazing back down.

'Are those yours?' asked Anna, nodding at the horses.

'Sadly, no. I had to let mine go when we converted the stables. I rent the paddock out to the people who bought the barn. Their daughter is a wonderful rider. She's won all kinds of ribbons and rosettes and what have you. Do you ride yourself?'

'I used to, a bit, when I lived in Lincolnshire. But that was a long time ago.'

Samantha nodded, as though suspecting there was a story in there somewhere, but too polite to ask. 'You don't have *en suites*, I'm afraid,' she said instead, 'but it's only you two down this end of the house, so the bathroom is all yours to share. I trust that's okay?'

'Of course,' said Anna. 'Do you have many people staying?'

'A fair few. The old stables are all taken. They always go first. People do like their privacy. And we sold the barn some years ago, like I say. But there are three other guest bedrooms down the other end, only one of which is occupied at the minute. Lovely Orlando, in the room next to mine.' She gestured vaguely at the passage then dropped her voice to a whisper, even though there was a heavy fire-door between here and there, effectively turning this part of the house into a self-contained two bed apartment. 'He's the perfect guest, to be honest – quiet as a mouse and always paying cash in advance without even having to be reminded. A writer, here to finish his latest book. Orlando Wren.' She raised an eyebrow to see if either of them had ever heard of him. They shook their heads. 'It's a time-travelling love story, from what I've been able to gather, set in Wiltshire during Edwardian times and the near future. But he hates to talk about it, and I'm not sure that it's going very well, to judge from the way he mutters to himself, so probably wisest not to ask. Not that you'll see much of him anyway, except maybe at breakfast.

He stays in his room all day, tap-tap-tapping away. Or he goes off on long walks, gesticulating like a madman. It would drive me nuts too, being alone all the time. Oh, and speaking of breakfast, it's downstairs in the dining room from seven-thirty onwards. Though I can do earlier on request.'

'Seven-thirty will be fine,' said Elias, heaving Anna's case up onto the bed in the back bedroom – the one, noted Anna with quiet appreciation, that offered her the view of Liddington Hill, rather than the front lane.

'You each have kettles and teabags and fridges, of course,' said Samantha, 'but you're also more than welcome to use my kitchen of an evening, if you don't fancy going out. I have a terrible weakness for buying all the latest gadgets I see on cooking programmes, so you'll find everything in there you could possibly want. Honestly, you could film your application videos for Masterchef in there – though I'd rather you didn't. All I ask is that people clean up after themselves. It's amazing that I even have to say this, but you wouldn't believe how many times I've come down in the morning to find the place a bomb site. People are strange, aren't they? Oh, and you mustn't mind me being in there, if I'm cooking for myself. I have to eat too. And you may have to put up with my dogs as well. Tristan and Gertie. It used to be Tristan and Isolde but then poor Isolde got hit by a car and I was so heartbroken that I couldn't bring myself to call her replacement Isolde. So Gertie it is. Shut them in the utility room if you don't want the company, but they're liable to whine piteously if you do. Though it's not much better if you let them in, to be honest, because they'll sit at your feet and stare up at you with the biggest, saddest, wettest eyes you've ever seen, beseeching you for treats. I beg you to resist. They have sensitive digestive systems, especially Tristan, my Lab. Solids I don't mind so much, they're part of the deal with dogs. It's scrubbing up all that melted chocolate after it's got deep into the carpets that gives me the shivers.'

'Message received,' Elias assured her.

'Good. What else? You each have keys on your bedside tables, along with codes for the Wi-Fi and my other house rules, which aren't terribly oppressive, I don't think. No curfews, exactly, though I do ask for consideration about making noise after it gets late. Honestly, that's about it. Though, before I go, may I be rude and ask what brings you down here? Is this some kind of *tryst*?'

Anna laughed. 'No. We're just friends.'

'But didn't I read in the papers that you were engaged?'

'I had to tell the hospital that,' said Elias, 'or they wouldn't have let me into the ICU to see her.'

'Oh,' said Samantha. 'How very disappointing.' But her eyes twinkled and she gave Elias an openly flirtatious look. 'Then what *does* bring you down here, may I ask?'

'I'm sorry,' said Anna. 'We really shouldn't talk about it.'

'Why not?' asked Elias. 'In fact, maybe Sam can help. I mean if this storm's going to be as bad as it sounds, going out tonight won't be much fun. How about we stay in and cook instead? If I buy enough for the three of us, we can pick Sam's brains while we eat.' He turned to her with a cocked eyebrow. 'If that's okay? Unless you're already doing something?'

'No. Free as a bird. That would be lovely, if you're sure?'

'Excellent. It's a date, then. Any allergies? Any foods you won't eat?'

'If there are, I haven't discovered them yet. But tell me, what sort of thing would you want to know?'

'Okay,' said Anna, dropping her voice a little. 'This mustn't go any further, but we're developing a series on lost British treasures for the BBC. The Time Detectives kind of thing, with me being the time part, and Ben here being the detective.'

'How thrilling!'

'Yes. Well. Nothing's been signed yet, so we shouldn't get ahead of ourselves. Our problem is that it'll take more than King John and Beowulf to make a proper series. And I've heard intriguing whispers about some discoveries being made on what I think must be the farm next door? I don't know if there's anything to them, but—'

'Oh, there is, there is,' said Samantha, seizing Anna by her arm. 'There absolutely is. I *knew* that was why you were here. I just didn't want to say. Come with me. Let me show you.' She led them through the fire-door to the far end of the house and her own bedroom, her pillows and duvet mussed up and a pair of field-glasses on the windowsill. She drew her curtains all the way open so that the three of them could see. 'That's Grove Farm there,' she told them, gesturing at the patchwork of fields the other side of a high hawthorn hedge that clearly marked the end of her own property.

The nearest two fields lay side-by-side, separated from each other by a drainage ditch and another, lower hedge, set at right angles to Samantha's own. Both were thickly carpeted by a straw of tall grasses, nettles and the like that had been mown down several weeks ago, to judge from their washed-out pallor. And each had a number of pits and trenches dug in it. A yellow mechanical digger with caterpillar treads and a large bucket on the end of its hydraulic arm was adding another trench in the right-hand field even as they watched, while half a dozen people stood around, eyes peeled in the hope of being the one to make some great discovery. There were two other men in the left-hand field, setting up a canopy with tarpaulins, rope and tent-poles, presumably in anticipation of tonight's storm. 'You won't believe this,' said Samantha, 'but they're planning to put up a whole lot of great big chicken barns right here. Incredible, isn't it? Just imagine the noise! The stink!'

'They're really building them that close?' asked Anna, startled.

'Not the first ones, no,' admitted Samantha. 'They're more over towards the house.' She pointed vaguely at a roof and a pair of brick chimneys just about visible behind a line of firs on the far side of the fields. 'But you know what these people are like. Once the first ones are up, they'll argue it isn't an area of outstanding beauty any more, what with all these hideous chicken barns. Before you know it, it'll be nothing but barns as far as the eye can see. And the cruelty of it! Don't get me started!

I can't bear to see animals mistreated. Look at my own run.' She pointed down and to their left, at a large wire-mesh enclosure in which a few chickens were pecking the ground. 'Only healthy, slow-growing breeds, with all the corn and space and water and sunlight they could wish for. And eggs to die for. You can have some for breakfast tomorrow. Talk about taste the difference. The only sad thing is having to cage them up at all. We used to let them roam completely free, only a fox took them, damn it to hell.'

'You were going to tell us what they've found,' said Anna.

'Oh. Yes. Not that they've seen fit to share anything with us. We've had to work it out for ourselves. So it all started a few weeks back when they were clearing ground for their first barn. They found skulls and bones and all other kinds of human remains. It was terribly exciting for a while. The police were everywhere. The farm's previous owner was murdered by his own brother, would you believe? So we all feared that he'd been at it for years, that we had our very own serial killer. But the bodies turned out to be ancient. Mid to late fifth century, so I'm told, or perhaps early sixth.' She raised an eyebrow at them. 'Though presumably you already know that, or you wouldn't be here.'

'Have they found much else?' asked Anna.

'They have, they have. You see that tent they're putting up? There's a bit of old wall down there, and some column bases, and a rather nice mosaic floor. Roman, apparently. I got rather excited for a while, what with it being so close; but then I looked it up online and it turns out that Roman villas are two-a-penny around here. Thirty odd in Wiltshire alone, and even more in Somerset next door. But they've been finding other good stuff too. At least I *think* they have. They keep scurrying back to the farmhouse with their plastic tubs, so I never get to see exactly what's inside them. And none of them are talking either, mostly because they're not even locals. They have to bus them in from Devizes and Swindon and other places, because no one around here is prepared to help them ruin the place. Except for that wretch Quentin Parkes, of course.'

'He's one of the people I was told to speak to,' said Anna. 'Is he really so bad?'

'No,' sighed Samantha. 'He's lovely, though I hate to admit it. Kind and gentle and one of my oldest, dearest friends. It's why I'm so angry with him, to be honest. Here we are, gifted a way to rid ourselves of these horrid chicken people once and for all, and he's only gone and joined them – which completely undermines our cause.'

'I'm afraid history comes first with us archaeologists. Anyway, if he does find something important, mightn't it spare you the barns?'

'I suppose. Except that they'll only put a bloody great tourist park next door instead. For god's sake don't tell Quentin, but I think I'd prefer the barns.' She gave a wry smile, torn between unhappy outcomes. 'I could call him for you, if you want? Let him know you'd like to visit?'

'Isn't he the enemy?'

'Oh, no. He's far too good a friend for that. I've had to put him in the doghouse for a bit, that's all. I'll let him out again the moment this is over, one way or the other. Though you mustn't tell him that. I do like a man to fret.'

'Then, yes,' said Anna. 'If you could call him, that would be great.'

'Good.' She patted her pockets, looked around. 'My phone. Where did I put it? I know I had it in the kitchen.'

They went down together. It was already warm from the Aga, and made warmer still by the welcome they were given by a border collie and a golden lab, jumping up on Samantha for a quick hug before she threw them off, then turning unabashed to Anna and Elias, to receive their loving there instead. Samantha's phone was on the table. She scrolled through its address book for Quentin's number, then touched a finger to her lips before dialling it and putting it on speaker.

'Sam?' said Quentin eagerly, when he answered. 'Is that really you?'

'It is.'

'It's so good to hear from you again,' he said, his voice bubbling over with pleasure and relief. 'I was afraid you'd—'

'This is business,' she told him sharply.

'Oh,' he said, deflating instantly. 'Business.'

'I warned you we intended to up the stakes. Now here we are.'

'What are you talking about?'

'You'll never guess who I have in my kitchen right now. Only Anna Warne and Ben Elias.'

'The King John and Beowulf people?' he asked, with just the right amount of puzzlement in his voice.

'The King John and Beowulf people,' confirmed Samantha. 'They're here to do a programme on lost British treasures for the BBC. I told them how you're helping your awful chicken farmer friends destroy a priceless piece of British history. They refuse to believe me. No true archaeologist would ever countenance such a thing, they tell me. I had to assure them it was really so. Now they want to see it for themselves.'

'They want to come here?' asked Quentin. 'When?'

Samantha turned to Anna and Elias. 'When?' she mouthed.

'Forty-five minutes?' suggested Anna.

'Forty-five minutes it is,' said Quentin, once Samantha had relayed this. 'Tell them I'll meet them by the gate. And to honk if they don't see me.' Then he added hopefully: 'Will you be coming too?'

'Not on your life.'

'Don't be mad at me, Sam. Please. I can't bear it.'

'You should have thought of that before joining the other side, shouldn't you? Have fun.' She ended the call, looked up at them with satisfaction. 'There you go,' she said. 'All set.'

FIVE

Anna and Elias still had a little time to kill before setting off for Grove Farm, so they put on boots and jackets more suitable both for an archaeological dig and the coming storm, then wandered out through the back garden to the paddock fence, where they could be sure of speaking freely without being overheard. There was a sack of horse nuts on the grass by the paddock gate. Anna grabbed a handful then held them out for the piebald horse to nuzzle and then gobble up, scraping its rough wet tongue across her palm.

'So we're seriously here for King Arthur, are we?' asked Elias. 'I thought the guy was a myth.'

'And so he is,' she said. 'Kind of.'

'Kind of?'

Anna gave a little sigh, aware that there was tricky terrain ahead. 'Historians really hate talking about "dark ages" these days. It sounds so judgemental. But, honestly, fifth and sixth century Britain really is a dark age for historians, in the sense that almost no writing from that time has survived. Even so, though, you'd expect any man as important and influential as Arthur is supposed to have been to have left *some* trace.'

'And he hasn't?'

'He really hasn't. He gets a handful of mentions in some Welsh poems that may not even have been that early. There's a peculiar surge in the number of people being named Arthur, suggesting there may have been a significant figure of that name. We also have a bunch of landmarks associated with him, though all of very uncertain date. And that's pretty much it.'

'Then where did the stories come from?'

'An excellent question,' she told him. 'And one we don't have a great answer to. We think he was already a bit of a folk hero by the first part of the ninth century, which is also when we get our first written reference to him. It's in a work called *Historia Brittonum,* which is usually attributed to a monk called Nennius, though we don't even know for sure that he wrote it. It credits Arthur with bringing the Britons together to fight the Saxons in a number of battles, culminating in the great victory at Badon Hill. But it was another three hundred years before Arthurmania really kicked off, thanks to Geoffrey of Monmouth's *History of the Kings of Britain.* As the title suggests, it's about far more than Arthur, but it does include a very extensive section on him. Geoffrey claimed that it was historical, or at least based on a number of genuine sources, including a mysterious book that has conveniently disappeared. It was a huge hit, and it provoked a clamour for more stories about Arthur and his court, which of course the bards and poets of the time were more than happy to supply – only these became more and more hopelessly romanticised and anachronistic, filled with sacred quests and chivalry and courtly love, none of which really existed in the fifth century, but which proved so popular that they're what most people think of now when they think of Arthur. So you can see why historians can't be bothered with it and write it all off as fantasy – though that swings in and out of fashion, to be fair. Largely because the question itself is wrong.'

'How so?'

'Well, what do we even mean when we say King Arthur? We call him king, but – assuming he even existed – he was much more likely to have been some kind of military figure. Nennius called him *dux bellorum,* a leader of battles, which is probably as good a description as any. And was Arthur even his name? He'd most likely have been a Romanised Briton of some kind, and Artorius was certainly a Roman name. In fact, we know of two Roman Artoriuses from around that time, including one who campaigned against the Picts in Scotland and the north of England. So it's certainly possible. But maybe it was a nickname instead. Artur was Celtic for bear, just like Beowulf in Anglo-Saxon. It's how the Arctic got its name, as it happens; after the Great Bear constellation. Or could Arthur have been a *title*? There's a case for it meaning something like "leader in chief". So we can't get very far with his name, but how about his deeds. Nennius says he led the Britons at Mount Badon, a battle we know for sure took place because Gildas wrote about it while it was still fresh in the general memory. Well, *someone* must have led the Britons there. Maybe that person is Arthur by definition. In which case, of course he existed. Except that he surely has to map at least somewhat onto the man described by Geoffrey of Monmouth, or the whole thing's a farce.'

'And no one does?'

'Not really, no.'

It was time to leave. They headed for the courtyard, climbed into the Leaf. They pulled a turn and were heading for the drive when they passed a man in his mid to late forties arriving back in the courtyard after a muddy walk, muttering and gesticulating to himself. He was tall and stooped with a long nose and thin lips, but otherwise well concealed by his bushy beard, his upturned collar and the plain dark blue baseball cap tugged down over his eyes. He stepped out of their way and stared at them with a rather unsettling intensity as they went by, before taking out a pencil to jot something down in his little black notebook.

Orlando Wren, no doubt, the lonesome writer.

A tractor was lumbering towards them from the right as they reached the junction with the lane, spewing straw from the hayrick on its trailer. Elias briefly thought about spurting out ahead of it, but his momentary hesitation meant that it was already too late, so he reversed a foot or two instead, to give it plenty of room to pass. He turned to Anna. 'You were telling me about Arthur,' he prompted. 'About how no one really fits

Geoffrey of Monmouth's description of him. But does anyone come close?'

She gave a shrug. 'There've been a few candidates over the years. The most promising is probably a guy called Ambrosius Aurelianus. We know for a fact he existed, which is a good start, and he lived at about the right time too, with the Saxons pressing west. He came from a leading Roman family, which fits, as does the fact that he seems to have been pretty much a naturalised Brit. Best of all is that Gildas, our one near contemporary source, implies that he was the man who led the British forces at Badon Hill, just as Nennius and Geoffrey tell us that Arthur did.'

'That seems pretty solid,' said Elias.

'Yes. Unfortunately, Geoffrey also tells us that he was brother to Uther Pendragon and thus Arthur's uncle, which would obviously rule him out. And we have to take Geoffrey seriously, as he's largely responsible for the Arthur we know today. Plus he gives lengthy descriptions of Arthur's campaigning across Europe, especially in France, and there's no record of Ambrosius Aurelianus ever doing anything like that. There is, however, another man called Riothamus, who did lead a British army of some kind into France at around that time. And we know for sure he existed too, because a letter to him survived. So was *he* Arthur? Maybe. Then there's another man who's been proposed, and who has the benefit of actually having been called Arthur – Artuir mac Áedán, to be precise. He fought the Picts up in Scotland, as Arthur was reputed to have done, though at far too late a date for him to have been involved in the Battle of Badon. So was that him? Or was it one of those Roman Artoriuses I mentioned earlier? Or was Arthur a kind of Robin Hood figure, a great big pot into which all stories of a certain type were tossed.'

'Huh,' said Elias.

'Exactly,' said Anna. 'Huh puts it perfectly. I'll make sure to credit you, if I ever write the book.'

'That's all I ask.'

Grove Farm was barely a minute's drive away, even

stuck behind the tractor. Elias slowed and indicated as they approached its drive. There was a kind of lay-by opposite, with an old wooden gate leading into a fallow field, in front of which a fifty-something man was sitting on a fold-up deck chair, a pair of binoculars on a cord around his neck, a sketchbook on his lap and a tartan thermos on the ground beside him. Without all that, they might have taken him for a tramp, what with his heavily-lined face, his unkempt long brown hair and three-day beard, not to mention his old boots, his ripped and dirty jeans, his tattered winter jacket and his ancient beanie. He toasted them ironically with his plastic cup when he saw them turning into Grove Farm, though the sourness of his expression made it clear he wished them anything but well.

A rutted drive led them up to a padlocked five-barred gate with a large PRIVATE PROPERTY: KEEP OUT sign on it, and another reading CAUTION: WORKS IN PROGRESS. A number of vehicles were parked on the concreted courtyard beyond, including a battered white van, a sky blue Honda Civic, a silver Audi A5 convertible and Ravindra Pandey's royal blue Rolls Royce Phantom that had somehow retained its showroom gleam, despite all the mud on the roads. There were pallets of concrete blocks and bricks, stacks of creosoted timbers and lengths of piping. And, in the open-fronted barn beyond, sacks of cement powder were piled up next to a cement mixer and a mound of building sand further protected from the elements by a huge green tarpaulin lashed down with orange rope.

The farmhouse itself was to their right – a pebble-dash Victorian box with a tiled roof and broken grey guttering whose once pale yellow paintwork had been turned a sickly grey by age, except for in the places where rude words had been sprayed, still just about legible beneath the whitewash they'd been painted over with.

Their arrival was noted. The front door opened and Quentin Parkes came hurrying out to meet them, rubbing his hands against the chill. He was very much dressed for an afternoon of excavation, with a waterproof jacket over his blue guernsey and lumberjack shirt, comfortable old jeans with mud-stained knees, and heavy black boots. He opened the gate to let them through, then padlocked it again behind them, and followed them over to where they parked. 'Clever of you to get Sam to call me,' he said, once Anna had introduced him to Elias. 'She'll never suspect you now.'

'It was all her idea,' Anna told him. 'I think she just wanted an excuse to talk to you.'

'Really?' he beamed, not even trying to hide how pleased he was. 'It was?'

They made their way together into the house, where Ravindra Pandey and Melissa Ward were waiting, he in a dark suit beneath his Astrakhan overcoat, she in an elegant ivory Verona jacket with matching trousers and a pair of high-heeled black leather boots, both of them looking as if they'd come to a cocktail party rather than an excavation site.

'I wasn't expecting you here,' Anna told Ravindra.

'I like to meet the people I hire,' he said, gazing Elias up and down. 'Especially the ones on two grand a day, plus expenses.'

'A word of advice, then,' Elias told him. 'You probably want to hold your interviews before awarding the contract next time.'

Ravindra gave an amused grunt. 'You'll do,' he said.

Quentin looked around to make sure there was no-one else within earshot. 'None of the other excavators or volunteers know about our little arrangement,' he said quietly, 'so we'll need to be discreet. We should be fine in here, though. All the others are out in the fields.' He ushered them along a hallway of stripped walls and ripped up carpeting into a spacious room in a similar state, its bare floorboards covered in places by small islets of hardened yellow underlay. The wiring had been ripped out, replaced and replastered, but the lights and other fittings hadn't yet been installed, so that taped up flexes dangled from holes in the walls and ceiling. A buzzy heater, a kettle and a standard lamp in the corner were all plugged in to a long orange extension cord, suggesting that there was at least some electrical supply; but there was no need for it right now, thanks to all the daylight flooding in through the large sash windows.

A pair of pine worktables had been placed end-to-end down the spine of the room, and a large number of blue acid-free boxes of various sizes were stacked on metal shelving against the walls. 'So this is our processing room,' said Quentin, somewhat redundantly. 'We'd normally have at least a couple of people in here, to log, photograph, catalogue and store the pieces as they come in. But it's a bank holiday, so…' He gave a shrug. 'You'll find this distressing, Anna, I know, but there are people in this world who actually put their families first.'

'Don't say such things,' said Anna.

'I know, I know, but there it is. They're a good crowd, actually. I'll take you out to meet them in a minute. They'll be thrilled. We career archaeologists are above such things, of course, but nothing stirs volunteer blood quite like the whiff of treasure.'

'Can we get on?' said Ravindra. 'They're here to find who pissed through Mel's letterbox. Not to admire your work.' He turned to Elias. 'Any thoughts yet?'

'Give us a chance,' said Elias. 'So far, we've met Samantha and her dogs, and I can't see any of them doing it. Though that charmer at the end of your drive…'

Melissa turned almost triumphantly to Quentin. 'See,' she said.

'Come on,' sighed Quentin. 'He's not that dumb. He'd never risk his parole over this.'

'Parole?' said Ravindra, startled. 'He's on parole? What the hell for?'

'He's the one who murdered his brother,' said Melissa.

'*What*? That arse at the end of the drive?'

'Come on, Ravi. You know all this. I told you when we bought.'

'You told me he was in prison.'

'He got released.'

'Bloody hell. Why didn't you say?'

'Because I didn't want you doing anything stupid. Not until

we know for sure.'

'Bloody hell,' said Ravindra again.

'It wasn't him,' said Quentin. 'He camps out there because he's angry about losing the farm. Which he's entitled to be, for god's sake.'

'No,' said Melissa. 'He's not. He forfeited that right when he killed his brother.'

'Except he didn't kill him,' snapped Quentin. 'How many times do I have to tell you? All those years inside, and then having the family farm taken from him too, for something he never even did. Wouldn't you be bitter?' He turned to Elias and Anna, as though this were some kind of trial, and they were the jury. 'His name's Wynn Grant. I've known him since we were kids. Our fathers were good friends, so we hung out here together all the time, along with his elder brother Caleb. But the farm's only big enough to support one family, and that was always going to be Caleb, so Wynn trained as a plumber instead. He was really good at it too. Knowledgeable, polite, honest, friendly, funny. People liked him. They *trusted* him.'

'Do we really need to know all this?' asked Ravindra.

'Yes,' said Quentin. 'How are they supposed to find out if he's behind all the shit that's been going on, if they don't know his story? And I won't whitewash it, I assure you.' He turned back to Elias. 'So anyway he was doing really well for himself when he got caught one morning in the middle of one of those dreadful motorway pile-ups, rear-ended by a lorry. He was in hospital for weeks, and he was never the same again. His back and his right knee both constantly caused him pain, which is the last thing you need as a plumber, of course, what with all that crouching in low tight spaces. So he started taking pills for it, and drinking in the evening. Only it got out of hand. He became unreliable.'

'Yes,' said Melissa. '*He* became unreliable. Because of the pills and drink *he* chose to take.'

'An accident like that could happen to any one of us,' retorted Quentin. 'And he tried all kinds of ways to sort himself out. But nothing ever took. He became increasingly angry and erratic. People stopped calling him. His doctors tried to wean him off his pain pills too, but that only caused him to turn to illegal drugs instead, everything you'd imagine, which he paid for by stealing from his parents, until finally they'd had enough of him. They owned a cottage a little way down the road that they rented out for some extra income. They put it into trust for him, so that he'd always have a place to live, and they set aside a bit of capital for him too, to ensure he had a modest income. But that was that. They washed their hands of him. And, after they'd both passed, the farm and everything else went to Caleb, which Wynn obviously resented. But they were still brothers. They got on fine.'

'Until he murdered him,' muttered Melissa.

'Stop saying that!' said Quentin. 'It was manslaughter, if it was anything. But it wasn't even that. He got railroaded, is all. There wasn't a lick of proper evidence against him. And I don't mean the case was thin. I mean they had nothing.'

'Nothing!' she scoffed. 'He confessed!'

'Only because they bullied him into it while he was still addled by drugs and feeling wretched about his brother. He retracted it as soon as he got himself together. And it was nonsense anyway. He confessed to stealing a silver photograph frame, for example. But Caleb had given it to him weeks before. I know, because I was there when it happened.'

'So you say.'

'Yes. So I say. But ask Vic if you don't believe me. He saw it in his home, at least two weeks before Caleb's accident.' He turned to Elias and Anna. 'That's Victor Unwin, the friend of mine Mel mentioned yesterday, who we've brought in as our nightwatchman here. So he'll be by later, if you'd like to check with him.'

'Maybe,' said Elias. 'But carry on. You were telling us how Wynn wasn't guilty.'

'Yes. It wasn't just lack of evidence against him in particular, it was that there was no evidence of a crime at all. Caleb was a heavy drinker too. It's the family curse. It's what saw both parents off so young. Anyway, they found so much alcohol in his blood that he'd have been falling-down drunk that night. Now come with me a moment. I need to show you something.' He led them out of the room and along a passage to a door that opened onto a steep and badly rutted set of steps that led down into a dank and musty darkness. 'He was found at the foot of these. I mean look at them. You could fall down them stone-cold sober. Try doing it with a litre of whisky inside you.'

'Why was he going down there at all?' asked Elias.

'It's where he kept his booze. He'd finished the bottle he was on.'

'And no sign of him being pushed?'

'None at all. But the police hated Wynn. He was always causing them grief of one kind or another. And he lives just down the road, like I said, so they went straight over there and found him in a haze. He had some banknotes on him that Caleb had just taken from a cashpoint. But that meant nothing either. Caleb always left a few in his wallet for him to nick. It was his way of topping up his allowance without him having to ask. But it was still enough for them to arrest and interrogate him, then charge and convict him.'

'Aren't you forgetting something?' said Melissa. 'He was seen leaving the farmhouse at the time his brother died, even though he'd denied being there at all. And, anyway, didn't he recently admit it all?'

'He admitted it because I begged him to, seeing as it's the only way you can get parole in this country, and why should he waste his life inside for something he didn't do? As for him being seen!' He turned back to Anna and Elias. 'The police got an anonymous call on their tip line from someone claiming to have seen him there, but honestly it was ridiculous. They played it in court. A breathy message left by someone clearly disguising their voice and refusing to leave their name.'

'Refusing to leave your name is hardly uncommon,' said Elias mildly. 'No one likes having a murderer know they've fingered them. But how the hell did it get played in court?'

'That was Wynn's barrister's fault,' scowled Quentin. 'He was useless. Worse than useless. He put it to one of the policemen that they had no evidence whatsoever of Wynn ever even having been at the farm that day. It went downhill from there. Especially as Wynn lost his head when they played that message. He knew it was a lie, so he accused the officer of fabricating it, then threatened to get him for it. That was the last straw, I suspect. He'd behaved okay until then; but suddenly the jury saw his potential for violence, and that was that.' He let out a long, frustrated breath, held up his hand. 'Forgive me, but he's my friend, and he's had years stolen from him for a crime that almost certainly was never even committed, not to mention having the family farm taken from him and awarded to some cousins instead. Wouldn't you be bitter?'

'Cousins?' frowned Elias.

Quentin shook his head. 'A couple on their dad's side from somewhere near Oxford, I think. Another lot out in Portugal. Though the idiots spent so long wrangling over who'd get what that half of it ended up with the lawyers. But all that's beside the point, which is that Wynn *hated* jail. I know because I visited him there. He's only out on parole, and he'd never jeopardise that over something so stupid as pissing through a letterbox. Anyway, he drinks himself into a stupor by ten each night. Even if he'd wanted to, he couldn't have.'

'This wasn't ten at night,' pointed out Ravindra. 'This was early hours, right around when alcoholics wake up with an aching bladder in need of emptying.' He held up a hand to forestall Quentin's response, then checked his watch again with a theatrical raise of the eyebrows. 'That's me out,' he said. 'It's our annual barbecue on Monday, and the wife's given me a shopping list ten feet long. If I don't get it done, it'll be me found next at the bottom of the cellar steps.' He shook hands with Anna and Elias then headed out, followed by Quentin, so that he could let him out the gate.

Elias turned to Melissa. 'Anna tells me there's been other stuff going on, besides your letterbox thing? Some death threats, even?'

'Death threats is putting it too strongly. Or so I thought before the other night. I mean everyone who works at Aston Farms risks getting abused by animal rights people, as I'm sure you can imagine, so we don't give out contact details. If people want to get in touch with any of us, they have to use a form on our website instead. After this all started, I got a few messages addressed to me personally. They weren't really threats at all, or they wouldn't have been passed on. But they could be read that way. Like one of them was one of those inspirational messages telling me to embrace each day as if it were my last. I got a link to a column advising parents to tell their kids they loved them as often as they could, because you never knew. And another to a review of a book called *The Unwelcome Visitor*. But the one that really freaked me out was when they said how scarlet suited me the day after I came here once wearing a scarlet blazer.'

'So they saw you here?'

'And scarlet's the colour of blood, isn't it?'

'I can see why you're anxious,' said Elias. 'Though do try not to worry too much. Making anonymous threats is easy. Carrying them through, not so much. But I'll need to see them anyway, along with whatever technical data your IT guys managed to collect. Anything else?'

'Some petty vandalism. They superglued the door of our digger and threw a couple of bricks through our windows. Oh, and they painted some vile words on the front of the house. I'm sure you can imagine.'

'No need to imagine,' said Elias. 'You can read them through the whitewash.'

'The bastards used black gloss,' sighed Quentin, as he came back in. 'You think you've painted them out, then a day later they're showing through again.'

'They dug some holes in the fields too,' said Melissa.

'That's an odd kind of vandalism,' said Elias.

'We think those probably weren't vandals,' agreed Quentin. 'More likely to have been treasure hunters trying their luck.

Though what they hoped to find on an ancient battlefield... But at least they didn't dig at any of the hotspots from our survey, so it seems to have been truly at random. And we've had no more visits since we put up cameras and brought Vic in as nightwatchman.'

'And you really think it was all the work of that guy at the end of the drive?'

'Maybe not all of it,' said Melissa. 'But some of it, yes. My letterbox for sure. You should have seen the smirk he gave me the next day. How pleased he was with himself.'

'I still can't see it,' said Quentin. 'He's got terrible impulse control, I grant you. He'll happily admit that himself. But none of these incidents were exactly impulsive, were they? Except maybe the threatening messages. They all took a certain planning and effort. Which gave him plenty of time to think whether they were worth losing his parole over.'

'Then who do you reckon it was?' Elias asked him.

'Isn't that your job to find out?'

'Yes,' said Elias. 'And the way I do that is by asking people who know more than I do.'

Quentin sighed, unhappy at having to point fingers at friends and neighbours. But it was a legitimate question, and he knew it. 'There's a family called the Millers in the Tudor house on Samantha's other side,' he said. 'They're as dead set against the chicken barns as anyone, but they have to be a bit more careful about it, because they're after planning permission of their own, so the arguments that were used against Aston Farms are the same ones they've been fighting themselves.'

'You think they may have resorted to dirtier tactics?'

'Not the parents, no. They're far too hoity-toity to go around pissing through letterboxes. But I could see their oldest boy Archie doing it, maybe. If you forced me to put down a fiver, I'd put it on him and especially his mates. Pissing through Mel's letterbox and smearing dog-shit on a windscreen are just the kind of mean-spirited stunts that would appeal to them, especially late at night after a few beers.'

'Do they have form?' asked Elias.

'Not Archie so much. But the gang he runs with, yes. They're always in the *Gazette* for one thing or another. One of them stole a car recently, then crashed it into a lamppost. Another was arrested for beating up his girlfriend. Then there are the usual drugs offences, some shoplifting and petty vandalism. A B&E or two.'

'Sounds promising. Where would I find him?'

'I just told you. He lives in that big Tudor house on the other side of Sam's place.'

'I'd rather do it without his parents around, if possible. Kids tend to clam up when the folks are about.'

'Ah. Yes. Of course. Then you might try the King's Head. They're not fussy there about serving the under aged.'

'The King's Head?'

'Sorry. Swindon town centre, between the mall and the cinema. That way, they get to jeer at the shoppers *and* the movie goers.'

'You have a photo of him?'

'I can find you one, sure. His parents are always posting their latest family snaps.'

'Thanks.' Elias handed him a card with his contact details. 'I'll be off, then. Get down to business before Mr Pandey moans about value for money again.' He turned to Anna. 'Text me when you need picking up. I'll be straight over.'

'No need,' said Quentin. 'I'll drop her back myself. It's only a minute.' He escorted Elias outside, to let him out the gate. He nodded through the line of fir trees towards Samantha's B&B as they went. 'So what did you make of your lovely hostess?' he asked.

'Lovely is right,' said Elias. 'I can see why you like her. She's pretty mad at you, though.'

Quentin gave a long sigh. 'Yes. So I've gathered.'

'But I wouldn't lose too much sleep over it. She says you're far too important to her to let this business ruin your friendship.'

'She said that?' asked Quentin eagerly. 'She actually said that?'

'She said she'd had to put you in the doghouse for a bit, but she's going to let you out the moment this is over, because you mean too much to her. Though she also said I wasn't to tell you that, now that I think of it. So best keep it to yourself, eh?'

'Thanks. Of course.' He tried to fight his smile, but it was hopeless. He gave in and beamed unashamedly. 'Honestly, you've no idea what a relief that is. I don't mind it so much when the others snub me. But Sam is different. I can't help but like her.'

'I imagine a lot of the men round here do,' observed Elias.

'Ha! Yes! We're a shallow lot, aren't we? Though it's not just her looks, to be fair. She's always so upbeat and warm and full of fun. When she smiles at you, it's like having the sun shine upon your face. I can't tell you how much I miss it.'

SIX

Quentin opened wide the gate for Elias, then closed and padlocked it again after he was gone. His feet were almost dancing as he did so. He felt ten feet tall suddenly, on top of the world – not least because he'd been so on edge these past few days, ever since Ravi had agreed to invite Anna and Elias here to investigate. It had been a rash suggestion on his part, because although he liked Melissa a great deal, and was appalled by the attacks on her and her two young girls, he was also a Badbury man through and through, fully aware that his friends and neighbours would consider it a betrayal that he'd helped bring in outsiders to investigate them all. Not that he much cared what most of them thought, as he'd just admitted to Elias. It was only Samantha's good opinion he truly valued.

It was only Samantha he loved.

He'd met her at Badbury's summer fete some years before, where she and her husband Graham had been manning the raffle stall. He'd fallen for her almost instantly, for her prettiness, for her smile, for her unstinting good cheer. He'd been so dazzled that he'd kept going back to their stand for more and more tickets, until he'd been loaded up with absurd prizes: a bottle of Slovenian red, a jar of green olives, a can of mushy peas and a signed copy of his own book, his one contribution to the event. He'd handed it straight back, of course, so that it could be raffled off again – only for the teenage girl who won it to give it a look of utter disgust and toss it in the nearest bin, which at least had made them all laugh.

An invitation to dinner had followed. The three of them had got on famously. But while he and Graham had become genuinely good friends, it was Samantha he'd fallen for. She'd known it too. They both had. They'd been fine with it, what was more, treating it more as her due than as some kind of breach. He was hardly her first admirer, after all, and he'd made sure never to cross the line. Their dinners together had become a regular Tuesday night event, until Graham's health had fallen suddenly and terminally apart. To Quentin's eternal shame – for he'd truly liked the man – he'd found himself gladdened by this, for it had sparked a perverse hope within him, while also allowing him to make himself useful to them both.

On the first anniversary of Graham's death, he'd gone to see Samantha with a couple of bottles of wine, in case she'd needed a shoulder to cry on. She had. The comfort hug they'd shared had ended in a kiss. He'd barely slept that night, so excited had he been to go see her again the next morning. But she'd texted him first thing to make it clear – sympathetically yet firmly – that the kiss had been a mistake. He'd been gutted, of course, but he'd accepted it too, retreating back behind his line and never trying for a repeat – for, rather to his surprise, her friendship had become as important to him as her love. Even her occasional flings with other men hadn't tormented him as they might have done, partly because of how she mocked those men behind their backs, making fun of their various shortcomings; but also because he'd come to accept that, while she might not have been the person he'd have chosen to fall in love with, she was the one he had.

In all their years of friendship, he'd only once seriously defied her. That, of course, had been by accepting Aston Farms' invitation to help them survey and excavate this place. But how could he have refused? It would have been a repudiation of everything he'd always stood for. Yet her disapproval had still tormented him. The fear that she'd cut him off for good. So it was little wonder, then, that he fairly bounced back into the processing room, enough for Melissa to eye him curiously.

'Have you had good news?' she asked.

'I have, rather,' he confessed. But he didn't elaborate, beckoning instead for her and Anna to follow him through to the next room along, which had also been taken over by the excavation, with more shelving against its walls and another pair of worktables in the centre, though these were side-by-side rather than end-to-end, and covered by an array of cork-boards to which a huge surveyor's map had been pinned, on which he himself had outlined Grove Farm in thick red felt-tip, before festooning it with colour-coded pins.

'Are these all your survey hits?' asked Anna, leaning over it.

'Not all of them,' he told her. 'If we'd done it that way, it would be nothing but pins. These are just the most promising ones. I had great hopes when I started, that it would give us an idea of how the fighting went. But it's chaos, as you can see. That's the trouble with battlefield archaeology, of course. It's overwhelming.'

'Battlefield archaeology?' asked Melissa. 'Is it its own discipline?'

'It is, rather,' he said. 'If you think about it, most field archaeology involves a *settlement* of some kind. A house, a village, a community. Our job as excavators is to find out how the people there lived, and how that changed over time. The ways they sheltered, what kind of pottery they used, which foods they ate. Their communal buildings, who they traded with, their burial customs. It's a kind of saga, if you like, unfolding over generations. Battlefields aren't like that. They were often chosen precisely because they were wide open spaces with nothing in the way. You'd have one furious explosion of activity that left debris everywhere. Broken swords and snapped off spearheads. Helmets and horseshoes and bits of armour. Medallions and brooches and lucky charms that hadn't exactly proved their worth. Teeth and bones and the rest, all swallowed by the mud. Then, just as quickly, it would have gone quiet again. "The moving finger writes, and having writ, moves on."' He turned to Anna. 'You know that line, of course? And who wrote it? Or translated it, should I say?'

'The Rubáiyát?' frowned Anna, surprised to be put to the test. 'And Edward Fitzgerald. But why do you ask?'

'He was an archaeologist too, did you know?' he told her. 'An amateur one, to be sure – they all were back then, of course – but a fine one nonetheless. His family owned huge tracts of land around Naseby, where the Civil War battle was fought. He excavated it himself, and he did such a fine job that he came to be known as the father of battlefield archaeology.'

'Now that I didn't know,' admitted Anna.

'Me neither, if I'm honest. Not until this project got underway, and I looked around for guidance. Precious few battlefields have ever been excavated, you see. Almost none from as early as this. Their locations have typically been lost, for a start. And what remains is a nightmare to decipher. But we're lucky here. If this really was Mount Badon, it was a siege first and foremost, and so went on for at least a few days. More likely weeks and possibly even months, because we've found traces of a well on the hill, suggesting they had their own water supply. Then you had the battle on top of that. Plus of course there's the clayey nature of the soil, which has preserved it all remarkably well.'

'But it's such a mess,' said Melissa. 'How can you even hope to make sense of it?'

'It's not easy,' he admitted. 'We have so little to go on. We don't even know for sure who the two sides were, or who was besieging whom. Not yet, at least. But that's precisely the sort of thing we're hoping to discover.'

'How?'

'Well, it's likely that the side nearest the hill was the one defending it. Sometimes you can find writing or symbols on their weapons. We haven't found anything like that yet, but you never know.' He went over to the shelves, checked several of the smallest of the acid-free boxes until he found the one he was after, brought it back over to show them. A small grey pellet shaped like a tiny lemon was lying on a bed of tissue paper. 'A lead slingshot bullet,' he told them. 'They used stones too, but the lead ones were best. Too small for the other side to see coming, yet still heavy enough to inflict real damage. They used to drill holes through some of them, so that they'd make a whistling noise as they flew. Must have been terrifying.'

'And how does that help?' asked Melissa.

He turned it over with his fingertip to show them the crude picture of a bird on its underside. 'Maybe this is just a bird, to represent how it flies through the air. But doves were also important early Christian symbols, which would make it Brittonic rather than Saxon. We can't be sure one way or the other with this, but people sometimes scratched short messages on them too, like gun-loaders with their munitions. You know the kind of thing: "Take this, Adolf." "Up yours."'

'Embrace each day as if it is your last?'

'Well, yes,' smiled Quentin. 'That's probably a little wordy for something this small. But you get the general idea. And the two sides used different scripts, you see, so anything like that would tell us for sure who the battle was between, and maybe even who was besieging whom.'

'Assuming it really is Mount Badon,' said Anna.

'Yes,' acknowledged Quentin. 'Assuming that.'

SEVEN

Elias drove down to the end of Grove Farm's drive then pulled in to the lay-by opposite. Wynn Grant gazed coolly at him as he parked and got out then came across to where he was still sitting on his camping chair, beanie on his head and his hands stuffed into the pockets of his winter jacket, zipped up to his throat against the increasingly chilly wind. 'Mind if I join you?' he asked.

'Public land, isn't it?' said Wynn, gazing Elias up and down. 'Police?'

'Not any more.'

'Why not? They catch you framing some poor bastard?'

'They don't fire us for that. They promote us instead.'

Wynn gave a snort. 'Fine. Please yourself.'

'Thank you.' He squatted down alongside him, the pair of them facing towards Grove Farm's drive. 'So I was talking with your mate Quentin just now,' he said. 'He tells me you used to be an addict.'

'Still am,' said Wynn, with mock piety. 'Just not using right now. Isn't that what I'm supposed to say?'

'You go to meetings?'

'God, no. They bore my tits off, those do. You need a bottle of whisky just to get through them. Anyway, what's the point? I'm off the junk, thank Christ. It messed me up. But I still need pills for the pain, and they'll only ever take the bottle out of my cold dead hands.'

'So was it you who pissed through Ms Ward's letterbox the other night?'

'Hah. You don't mess about, do you? No, to answer your question. That wasn't me. Why would I? Woman's only doing her job. It's that arsehole Ravi Pandey I'd go after, if I was to go after anyone. He deserves all the shit he gets. But I couldn't have managed it, even had I wanted to. I mean, come on. That time of the morning, it's a miracle if I can hit my own bowl, which is a good foot around. If you think I'm going to hold my bladder while trekking five miles through the darkness to piss on some bird's doormat… Come on. Don't make me laugh.'

'What about the other stuff?'

'What other stuff?'

Elias nodded across the way at Grove Farm. 'Painting graffiti on the walls. Supergluing equipment. Smearing shit on Quentin's windscreen.'

This last one made him scowl. 'No,' he said angrily. 'I'd never mess with Quentin like that. He's the only one of these bastards who ever stood up for me, or came to visit. Anyway, why would I make it that easy for them?'

'Make what easy? For whom?'

He waved a hand. 'For them, for them. To yank me back inside. Sitting here's one thing. It's public land. They'll never revoke my parole for that, not with the prisons so full. But the kind of shit you're talking about…? I mean life outside isn't all sunbeams and rose petals, but it's the Seychelles compared to being inside.'

Elias nodded. 'That's what Quentin said. He said you never killed your brother either. That you were railroaded.'

Grant's eyes filled with moisture. He wiped it irritably away. 'And so I was,' he said. 'I was bombed out of my mind when they told me about Caleb. I felt sick and confused, guilty and devastated all at once. I was on the junk back then too. Aching for my next fix. They came at me in teams, painting this picture of how it had happened, repeating it and repeating it until it felt like a proper memory. Then they told me I could go if I signed their piece of paper, at least for the moment. And that's the thing about junk. It becomes all you ever think about. So I signed their bloody piece of paper, and they promptly arrested me and locked me up. Bastards. But at least it cleared my head, enough for my memory to come back. And I never touched Caleb. I never pushed him down those sodding steps. I wasn't even in his house when they said. I know it for a fact.'

'How so?'

'I used to lie on my sofa with the TV on. Not watching it exactly. For the company of voices. So I thought to check the listings for the time I was supposedly seen coming out of Caleb's house, and they had one of those Channel 5 movies on. You know the ones – awful yet somehow impossible to turn off. And I'd watched it all the way through. I even remembered how it ended. So it couldn't have been me, could it? But it was too late by then. No one believed me, not even my own bloody mouthpiece, useless streak of piss that he was. Getting them to play that bloody phone call! How were the jury supposed to believe me after that? Then letting them steal my farm from me too.'

'No one stole it. Aston Farms bought it fair and square.'

'From people who had no right to it. Caleb left it to *me*, not some arsehole cousins we'd never even met.' His eyes went distant; his jaw set hard. 'So it's still mine, isn't it? By rights it's still mine. As is all that shit they're digging up. I'll get it back too. I swear to god I will. I'm going to clear my name and make the bastards pay.'

'How?'

'That'd be telling, wouldn't it? But just you watch. Just you watch.' He drained his cup then unscrewed his thermos to pour himself a refill. Gin from the smell of it, though so little left that he tossed it straight back in disgust. He laboured to his feet, made his way over to the gate behind them with an oddly rhythmic walk, rising up onto his tiptoes to protect his bad right knee. There was a bike tucked away on the other side of the hedge that Elias hadn't noticed. An e-bike at that, fitted with a front hamper and a rear basket, enough to carry a decent sized shop, and likely his only transport, on the fairly safe assumption that he'd have lost his licence somewhere along the line. He took a fresh bottle of cheap gin from the hamper, held it up. 'Keeps it out of the sun,' he said.

'What sun?' asked Elias.

'It was there when I left home.' He made his way back across with the same peculiar limp. 'Tastes like dog's piss when it's warm. Pretty much tastes like it straight out of the freezer too, if I'm honest, only you don't notice it so much.'

'Then why not vodka?'

'Costs more.' He unscrewed the cap and poured himself a generous slug before tucking the bottle away beneath his chair. 'I'd offer you a nip too, if only you weren't driving. Wouldn't want to cause an accident, would I?'

'How very public spirited of you.'

'Yeah. What can I say?' He raised his cup in farewell. 'Always thinking of other people, that's me.'

EIGHT

Melissa might look dressed for a garden party, but she'd also come prepared for a spot of fieldwork too – not least because she hadn't yet seen the villa, or its famous mosaic. She replaced her Verona jacket with a far more practical hooded green Barbour from the boot of her Audi, then sat sideways on the passenger seat to trade her high heeled black leather boots for a pair of tall green Hunter wellies. Anna, meanwhile, shared an anxious glance with Quentin, for the sky had turned an ominous battleship grey, while the wind was growing both colder and fiercer, coming down from the north in biting hard gusts.

They crossed the courtyard to a dirt track that – just a month or two ago – would have passed between a pair of large outbuildings; but both of these had since been torn down and their foundations ripped up, great slabs of brick and concrete half buried in the roiled earth. Quentin pointed out to her the site of the body-pit as they passed it, not that it was necessary, for shreds of blue and white police tape still fluttered from a cordon of metal stakes. Then they passed through the line of firs into the nearest of the fields. 'You should have seen all this before they got the mowers in,' he told Anna. 'It hadn't been farmed in years, what with all the legal wrangling going on, and then the planning disputes. It was a jungle. Wild grasses everywhere. Nettles and brambles up to your chin. We even had a few saplings and some patches of bamboo. Honestly, you needed a machete even to take the dog for a walk. Wonderful for the wildlife, of course. We had all sorts. Hares and muntjacs and badgers. And rabbits too, of course. They bred like... well, I'll leave it to you to fill in the blank. And so colourful too, particularly at this time of year. Like a great big Monet canvas, dotted with dabs of bright spring flowers. Huge daisies and wild garlic; bluebells and cowslips; primroses and lady's smocks and those prickly mauve thistles. And the butterflies! My god, the butterflies! But it all needed to go, sadly. I thought it would take them weeks, but they brought in a pair of huge industrial mowers and got it all done in a day. Necessary, of course, but still terribly sad, particularly for all those animals. I hate it, being the cause of suffering like that.'

Anna stopped a moment, to scrape off some of the mud that had already clumped to her boots. 'And your ground penetrating radar worked okay?' she asked.

'It was brilliant,' nodded Quentin. 'But it's a huge area, as you can see, so we had a ton of data to go through. And while the GPS it's fitted with is far better than the one you'll likely have on your phone, even that is only really accurate to about a yard or so. Then you have to remember that each rainstorm over the past fifteen hundred years has brought a little more mud down from off the hillside to lay upon these fields, burying all our artefacts that fraction deeper, meaning that everything is at least four feet underground, usually a fair bit more. Thankfully, we already had a mechanical digger on site, which Ravi has very generously kept on, and which makes amazingly light work of it. I can work it myself, if push comes to shove, but he's also very generously paid for our operator Nigel to come in on any days when he's not needed elsewhere. And we've got him so hooked that he's volunteered this weekend for free.'

'Ha!' laughed Anna. 'We get them all in the end.'

'Quite. Though frankly his job is much more exciting than mine. I'm mostly stuck indoors, trying to identify promising sites for him to work. What he does is, he skims off six inches of earth at a time until my two metal detectors can pick up whatever it was that our survey flagged for us. Then it's over to our volunteers to get busy with their trowels and brushes. All a bit crude, I know, but we have a crazy amount of ground to cover, and so little time. I promised Ravi we'd be out within a month, you see, one way or the other. And he's been so helpful that I mean to stick to that. Besides, our volunteers won't keep coming forever.'

They trekked diagonally across the field along a footpath helpfully trampled for them by a multitude of previous feet, eventually reaching the tarpaulin tent she'd watched being put up earlier, its sides already being pressed taut by the wind. Quentin untethered a rope then pulled back a flap to let them see inside, proud as a smallholder showing off his prize pumpkin. Anna ducked her head to go within. The tent was only a little longer and wider than the trench it was there to cover, so that the struts and frames holding it up were awkwardly set, making her worry for it if the night's storm proved as fierce as predicted.

A little daylight filtered through the open mouth, but it was still gloomy enough that she took out her phone for its torch and shone it down at the foot of the trench some four feet beneath her. The base of an ancient wall ran alongside a line of flagstones and then part of a pebble mosaic showing the lower halves of a man and woman seated side by side on a pair of thrones, wearing matching sandals and white togas with a coloured band near the hem.

Anna had excavated a Roman villa herself once, and so was somewhat familiar with their mosaic styles. This one had a geometric border of a kind that had become fashionable in London at the turn of the fourth century CE, though it had likely taken longer to make it all the way out here. Mid fourth century, then, give or take thirty or forty years, and in a wonderful state of preservation, the tesserae gleaming and glistening in her torchlight.

'I had no idea,' said Melissa, turning to Quentin. 'Those photographs you sent. They didn't remotely do it justice.'

'We've given it a clean since then,' he said, chuffed by her reaction. 'Though mostly it's luck, to be honest. These old villas were typically abandoned after the Romans left, because they were such easy targets, and impossible to defend. So they quickly fell into disrepair. Their roofs fell in, opening their floors up to the elements. They cracked and grew dull. Not this one. This one was burned instead. You'd think that would cause more damage, wouldn't you? Not a bit of it. Its thatched roof would have gone up wonderfully, laying a carpet of ash over the floor. And then the first rains would have turned that ash into a hard shell that has protected it ever since. Wonderful, isn't it?'

'Amazing,' said Anna. 'How far does it extend?'

'We don't know yet, not for sure. We don't have the resources to excavate it properly right now, not with everything else that needs doing. And we can always come back. But we've found suggestions of structures of one kind or another in pretty much every direction from here. This was a big place, it turns out.'

Anna nodded and reached her torch a little further down into the pit, to spotlight the two seated figures. 'Those coloured bands on their hems,' she frowned, looking back up at him. 'They're not porphyry, are they?'

'What an excellent eye you have,' grinned Quentin.

'Bloody hell,' said Anna.

'I told you, didn't I?'

'What is it?' asked Melissa, looking back and forth between the pair of them, sensing the excitement but without understanding its cause. 'What am I missing?'

Anna hesitated, for it wasn't her place to say. But Quentin nodded for her to go ahead. 'Porphyry is the stone the Romans used to indicate the colour purple,' she said.

'Purple?' said Melissa. 'But wasn't that the colour of emperors?'

'Well, exactly,' said Anna. It hadn't been the colour itself that had so appealed to them, so much as the difficulty of making the dye, which had come from a species of sea snail called murex found almost exclusively around Tyre. Vast quantities of these snails had been gathered up and tossed into huge tanks where they'd been left to rot and liquefy, producing both a gorgeous rich dye and a stomach-turning stench. The amount of labour involved in producing even small quantities had given Tyre a monopoly of the trade, making the dye so absurdly expensive that only the very richest or most powerful could afford it. Emperors grew so jealous of the prestige it conferred that they passed laws banning others from wearing it. But those laws soon enough frayed around the edges. Their children and grandchildren began embroidering the hems of their robes and togas with it. Then tribunes and senators and even the leaders of military units had taken to wearing it too. It had still remained incredibly expensive and exclusive, however, though that wasn't the reason finding it here was so significant. The reason finding it here was so significant was that one of the very few things known for sure about Ambrosius Aurelianus – the most promising of the real-life candidates for King Arthur – was that his parents had worn the purple.

NINE

As a fellow detective had once joked to Elias, if you couldn't trust a junkie, who could you trust? Yet he'd found Wynn Grant oddly convincing, particularly his anger at being accused of smearing dog-shit on Quentin's windscreen, one of the very few people who'd stayed loyal to him. And if someone else had been responsible for that, then they surely made a far better suspect for Melissa's letterbox, even discounting the five mile trek that Wynn would have had to make with a bursting bladder on an e-bike in the dark. It was still possible he'd been behind the graffiti and the vandalism, of course, as well as the anonymous threats – though what big risks to take for such limited satisfaction. As for digging holes in the fields, that was surely far too much like hard work. As Quentin had suggested, those were more likely the work of some random nighthawk after treasure.

The afternoon was pressing on. The storm was drawing closer. He drove back over the M4 and into Swindon, then found an underground car park for the Leaf. The King's Head was indeed situated between a mall and a cinema, its small front garden given a little shelter by the brick walls on either side and the retractable awning above. Three young men were drinking at one of its outside tables, warming themselves on a space heater, but they seemed peaceable enough. He checked them against the photos of Archie Miller that Quentin had sent through, but none were a match. Nor was anyone inside.

He needed to buy dinner, so he took a trolley for a walk down the aisles of a supermarket in search of inspiration. Pasta was his go-to, but he rarely got to eat with Anna, and wanted something special. She'd raved about a seafood broth they'd been served at the Anglo-Saxon feast they'd attended during the Beowulf affair, so he searched for recipes on his phone until he found one that closely matched it, then went hunting for ingredients. He bought cuts of salmon and haddock from the fishmongers stall, added bags of scallops, mussels, king prawns and crab legs. Some shallots, a tub of cream, butter, olive oil, fish stock, parsley, garlic, lemongrass, fennel, a small pack of hot chillis and a loaf of crusty bread. The aim of the dinner was to get Samantha to dish dirt upon her neighbours, and it was on expenses anyway, so he added three bottles of Rioja and another three of Chablis. Then he settled up and packed it all away in his boot, and was about to set off back to base when he thought to give the King's Head another try.

Four more young men had joined the previous three at the outside table, somehow turning them into a gang, brasher, rowdier and more intimidating. He checked Quentin's pictures again. One of the new arrivals was indeed Archie Miller, though he looked different from the family shots, his hair cut into a high-top fade, a little teenage fluff on his chin and upper lip, and hunched inside a ski jacket two sizes too big for him. A movie was about to start. They began jeering at the cinema-goers as they arrived. 'Oi, babe,' one yelled at a woman meeting her date upon the steps. 'Dump that ugly loser and come talk to us. We'll show you a proper time.'

Elias watched them for another minute or so. They were of that unsettling age: Children in their laughter, adult in their menace. He found himself growing pleasantly nervous, like when he'd touched gloves with some unknown opponent before the first bell. There was a swagger he'd used as a detective that had announced his status better than his warrant card had ever done. He adopted it now as he strode up to their table. It did the trick beautifully, for they mistook him instantly for authority, quietening at once, looking anywhere but at him, no doubt wondering which of their petty crimes had brought him here. He stared at the Miller boy until finally he looked up and met his gaze. 'Archie, isn't it?' he asked. 'Archie Miller?'

'What's it to you?' asked one of the others. He looked to be the oldest, maybe nineteen or twenty, wiry of build and wearing an expensive leather jacket, jeans and trainers, a black motorbike helmet with bright red flashes on the floor beside his chair. His features and complexion suggested a mix of ethnicities much like Elias's own, yet – unlike Elias – he'd come out of the blender blessed with uncommon good looks, his high cheekbones and shrewd dark eyes given a little theatrical menace by a scar on his upper lip. The leader of this little gang, if Elias had to guess, and for sure the one Archie Miller was modelling himself on, if their matching haircuts were any guide. That said, the one next to him needed watching too. Tall and powerfully muscled, with bright red hair, a broken nose and uneven teeth. He had the look of an enforcer. Ready to supply the bite whenever the other barked. 'My name's Elias,' he told them. 'Detective Ben Elias. And yours?'

'Piss off.'

'You want to turn out your pockets for me?' he asked. Then he looked around at the rest of them. 'Anyone? No? Then shut up.' He turned back to Archie Miller. 'I need a word. Let's take a walk.'

'Are you some kind of paedo?'

'Are you some kind of rent boy?'

'Screw you. I've got nothing to say.'

'Yeah, you do. And you either give me five minutes now or we can spend the evening down the station. I'll bring in all your mates here too, just to make them hate you for ruining their night. Your call.'

'What's this even about?'

'About how you used Melissa Ward's letterbox as a urinal.' He glanced around as he said this, to gauge the general reaction. The one with the bike helmet gave a snort, his sidekick stared impassively, but two of the others looked away in shame, giving Elias all the confirmation he needed. He took advantage of their discomfort to make his way around the table, grab Miller by his shoulder and haul him to his feet. The two dangerous ones half stood up, but he sat them back down again with a glare. Then he led Miller away off down the pavement until they were out of sight.

'This is battery,' protested Miller. 'This is police brutality.'

Elias laughed. 'Seriously? Just how soft are you? Anyway, I'm not police. Not any more.'

'You're not? Then what the hell?' He tore himself free and doubtless would have returned to the King's Head, except that Elias stepped across his path. So he turned and set off the other way instead.

'Two minutes!' said Elias, following close behind. 'Just two minutes. Then you can go back to your mates.'

'Sod off.'

'I only want to talk. Melissa's my friend, you see. She just wants to know why you and your mates did that the other night.'

'Did what? We never did nothing.'

'Come on. Don't bother denying it. The family across the road have a doorbell camera. You're all on it, clear as day.'

'Bollocks, we are.'

'You are, I'm afraid. But I'm the only one who's seen it so far. And I won't give it to the police if you just talk to me. I won't even show your parents. You have my word.'

He slowed at that, but shook his head. 'Nothing to talk about. It wasn't us.'

'Her kids were asleep upstairs. Did you know that? Her two young daughters. Now she can't sleep at night. She's terrified they're going to burn.'

He turned around to face Elias, though still walking away, hunched in his hoodie and with his hands stuffed in his pockets so that Elias could see how he'd shaped them into fists. 'It was only a bit of piss, for god's sake. How's piss going to burn?'

'She didn't know that. Not when you dropped in that match.'

'That wasn't me. I never did that.'

'I believe you. I do. But it doesn't matter which one of you it was. What matters is that it happened. Come on. You seem like a nice enough kid. Look at it from her point of view. How is she to know it wasn't a threat? How is she to know it won't be petrol next time?'

'Don't be daft. It was a bit of fun, that's all. We're not murderers.'

'Yeah. But like I say: how's she to know that?'

'Tell her, if you like. Tell her from me.'

'It won't mean anything, coming from me. It has to be from you.'

'Screw that. No way.' He turned around again, making sure to keep a good few steps ahead. He had a rocking way of walking, as if talking to himself, building himself up. The rain finally started, but only in a light mist that swirled in the car headlights and put a sheen on each of their faces, slowly turning the pavement a darker shade of grey. The streets had largely emptied, too, and some of the lanes and alleys they were taking were narrow, poorly-lit and just a little bit menacing, so that Elias began, perhaps belatedly, to wonder if he wasn't being deliberately led somewhere.

He began to wonder if he wasn't walking into some kind of trap.

TEN

Anna and Quentin were still explaining to Melissa the significance of the purple band on the hem of the two togas when a tall, ruddy-faced, middle-aged woman in gumboots, baggy blue jeans with worn knees, a cream sweatshirt and a blue waterproof jacket came striding towards them across the field. 'There you are, Quentin!' she cried. 'I've been looking for you everywhere.'

'Whatever for?' asked Quentin, with enough exasperation to suggest that she was always looking for him, for one reason or another.

'You have to come with me,' she said. 'There's something you need to see.'

'I'm busy, Betty,' he sighed. 'Can't you just tell me?'

'No.' She was close enough now that Anna could see that it wasn't just cold that had put such colour into her cheeks. It was excitement too. 'You have to see this for yourself. Dave said I absolutely wasn't to come back without you. He needs your advice, before the rain starts.'

'Fine,' said Quentin. He lashed the tarpaulin back down then they all set off together for the gap in the hedge that took them into the next field, in the far corner of which the yellow mechanical digger sat with its engine turned off and its bucket raised high, having backed away from the trench it had dug in the ground, around which a small group of archaeologists and volunteers were gathered, and within which a middle-aged man was sitting or kneeling, so that they could only see his head and shoulders.

It was still only mid-afternoon, but it had grown so heavy with cloud that the upstairs lights shone brightly from Sam's B&B. Anna could see Orlando Wren pacing back and forth past his window, no doubt suffering under the tyranny of the empty page. Yet now he paused to stare out. With his light behind him, however, it was impossible for her to tell whether he was watching what was going on below, or merely gazing out into the distance, lost in a brown study. Then the curtains next door twitched too. Samantha was clearly watching as well, though anxious not to be seen.

This field was muddier than the last. Their boots kept clumping so heavily that they kept having to stop to scrape or kick it off. They arrived at the trench to see that it was maybe two feet deep by three feet wide and six feet long, with all the spoil being dumped on the left-hand side for the volunteers to run Quentin's two metal detectors over it, while others squished the clumps between their fingers in search of shards of pottery or anything else non-metallic, the soil being too wet and clayey for sieving.

The man inside the trench proved to be the local museum's David Connelly, kneeling on a strip of soiled matting. He was shaven headed and solidly built, his hands, forearms and face all so smeared with mud that he looked less the distinguished archaeologist than a weekend warrior playing at Special Forces. He'd dug out a smaller pit within the larger with his excavation trowel, exposing the cause of the excitement – the top few inches of a fin of tarnished metal with just a hint of green to it, as though a sickly shark had somehow got trapped beneath the surface. Anna's immediate thought was that a plough or scythe blade had broken off and got buried, and wondered why it warranted such fuss. But then she saw the scratch that had been scored in it, and the silvery metal it had exposed. It had a raised rim, what was more, so smoothly curved that it had surely once been part of a large round object like a platter, only to have been cut up since into smaller parts, as had often happened with such artefacts when they'd come to be valued less for their beauty than for the precious metal they contained, the weight of which had then typically been scratched onto the back of each piece so that they could be used in payment like bulky, misshapen coins.

Silver platters were about the last thing you'd expect to find in the middle of a battlefield – though the nearby villa made it less surprising, of course, for householders had often buried their valuables when enemy armies had drawn too close. Yet that didn't make much sense either, for any such hoards would surely have been buried beneath the battlefield layer, not above it, as this seemed to be.

'Dear god,' muttered Quentin. He tore his eyes off it to look up at the sky instead, the ever darkening clouds, the furious storm they heralded. 'Dear god,' he said again.

'Well, quite,' said Dave, wiping a weary forearm across his brow, rearranging the sweat and mud upon it. 'So what do we do? Stop or go on?'

Quentin gave himself a moment to think. It was one thing for silver to remain buried for centuries. The damage from that was long since done. Moreover, oxidisation had given it a protective patina, much like the ash over the mosaic. But, now that it had been exposed, it was vulnerable once more. Who could say how much additional damage tonight's storm might not do? They could refill the pit with earth, of course, but that would likely do even worse, and was sure to disrupt the context too. Perhaps they should cover it with a canopy, then, as with the mosaic; except they lacked the time to do it properly, if the storm proved anything like as fierce as was predicted, and the rain was certain to seep in anyway. And what if one of the pegs came loose, to be set flapping this way and that by the wind?

There was another risk too. An unlikely one, to be sure, yet potentially devastating. For it seemed probable that treasure hunters had dug up these fields several times already over the past few weeks. And what if they learned of this discovery somehow, and returned in the small hours to steal this for themselves?

'No pictures,' said Quentin abruptly, clearly realising this danger for himself. 'No texts, no social media, not a word to anyone, not even your families. I mean it. This can't go any further.' Their sheepish looks made it clear it was too late, however. Then Melissa made it worse, crouching down right in front of him to take a photograph on her phone then send it off.

'Sorry,' she said, though she didn't sound it. 'This is Ravi's property. He has a right to know.'

'Okay,' sighed Quentin. 'But nothing more, I beg you. We need to keep this to ourselves until we've got it out. I'm serious. I need you all to give me your word. Now.' He looked at them each in turn, even Anna, until they'd nodded or made their pledge some other way. 'Thank you,' he said. But he still looked worried. And little wonder. People who gave up their bank holidays to go excavating made for unlikely antiquity thieves. But what about their friends and families? What about all the people who'd been passing by on the lane, from which this was clearly visible? What about Orlando, or Samantha, or the hikers on the hilltop? What about Wynn Grant, indeed? Any one of them could come back during the night. And while they could perhaps post a guard, what a miserable job *that* would be, and certainly not something they could ask of an elderly nightwatchman. One or more of them would have to camp out here themselves in what was liable to be a particularly vicious electric storm. Even then it might not be enough.

'Well?' asked Dave.

'How deep does it go?' asked Quentin.

'It feels pretty well anchored,' shrugged Dave. 'But I can hardly pull on it, can I? Honestly, your guess is as good as mine. Another few inches, maybe?'

'Can we get it out before the rain starts?'

'If we work fast enough, sure. But how much damage will we do it? How much context will we lose?'

'We'll lose it anyway, once the rain starts. We just need to get it out.'

'We go for it, then?'

'We go for it,' nodded Quentin, happier now that the decision was made. 'You and me. But carefully, carefully.' He picked up a trowel, turned to the volunteers. 'I need two of you filming us as we work. The rest of you, go get that tent off the mosaic. This is more important right now. But see if you can't replace it with a tarpaulin or something. Oh, and we'll need some proper lighting, if there's any in the house.'

'My digger has some lamps,' said Nigel. 'I can bring it in closer.'

'Great,' said Quentin, clambering down into the trench, then stepping carefully over the silver fin to attack it from its other side. 'Then let's get to it.'

ELEVEN

It was indeed a trap, of sorts. Only it was Archie Miller who walked into it. He turned down another alley, presumably expecting it to be open at its far end, only to discover that some utility company had fenced it off to dig it up and get at the pipes beneath. He turned to face Elias, looking like a boy again. 'Stop following me,' he said. 'I'm warning you. Don't come any closer.'

'Or what?' asked Elias.

'I'll smash you,' said Miller. 'I mean it.'

'Don't be an arse. I only want to talk.'

'Yeah. Well. I don't.' He came running towards Elias, as if intending to pass him on his left before sidestepping sharply right. But the alley was narrow and Elias had been a boxer too long to fall for so obvious a feint. He grabbed him by his arm as he went by, swinging him a full 360 degrees until he tripped over his own feet and went down. He jumped straight back up, fists clenched and held up in front of his chin, like he'd seen the pros do. He stepped forwards and threw a roundhouse so laboured and crudely telegraphed that Elias could have cooked dinner in the time it took to arrive. He swayed back to let it scythe the empty air, then stepped in again, while Miller was still off balance, and gave him a tap to the midriff that folded him up like a laptop and dropped him back to the ground. 'Ow,' he said, wheezing and clutching his stomach. 'What was that for?'

Elias laughed. 'Come on. You tried to take my head off. If

you're going to start throwing punches, you need to learn to take them too.'

'What would you know?'

'Enough. I used to box for England.'

'You did? Hell.' But it clearly made him feel better, having a war-story to tell the others.

Elias helped him back to his feet, keeping a hand on his arm, just in case. 'So whose idea was it the other night, then? Yours or your mates? Not that they're up to much as mates, I have to say. Proper ones wouldn't have let me march you off like that.'

'They thought you were police. Anyway, isn't that an offence? Impersonating an officer?'

'You watch too much TV. And we're not talking about me. We're talking about you and Melissa Ward. Because it wasn't you that came up with the idea, was it? You're not mean enough. Don't look so sour. It's a good thing. The way I see it, you were shooting your mouth off about how unfair it all was, these big corporations coming in, screwing you over. Then one of them called you on it, right? Asked you what you were going to do about it. The pretty boy with the red flashes on his helmet, I'd guess? Born troublemaker, that one. And those new trainers, so good for running away on. But it wouldn't have been him who dropped in the match, would it? He's too sly for that. He'd have left it to his red-headed mate.'

'No.'

'You need to put more oomph into your denials, if you want them to be believed. Did you know they were going to do that? When you went over there, I mean?'

'It wasn't like that. We were in the pub having a few beers. I told them what those bastards from Aston Farms are up to. We talked about how someone ought to do something. But it was just talk, you know? Only... only one of the others found out on his phone where that... where Ms. Ward lived. He said we should go over there and foam her car. But none of us were sure what car she drove, so we ended up doing the letterbox thing instead.'

'Who did the actual pissing?'

'None of us. All of us.' He gave a sigh. 'The thing was spring-loaded like a jungle trap. I'd sooner have put my dick in a crocodile. But we had a couple of bottles with us, so we necked those and pissed in them instead, then poured them through that way.'

'Nice.'

'We were drunk, okay. We never meant to scare her.'

'Sure you did. At least have the balls to own it.'

He let out another sigh, so long and heavy that it punctured him like a tyre. 'Yeah, okay. You're right. It was dumb and mean and I've felt like shit about it ever since. Is that what you want to hear?'

'It's what Ms Ward needs to hear. So how about this? Tell her how it happened, admit it was dumb and apologise for it. Apologise properly, I mean. You do that and I'll do my best to make sure that's the end of it.'

'Apologise?'

'Yes, you little brat. Apologise.' The rain had been growing harder all this time, and was now threatening to come pelting down. He had better things to do than drive around Swindon in a storm, searching for a house. 'We'll do it tomorrow morning,' he said. 'Meet me by the gate of Grove Farm, nine-thirty sharp. If she's not there, I'll find out where she is and take you over to see her. Do your bit, do it properly and sincerely, and the police won't ever need to know. Oh, and you can apologise to Quentin Parkes while you're at it, for smearing that dog-shit on his windscreen.'

'No way,' protested Miller. 'I'm not apologising for that.'

'Are you really going to stand there and pretend that wasn't you?'

'No. That was me, all right. I'm just proud of that one, is all. The man's a prick.'

Elias laughed, he couldn't help himself. 'Fair enough,' he said. 'What about all that other stuff? Supergluing the equipment? Painting graffiti all over the house.'

'Nah. Not apologising for those either. They'd only make me pay.'

'Can I tell Aston Farms it won't happen again?'

He considered a moment. 'Yeah. Wouldn't be me, at least. Wouldn't have been anyway, not since they brought Vic in as their nightwatchman. He's always been good to me, Vic has. Wouldn't want to get him into trouble.'

'How about those holes in the field? Did you dig those?'

'Do I look like a bloody navvy?'

'The threats on Aston Farms message board?'

'Nah. Never thought of it, to be honest.'

'How about your parents? Is that more their kind of speed?'

'You want to ask them that, not me.'

'Okay.' It was much as Elias had expected. He gave him a card from his wallet, to contact him in case of problems. 'Tomorrow morning, then. Are you on?'

'Yeah. I guess.' He hesitated a moment, almost shyly, then asked. 'Did you really box for England?'

'Look it up on your phone, if you don't believe me. Name's Ben Elias. Almost made the Olympics once, only it turned out I was a cocky little shit, just like you. I didn't take my opponent seriously enough, so he put me on the floor. Just like I did you.'

'You certainly know how to punch,' said Miller.

'That?' scoffed Elias. 'That was barely even a love tap. You want to know what a proper punch feels like, go down your gym. I'll take you, if you like?'

'What? Why?'

'Because it'd be fun watching you get the shit kicked out of you by a kid half your size. Might also do you some good as well. I was an arse, too, when I was your age.'

'So it doesn't always help, then?'

'Oi!' laughed Elias, turning to head back to his car. 'Grove Farm. Nine-thirty sharp. See you there.'

TWELVE

The rain arrived in a gentle mist that allowed Anna, Melissa and several of the volunteers enough time to steal the tarpaulin tent from over the mosaic and set it up above the trench instead, working around Dave and Quentin as they pared the mud away from the silver platter. No one could find a mallet, so they twisted the poles in with their hands instead, and stamped down the pegs with their boots. The clayey soil was yielding enough that everything went in easily enough, though Anna couldn't help but worry what would happen once the storm began in earnest.

They pinned back the flaps to allow in light from the digger's lamps, then crowded into the tight space, filming Dave and Quentin at work, checking the spoils as they were peeled away. Despite the growing chill, exertion and the press of bodies kept them warm – at least until the storm properly arrived, its fierce cold gusts pressing the tarpaulin walls hard against the struts, making them bow alarmingly. One of the tent's flaps became unpinned, plunging them into darkness before Anna fixed it back again. The rain became a deluge, thundering like a waterfall around them, sweeping in through the tent's open mouth and oozing beneath its walls. They looked uneasily at one another, wondering whether they were doing the right thing. Yet it was too late to stop now, despite the platter being plugged deeper into the ground than any of them had imagined possible, and trickier to clear too, for it was ripped around its edges in places, and crumpled in others, demanding far greater care than the conditions allowed. Quentin and Dave did their very best, striving not to touch the platter itself, but rather working like sculptors, peeling away the clay around it to reveal the shape inside. Perfection was impossible, however. The earth was too infused with the silver oxide that had bled into it over the years, making it hard to see what was artefact and what was soil. To complicate matters still further, Quentin came across a lump in the platter's surface, as though a tractor wheel had driven straight over it at some point, embedding a small pebble deep in it. He licked his thumb and gave it a rub before shining a torch upon it at an angle, causing all their hearts to skip a beat when it gave off the bright blue twinkle of a sapphire. And it was only the first of many such gemstones, some scratched or dulled with age, but others glittering with rainbow colours.

The rain by now was pooling heavily in their tarpaulin roof. They had to keep pushing it up from beneath to clear it, so that it splashed noisily down the sides then ran in beneath the walls and into the trench itself. Betty ran back to the house for a pair of mugs and a small saucepan to bail it out with, but it still filled up faster than they could clear it. The platter, meanwhile, was growing ever larger and more complex in shape, until finally it became clear that it wasn't a platter at all, but rather a bowl made up from a number of different leaves, most of which had ripped along their seams before being flattened into a kind of starfish shape by the weight of earth, so that—

'Dear god!' muttered Melissa.

Anna looked across the trench at her. She was kneeling on the ground, indifferent to the mud seeping through the knees of her designer trousers, checking the spoils as Quentin and Dave peeled them away to make sure that nothing was being missed. Just as well, for now she was holding up a small round object that she'd found in one such discarded clump, and had rinsed off, the better to see. A coin, the size of a thumbnail, with an unmistakable rich yellow gleam. And suddenly the possibility that had been floating around unsaid took solid form. For this new discovery surely meant that there wasn't just a bowl down there, but rather a hoard of some kind.

This supposition was confirmed barely a minute later when Quentin exposed the top of an earthenware jar overspilling with more coins, some small and fat and gold, others broader yet thinner and with the distinctive greenish-black patina of Roman silver. The excavation went on. Melissa gave a cry of frustration when she could no longer put off going to collect her two girls from her parents, who were already running late for an important drinks party of their own. But it would have taken the outbreak of a small war to get any of the others to leave.

Earthenware was far more robust than silver. Quentin therefore allowed himself rather more licence as he worked to free the jar, scraping away the earth from around it with quick bold strokes until he could get his hands on either side of it. He lifted it carefully up and out, then passed it up to Anna, taking her by surprise with its weight; for though it was barely the size of a small loaf, it was so packed with coins that it made her arms tremble.

Quentin shone his torch into the hole it had left behind and gave a grunt of disbelief. A jewelled brooch was lying there in plain view for all to see, along with what looked like a crumpled golden goblet and the edge of a small silver plate. Again the question was forced upon them – to carry on with the excavation or wait for morning. But their improvised tarpaulin tent looked less and less likely to survive the storm; and, besides, none of them had any appetite for stopping now.

'We need someone in the farmhouse,' said Quentin, looking meaningfully at Anna. 'To log it all as it comes in. Photograph it, box it, maybe even start on basic conservation.'

'You want me to do it?' asked Anna.

'You're the next most experienced.'

'No worries. However I can help.'

The rain was still thundering down. She snuggled the jar of coins to her chest and zipped her jacket up around it to protect it as best she could. Then she set off for the house, walking as steadily as conditions allowed to make sure she didn't spill anything, letting herself get absolutely drenched in the process. Betty came with her, hurrying ahead to hold open the front door. They made their way through to the processing room, then found a hand-towel in the downstairs bathroom with which to dry themselves off a little before getting down to work.

Some more coins arrived. Then rings, brooches, clasps and other small items of jewellery, followed by the golden goblet Anna had glimpsed, and the silver saucer too. She photographed each piece on one of the work tables, dabbed off the worst of the clayey wash before logging it on a form then packing it away on a bed of tissue paper in its own acid-free box. The stream of artefacts finally slowed and stopped. Only the silver bowl itself now remained, proving to be far larger and deeper than any of them had at first imagined, and which now seemed to have been used as a kind of basket into which all these other artefacts had been gathered before being buried – except that it had tipped onto its side somehow, before being torn, twisted and crumpled by the weight of earth upon it, and the passage of fifteen hundred years.

The front door banged. Betty hurried breathlessly in. 'They want one of our tables,' she cried.

Anna looked at her in bewilderment. 'A table? What for?'

'For carrying the bowl on. And hurry, hurry! The tarpaulin's about to go. The pegs are all pulling out.'

Anna nodded. She cleared the left hand worktable, turned it onto its side, folded up its legs. They took an end each and hurried outside with it, the wind howling and the rain coming down with astonishing force, as though some sky god had tipped over his bath. They splashed between the outbuildings then through the gap in the hedge. Lightning lit up the northern sky. Instinctively, Anna started the count in her head, reaching eleven before she heard the first low rumble of thunder. The digger still sat there with its bucket up and lamps on, light glittering off the puddles that had formed everywhere, already joining into small lakes. As Betty had feared, the tarpaulin was indeed collapsing, the wind turning it into a great sail, plucking the pegs from the muddy ground as fast as the volunteers could grab them and stamp them back in.

She let go of the table to run ahead. It was mayhem inside, the trench several inches deep in rainwater with more pouring in all the time, the tarpaulin bellying dangerously far inwards, its loose flaps cracking like whips. A pair of volunteers were on their knees beside the trench, holding the bowl steady as Dave and Quentin worked to free it fully from the mud. Anna knelt beside them. The bowl was huge and largely still intact. A base plate at its heart looked to be some ten inches across, with eight cambered edges, from each of which a leaf would once have risen up to create an eight-sided bowl. Seven of these leaves were still attached – though mostly torn from one another – but the eighth was missing, presumably still buried somewhere else in all this mud. The lower part of each leaf was studded with beads or gemstones, though they were all too covered in slurry right now for her to be sure which. And some kind of design had been engraved into their upper parts, though again it was impossible to make out beneath the muck.

'What a disaster,' muttered Quentin, when he saw Anna arrive. 'What was I thinking?'

She gave his shoulder a squeeze, but no real comfort was possible, not until the bowl was safely out. He and Dave returned to their task once more, splashing water aside simply so that they could see what they were doing. Anna tried to bail it out with a cup, but it poured back in just as fast. At last it was almost out, however, with only a tiny bit of rim still trapped, at which point Dave simply lost patience and pulled it free.

The tarpaulin had by now almost completely collapsed, with the volunteers themselves holding it up above their heads. Quentin, Dave and Anna lifted the bowl out of the trench between them. It wasn't heavy so much as awkward: twisted and fragile with its seams barely holding together, so that they had to support it carefully from beneath. They took it outside to the table, which had been laid upside down on the ground with its legs extended once more, serving as props to hold up a groundsheet that someone had found, creating as dry and sheltered a space as the dreadful conditions allowed.

They were just in time, for the tarpaulin now collapsed behind them before being caught like a hot-air balloon by the wind, dragging it off across the field, trailing pegs and poles. A pair of volunteers grabbed it before it could do any damage, gathering it up in their arms then carrying it off to the house. Quentin and Dave, meanwhile, briskly ran the two metal detectors over the exposed pit, to make sure they'd got everything. The silence, perversely, came as a relief rather than a disappointment. The field was too waterlogged and pitted with trenches to be driving the digger, and they had far too much to carry already, so they stowed the detectors and some other equipment away in its cab, turned off its lamps. Then they gathered up all the remaining gear before lifting the table like so many casket bearers and carrying it back through the storm to the house, tipping the rainwater from the groundsheet every so often before it could pool and cause problems.

More lightning shuddered away to the north, closer than before. They reached the courtyard even as the last peal of thunder died away. The tabletop was a fraction wider than the front door. They had to tip it slightly and fold down its left-hand legs a little way to fit it through. But then they were inside, laying it on the hallway floor, passing around the towel from the downstairs bathroom to wipe off their hands and faces.

Quentin stripped back the groundsheet so that they could all gaze upon the torn and twisted bowl, still coated in its wash of watery mud, yet magnificent even so. 'What the hell do we do now?' he muttered.

'We can't keep it here,' said Dave. 'We just can't. It's too wet and fragile and important.' He gestured towards the nearest sash window and then the front door, the lock on which looked as if it would give way to a good firm kick. 'Not to mention too insecure. We need to get it safe. We need to start on conservation. And not tomorrow morning. Now. Tonight.'

Quentin gave a grimace. He wasn't just the most experienced archaeologist here, he was also the on-site representative of Ravi Pandey, legal owner of these pieces, at least for the moment. Ceding possession by allowing their transfer to the museum could open him up to serious personal consequences. Yet his sense of duty was too strong. 'Can you even get people in tonight?' he asked.

'Sure. Pam and Anish are both around.'

'What about their bank holidays? Don't they have families?'

'Come on. They'd sacrifice them to the great god Ba'al for a shot at this.'

'Okay,' said Quentin. 'Let's do it.'

Dave nodded then ran back out into the rain, backing his van up against the farmhouse then throwing open its rear doors. It was designed for freight as well as people, with fold-up benches on either side. They began by laying the boxed-up artefacts upon its floor like a flagstone patio, the better to keep them still in transit, and were still at it when a battered Fiat 500 came bumping up the drive, its driver stopping by the gate to unlock it and haul it open before driving on in and parking.

'Vic,' Quentin told Anna, as he came hurrying over. 'Our nightwatchman.'

He had his waterproof hood pulled up over his head, yet she could see enough of his face to enjoy his reaction when he saw the silver bowl being carried out to the van, still on its upturned table. 'My god,' he said.

'I know,' grinned Quentin, clapping him on his back. 'Isn't it amazing? And it's not just this bowl. We've found a whole hoard of the most wonderful stuff. Just astonishing. But it's possible there are more pieces still down there, or close by – so not a word to anyone, okay? We can't afford even a whisper to get out. Not until we've checked the whole area.'

'Of course,' said Vic, still looking stunned. 'Of course.'

'We're taking it all off to the museum tonight. Not a reflection on you in any way. It's just far too important to risk. And we need to start on conservation.'

The van was loaded and ready to leave. It was not a night for prolonged farewells, so Dave and his volunteers waved goodbye even as they clambered into the van. Then they set off through the open gate, their headlights jolting wildly as they bumped down the potholed drive to the lane.

THIRTEEN

The heavy rain had turned into a deluge even as Elias had been making his way back to the Leaf. He'd had to sprint the last hundred yards to the underground car park. Even so, he'd brought so much dampness inside with him that his windscreen promptly misted up, as it was prone to do. He put the heater on full blast and lowered his windows until it had cleared; but it still misted up again the moment he drove out into the rain, so that he had to make a mitten of his sleeve and rub himself a viewing hole through which to see.

He took it slowly, as did all the other traffic. He made it safely home, parked as close to the Manor's back door as he could get. He got his keys ready then waited for a lull before hurrying around to his boot to collect his shopping then running with it for the house. The sight of all those bags sent Tristan and Gertie into a mild frenzy. They snuffled their noses against them and jumped up on him, wagging their tails in the hope of treats. He pushed them off then unpacked everything into the fridge and pantry, making sure it was all well out of their reach. Then he went upstairs for a shower and a change of clothes.

There was no sign of Anna in her room, or when he went back down. He texted her to renew his offer of a lift, but didn't get a response. He took a tour of the kitchen, flipping through Samantha's impressive collection of cookbooks then checking her drawers and cupboards to scout out the pots and pans and cooking implements. A cork-board next to the Aga was crowded with overlapping postcards, invitations and photographs, including one of a much younger Samantha with a tall, slender and strikingly handsome older man that Elias would probably have taken for her father except for the salty look she was giving him, and the way he had his hand upon her backside.

The door opened and Samantha herself came in, no doubt having heard his return. She'd changed too, into a low-cut, tight-waisted, dark blue dress whose skirts swirled out like a cocktail umbrella whenever she turned sharply. She'd put on a little makeup: dark red lipstick, eyeliner and mascara, along with pendant gold earrings and a delicate silver bracelet that jangled loosely around her left wrist. The comfortable grey socks were gone too, replaced by silk stockings and elegant navy heels. 'You look nice,' he said, with rather more feeling than he'd intended.

'Having dinner cooked for me is such a rare treat,' she told him. 'I mean to make the most of it.' She crouched down to give each of the dogs a quick hug, careful not to get their hair on her dress. 'But your friend Anna – do you know what she's found?'

He shook his head. 'How do you mean?'

'She's been digging away in that field all evening. They only just stopped a few minutes ago. They must have found something extraordinary, don't you think, to have still been at it in this?'

'She does seem to have the knack.'

Samantha came over to where he was standing, took his arm. 'My husband Graham,' she said, when she saw which photograph he'd been looking at. 'I was his personal assistant, fresh out of college. He was the managing partner, successful and vigorous and powerful. And beautiful. My god! Well, you can see for yourself. All those long days and late evenings we spent together, I suppose it was kind of inevitable. I was single at the time, but he was married, of course. Men like him always are. He was loyal too. He stayed faithful to her for the longest time, which I both admired him for, and hated. But in the end...' She gave a shrug. 'And honestly they'd grown so far apart that I think it was a mercy to them both, especially after their kids left home.'

'It's a nice photo,' said Elias.

'Thank you, yes. A friend took it for us, the day we got back from our honeymoon. The start of four wonderful years. Then one afternoon he complained of an ache in his shoulder. He was in hospital for a bypass the very next day. After that, it was bang bang bang. Like sniper's alley, as a friend of mine put it. A stroke slowed him down so much that he decided to give up work to concentrate on his rehab. Then his lungs began playing up. Then it was his kidneys, and blood, and god knows what else, as if all these horrible conditions had been queuing up outside, waiting for their chance. He needed nursing around the clock, which is when we sold off the barn and had the stables converted for the live-in help – and for his mum, too, because she was increasingly frail herself. Only she died before moving in, and then Covid hit, at which point our nurse fled back home, leaving me to deal with Graham by myself. I put him into quarantine, even before the lockdowns started, and way before the vaccine. Back when we were still washing our hands twenty times a day, but no-one had even yet warned us that it was airborne or that you could be contagious without showing symptoms. And someone had to do the shopping. Someone had to pick up the prescriptions. So I caught it myself, somehow, and passed it on to him before I even realised I was sick.'

'I'm sorry,' said Elias.

'Thank you. Graham... He didn't want to go into hospital. He'd spent far too much time in there already. And he really, really didn't want to die alone. But it got so he couldn't breathe. It was the most horrible thing I've ever had to listen to. Unbearable. There were no ambulances by then, of course, so I drove him in myself, even though I was feeling like death myself by then too. They put him on a ventilator, but...'

'I'm sorry,' said Elias again. 'It must have been brutal.'

'Well, what are you going to do? And I was hardly the only one to go through it, was I?' Her eyes had moistened from the memory. She tore off a sheet of kitchen paper to dab them gently dry, making sure not to smudge her makeup. 'But, anyway, there I was, a widow with three granny flats and a ton of debt, because you wouldn't believe how expensive the conversions and the round-the-clock care all was. I mean I loved him, I did, whatever some of the horrible people around here might tell you. But we'd gone in no time from being rich to comfortable to okay to broke. Hence the B&B. Not that I don't enjoy it,' she added hurriedly, before he could take offence. 'I'd go crazy without the company. But still, you know. Cleaning up after people, and all the damn ironing. You've no idea how much ironing there is. It's just not what I expected my life to be.'

'No.'

She dabbed her eyes a final time, then shook her head to declare the subject closed. 'So dinner,' she said. 'What are we in for?'

'Seafood chowder with crusty bread followed by lemon cheesecake. Hope that's okay?'

'Sounds amazing. Is it your speciality, or something?'

'God, no,' said Elias. 'Never tried it before. I'm a carbonara and bolognese man myself. Frozen pizzas, takeaway chow mein and the odd kebab. But I found a recipe on my phone, and how hard can it be?'

'Oh god,' said Samantha. 'A recipe on your phone, in a kitchen you've never used before, and only ever cooks pasta. Here's an idea: How about I act as your sous, so that I can learn from the master?'

Elias laughed. 'Maybe that would be best.'

She nodded happily, glad of the company. 'So how was your afternoon?' she asked. 'I didn't see you at the farm with the others.'

'I was only there for about twenty minutes, to be honest. I tend to get in the way when I'm around archaeologists, asking my dumb questions. There's this glazed look that comes over them, you know. As if it's an effort not to pat me on the head and send me out for an ice-cream.' He vanished into the pantry for a bottle of Rioja, popped its cork and poured them each a glass.

'Though I did have a nice chat with your mate Quentin while I was there.'

'Oh,' she said, pretending indifference, but not very successfully. 'And? How was he?'

'Good, I think. All the better for hearing that you'd be letting him out of the doghouse soon.'

'What?' She looked at him aghast. 'You told him? I can't believe you told him.'

'Why not? It's what you wanted, isn't it?'

'But I said the exact opposite.'

'Yeah, but you didn't mean it, did you? You like him. He likes you. I mean he *really* likes you. You should have heard some of the things he said.'

That stopped her. 'Like what?'

'Ah, but he asked me not to tell you, you see. And seeing as you're so scrupulous about not revealing—'

She laughed and slapped him on his arm. 'Stop it! What did he say?'

Elias grinned. 'He said he didn't give a hoot when any of his other old friends snubbed him, but it hurt like hell when you did.'

'Good. What else?'

'He said that you're lovely, but it wasn't your loveliness that he most missed. It was how kind and cheerful and full of fun you were. He said that when you smiled at him, it was like having sunshine upon his face.'

'He said that? Really?' Then she added, more softly: 'He never said anything like that to me.'

'Of course not. He's shy. What do you expect? That's why he told me instead, so that I'd pass it on. Just like you did.'

'I'm not shy. Believe me.'

'No. But you're proud. Which comes to the same thing.'

She shook her head at him. 'Bloody detectives.' But the flush of her skin showed how pleased she was. 'Anyway, who are you to talk?'

'What's that supposed to mean?'

'What do you think? Anna. You like her, don't you?'

'Of course I do. She's probably my closest friend.'

'Not that way. The other way. I saw you earlier. The way you didn't look at her.'

'The way I didn't look at her!' laughed Elias. 'That's a new one.'

'Don't give me that. You know exactly what I mean. Constantly fighting not to stare. I wish I had men fighting like that not to stare at me.'

'Come off it. I bet you have half the men in Badbury fighting not to stare.'

'Yes,' she said. 'But it's never the right damn half, is it?' She gave a sigh then reached out to touch the photograph of her husband gently with her thumb. She looked about to say something further, only to hesitate for a few moments before deciding to push on through. 'After Graham fell ill, and even more so after he died, you wouldn't believe how many people asked me if I regretted it. Regretted marrying a man so much older than myself, I mean, now that it had all turned to shit. Kind of rude, don't you think?'

'I guess.'

'The answer is no, in case you're curious. In fact, it's not even no. The true answer is that those people completely misunderstood how I felt. I *couldn't* have said no to Graham, even had I known all the horrors yet to come. In fact, if I'd known all the horrors yet to come, it would have only made me more determined to marry him, so that I could face them alongside him, so that he wouldn't have to go through them alone. I loved him, you see. I loved him with all my heart. To have said no just because we'd been born a few years apart, or because we'd face some troubles down the line...'

'Is that supposed to be some kind of lesson for me?'

'She likes you that way too, you know. Maybe not quite as much as you like her, but still plenty.'

'Yeah, maybe.'

'There's no maybe about it. I'm telling you as a woman. I bet

I can prove it too.'

'How so?'

She gave him one of her trademark sunshine smiles, overflowing with happy mischief. 'Just you watch,' she said.

FOURTEEN

Anna and Quentin watched the museum van out of sight before running across the courtyard to Quentin's car and setting off themselves. 'Poor Vic,' said Anna, looking back over her shoulder as he closed and padlocked the gate behind them, hunched within his waterproofs. 'Hell of a night he's got in store.'

'Don't worry about him,' Quentin told her, squinting through his windscreen as he weaved his way slowly up the drive, so completely flooded that it was a challenge to tell what was track and what was pothole. 'He'll be happy as Larry now that we're all gone. No-one's going to expect him to do rounds, not on a night like this. He'll sit in the warm, read his book and bank ten hours pay. Money for old rope, as far as he's concerned. Never stops thanking me for getting him the gig.' They reached the end of the drive. 'Sam's place, yes?'

'Please,' said Anna.

'What a night! What a night!' He turned to her with a shake of his head, as though the enormity of their find was still sinking in. 'Talk about having the magic touch,' he said.

'Don't look at me,' said Anna. 'This one's all yours. I'm just thrilled that I was here to see it.' She turned to him with a question, only to think better of it and stay quiet instead.

'What?' he asked.

'Nothing. It's nothing.' But then she smiled and shook her head. 'You were one of archaeology's rising stars. You wrote a brilliant book, packed with fascinating new ideas and insights. Then suddenly you vanished.'

'And you're wondering what happened? But you're too polite to ask, in case it was because I did something shameful or dishonest. That wasn't it, I assure you. Though it was a comeuppance of a kind, I suppose.' He took a long, bracing breath before setting out on his story. 'I was a lucky young man, blessed with robust good health. I didn't just take it for granted, I was a little cavalier with others who weren't so fortunate.' The rain was coming down so hard that the windscreen was a virtual waterfall. He never even tried to get out of third gear, but rather made his way cautiously down the middle of the lane. 'Whenever any of my students came to me complaining of stress or depression or ME or any of those other chronic but nebulous conditions, I like to think that I was sympathetic and helpful enough, but there was always this impish small voice whispering in my ear that what they really needed was a good swift kick up the arse – and I've no doubt that it showed through from time to time.'

'Ah. Don't tell me. And then it happened to you?'

'And then it happened to me,' he agreed, with a rueful smile. 'I'd had a bad bout of flu a little while before, so maybe it was post-viral fatigue. But I'd also just come through a difficult personal experience. I'd testified in support of Wynn Grant, the man you saw sitting across the drive from Grove Farm when you arrived earlier. He was my friend. No. Sorry. He *is* my friend. I was as sure as can be that he was innocent of his brother's death, or, at the very least, that there had to be very considerable doubt, so I was happy to speak up for him at his trial. But they convicted him anyway. I don't know why exactly, but it hit me hard. I felt like I'd let him down, that there was something I could have said or done...'

'I'm sure there wasn't.'

'Yes. Well. You never know, do you? You play it round and round in your head. And you also kind of lose faith in the whole system, you know? In the way the world works. What's the point of it all, and all that. Like depression, only I think arrived at from the other side, if that makes sense? Anyway, it was just a few days later that I found I couldn't get out of bed one morning. It wasn't just mental. It was physical too. I literally had no strength. I had to crawl to my phone to call in sick. I assumed it would pass in a day or two, but it went on and on and on. I tried to fight my way through it a few times, but it always left me so exhausted that eventually I decided I needed a proper break. As long as it took. That meant resigning, of course, partly because it felt wrong to cling on with so many other fine candidates desperate for a job, but mostly because it added to my stress, thinking I was letting down my students and the university. I broke with my girlfriend too. She was wonderful, considering we'd only been going out a few weeks at the time, but frankly it was exhausting trying to be upbeat for her. It did me more harm than good. Especially as I could see in her eyes the exact same sentiment I'd had towards my students: that what I really needed was a good swift kick up the arse.'

'Ouch,' said Anna. They'd arrived outside Samantha's B&B by now, but she made no effort to get out, too involved in Quentin's story. 'So how did you get by?'

'It wasn't easy,' he admitted. 'I hate relying on the kindness of friends. I'm too independent of spirit. But I was lucky. Vic heard I was struggling and came to see me. I assured him I was fine and could manage by myself. He nodded agreement then completely ignored me. He did all my shopping for the next few weeks, and cleaned my gutters, and did my hoovering and countless other bits and pieces around my house to make sure my life didn't fall completely apart. He'd have done it for free, of course, because that's the kind of man he is. But I hate being under an obligation to anyone, so he was thoughtful enough to accept payment – though I know for a certainty that he undercharged me horribly on the hours.'

'A true friend.'

'The best,' agreed Quentin.

'And you're better now?'

He hesitated before answering. 'I'm much improved, thank you. As you can see for yourself. But I'd never say I was better. It would be too much like tempting fate. I still get far more tired than I ever did before, though some of that is surely just age. And my health feels much more precarious now. Like living on the edge of a cliff, forever aware of the fall. I'm fine where I am, but the drop is always there, waiting to snatch me if I should put even one foot wrong. And the devil of it is that I don't even know what wrong is. So I make sure to get my eight hours, or I'd be off to Devizes with Dave, to spend the night with all our treasures. I try to avoid undue excitement. Most of all, though, I gave up on my career ambitions. My old department hired a replacement ages ago, and it would be unfair on her to try to get it back. Futile, too, for I hear she's very good. Far more popular with her students than I ever was. And I couldn't face the prospect of applying for posts elsewhere, having to explain the gap in my résumé, only to be rejected at the end of it all anyway. I was also lucky enough to have inherited the place in Badbury in which I grew up, along with enough money to get by. But I didn't want to become completely isolated, either, because that's no kind of life, is it? So I've gradually taken on some modest activity. I volunteer at the local library, and I consult for the county's archaeological service, and I plug away at my next book, though that's more for my own—'

'Another book!' cried Anna. 'Excellent. What on?'

'Oh god!' he said. 'I shouldn't have mentioned it. It's more a hobby than anything. A way to keep my hand in. I've been at it three years already, would you believe? And at least that much more ahead, at the rate I'm going. Especially after our finds tonight.'

'Now I'm really intrigued. You have to tell me more.'

'Oh god,' he said again, though he looked undeniably gratified by her interest. 'I suppose you'd say it's on Arthurian Britain. Or more exactly on Arthurian Wiltshire and Somerset. I'm not one of those sceptics, you see, who have taken over academia these days, and who seem to fear nothing more than being thought credulous. The man existed, I'm sure of it. And I'm equally sure that this right here is where he lived and fought and flourished and died. It's why I put my consortium together, to buy Grove Farm. Because Liddington Hill used to be Mount Badon; I know it in my bones. And those fields we tramped today were where the battle was fought. It's not just wishful thinking, I assure you. Even before our recent finds, I had good reason for thinking it. My dad used to go out shooting with old Mr Grant, bagging rabbits and wood pigeons with their twelve bores. I used to tag along with them, though even then I was far more interested in the bits and pieces I kept finding in the ground, particularly after a good ploughing. It's what got me interested in post-Roman Britain in the first place, as it happens. And I'm hardly alone in my thinking. People have been suggesting the same forever. Serious historians, I mean. Not cranks. But there's never been enough hard evidence to prove it. Only folklore and tradition. Though what an abundance we have of that!'

'You should visit Wales,' Anna told him dryly. 'They have a fair stock of it too.'

'Ah, but that's the thing. Wales can be explained, as can Cornwall. Arthur was the great Celtic hero, so when the Britons got pushed back into those places by the Anglo-Saxons, they took their knowledge of him with them, their stock of stories, poems and the rest. So *of course* they named their landmarks after him. *Of course* they claimed that that was where he'd lived and fought and flourished. It was their way of keeping him alive. But there's no such easy explanation for the mark he's left around here. Think how closely associated he is with our West Country sites. Not just Mount Badon, where he won his greatest battle. But Cadbury Castle too, by far the most likely candidate for Camelot, and a fair shout for Camlann too, the site of his final battle against his nephew Mordred, the one in which he took his mortal wound. Then there's Glastonbury, our traditional Avalon, where Arthur was supposedly taken to recover. And it's not just folklore that links him here. We have real history too, not least in the shape of Ambrosius Aurelianus, who we're told gathered his fellow chiefs together at Stonehenge to start the British fightback. Amesbury is surely named after him, and I'd argue that Avebury very likely is too. Plus you have the Wansdyke, of course, the great earthen wall that marked the border between Briton and Saxon, surely built in the aftermath of Badon. All that and now this too.'

'Well, you'd better get on with your book, then,' said Anna, unbuckling her seatbelt and bracing herself to dash out into the deluge. 'Because I'm not waiting three more years to read it!'

FIFTEEN

Elias was refilling Samantha's glass with Rioja when the back door opened, only to be slammed shut again by the wind, eliciting a loud curse from Anna, who came hurrying into the kitchen a few moments later, her hair plastered to her face, her jacket soaked, her jeans and boots drenched and muddy. 'My god!' cried Samantha. 'Look at the state of you! Upstairs at once. Change into something dry before you catch your death. Then bring me down those clothes. I'll run them through the wash.'

'Would you?'

'Of course. Don't be silly.' She found a fresh glass, filled it with Rioja, handed it to her. 'Now be off with you. A nice hot bath, that's what you need. Give us forty minutes and we'll even have dinner waiting.'

Elias followed Anna upstairs, then stood awkwardly outside her bedroom door as she stripped. 'So?' he asked. 'How was it?'

'Incredible,' she said. 'But later, okay? Sam's right, I need a bath. You?'

'Not too shabby,' he told her. 'I found Melissa's letterbox charmers.'

'Already?' She came to the door, clutching her unbuttoned white blouse close around her chest. 'That's amazing. Who?'

'The Miller boy and his mates, just like Quentin said.'

'They admitted it?'

'Archie Miller did, yeah. After a little coaxing. He's agreed to apologise to Melissa too. And he's given me his word there won't be a repeat.'

'Do you trust him?'

'I do, actually. Which means that's pretty much that, at least for my bit of it.'

'You want to go back home?'

'God, no. Not as long as I'm on two grand a day. Though I expect Melissa and Ravi will see it differently when I tell them in the morning.'

He went back down to find that Samantha had taken his ingredients from the pantry and the fridge, to line up upon the central island. 'Let's have a look at this recipe of yours, then,' she said. He brought it up on his phone, passed it across. She studied it for a minute or so, frowning and biting her lip. Then she rearranged the ingredients in the order they'd be needed, and fetched out various pans and implements from her drawers and units.

'You're so organised,' said Elias. 'I was just going to toss everything into a great big pot and let it work out the details for itself.'

'You don't say,' smiled Samantha. 'Why am I not surprised?'

A pair of matching blue and white aprons were hanging from some hooks by the Aga. Samantha handed him the larger, took the smaller for herself. She oiled a large pan, put it on medium heat, tossed in the pancetta to brown. Then she took out a huge sharp knife to peel and dice an onion, a garlic bulb and a red chilli, her hands flashing with impressive speed and skill, before scraping it all from her chopping board into the mix.

'I thought we were doing this together,' murmured Elias.

'We *are* doing it together,' she assured him, finding a wooden spoon for him in a drawer. 'You're in overall command of everything, and you also have executive control of the stirring and the seasoning, *by far* the most important bits.' He prodded and pushed the bacon, onion and the rest around the pan with his spoon while Samantha scrubbed the mussels and the crab legs, pausing every so often to check on how he was doing, adding the fish stock to his pan once she judged that everything was sufficiently browned, then sprinkling in a spoonful of flour. She briskly quartered several new potatoes and tossed them into the pan as the stock came to the boil, then turned her attention to the fillets of fish, cutting them into manageable cubes that she quickly browned along with the scallops on a skillet.

Tristan and Gertie came to sit at her feet, gazing devotedly up at her with lolling tongues and hopeful wet eyes. For all her earlier admonitions about not feeding them, she couldn't help but toss them the occasional treat that they snapped up in midair like performing seals. 'I know,' she said, when she caught Elias smiling. 'But look at them! How am I supposed to help myself?' She scraped the chunks of haddock and salmon into the pot, then added the mussels and the crab legs and half the pot of cream, all while he stirred rhythmically away. It began to look and smell like chowder. She leaned over it and inhaled deeply through her nose, then sprinkled in some mace and cayenne pepper. He took a taste on his wooden spoon, added a pinch of sea salt. Samantha dipped in a finger. 'Delicious,' she said. 'Though perhaps a touch more.'

'I thought I was in charge.'

'You are, you are,' she assured him. But then she dipped her finger back in and held it to his mouth. 'Take another taste. Tell me I'm wrong.'

He licked her finger, gave a shrug. 'I always worry people won't like salt as much as I do. You can always add more, as they say. But you can't take it out.'

'Oh. We all need our salt, believe me. Otherwise it's just tasteless gloop.'

'Hey! I thought you said it was delicious.'

Samantha laughed. 'Never insult a man's cooking, that's what I've learned. Cooking, driving and in bed. The holy trinity.' She gave him a sideways glance. 'Though I'm sure you have no cause for worry. I'm sure you know *exactly* what you're doing behind the wheel.'

'I've put in some miles.'

'I'll bet.' She nodded at his hand. 'How come no ring?'

'There was. I screwed it up.'

'Ah. I'm sorry. Kids?'

'Two. Twins.'

'See them much?'

He put the crusty bread in the oven to warm. 'Not as much as I'd like.'

'That must be hard.'

'Yes.'

'That's what I love about men. Always so ready to open up.'

Anna came back in, wearing trainers, cargo pants and a baggy navy blue guernsey. Her hair was still shining wet from the bath, and she was carrying her muddy clothes in a bundle, as well as her empty wine glass. Samantha took her clothes from her then went through to the utility room to set a new wash going. 'You have to tell us what you found,' she said, coming back in. 'It must have been spectacular for you all to carry on in that filthy weather.'

'It was, rather,' admitted Anna.

'And? You can't stop there.'

'I have to, I'm afraid. I gave my word.'

'Oh, come on. Don't be such a spoilsport. It's so close to my own property, surely I have a right?'

'You do, you do, you absolutely do,' agreed Anna, as she wandered over to the Aga. 'What *is* this you're cooking? It smells delicious.'

Samantha laughed good-naturedly and let it go. 'Seafood chowder with crusty hot bread, all followed by lemon cheesecake.'

'My god. It's like you've been reading my dreams.'

'Not me. Your friend here. Your pleasure is his pleasure, so it would seem.'

Dinner was soon ready. Samantha laid places on the island, lit some candles, dimmed the lights. Elias spooned chowder into three large bowls, topping each with a pinch of fresh parsley. He fetched the butter and a bottle of Chablis from the fridge to pour them each a glass, then took out the bread from where it had been warming, cutting them a fat wedge each.

'Dear lord,' said Anna to Samantha, after taking her first mouthful. 'This is amazing.'

'Don't look at me,' said Samantha. 'It was all Elias.'

'I did the stirring,' corrected Elias. 'And added a bit of salt.'

'The most important bits,' said Anna.

'That's what I told him!'

Lightning shuddered outside the window, violent enough to stop their conversation dead. Samantha hurried over to her dogs, hugging her arms around them both before the boom arrived, which it did barely six seconds later, setting them barking and whimpering. 'I *hate* storms,' confessed Samantha, once she'd soothed them enough to return to her chair. 'I used to love them. That feeling of being warm and dry and safe, yet with a whiff of danger too. Like a fairground ride, only with less vomit. Now all I can think about is which bit of my roof is going to leak next, and how much it will cost to fix. It used to be so simple. I'd give lovely Vic a call and he'd zip up his long ladder with a tub of muck. But he's got arthritis in his hands now, so he can't do that any more. And the people I've asked about it since just jabber on about health and safety and how they need to put up scaffolding and strip off all my tiles to see what's underneath. Tens of thousands of pounds they quote me, rather than a hundred or two. I mean, come on. Where am I going to get that?'

'It must be difficult,' said Anna.

'I love this place, I really do. It will break my heart to sell, but I don't think I have much choice. Except that I can't even do that right now, with the market as it is, and those bastards next door building their wretched barns. I mean who's going to buy with all that going on? I don't have a prayer of getting what it's worth until it's resolved, one way or another, and who knows how long that will be? So I soldier on instead. Not that I mind,' she added hurriedly, lest they take it amiss. 'I'd go crazy without the company, like I was telling Ben earlier. And most of my guests are wonderful. But the ones who aren't, really, really aren't. They expect everything for nothing, then they leave horrid reviews anyway.' She looked a touch anxiously at Anna. 'I suppose you saw?'

'There were a couple,' admitted Anna. 'But mostly they were nice.'

'Mostly, yes. Though it only makes the bad ones stand out more. My heart sinks whenever I see I've got a new one, even before I know whether it's good or bad. It hurts so much when they're mean, after I try so hard.' She dropped her eyes, ashamed to be engaging in such obvious lobbying, but pushing through with it all the same. 'And it does such damage to my business. You can actually see the bookings fall off.'

'We'll leave good ones,' promised Elias, coming around with the pan of chowder to give them each a second helping. 'About how charming it was to have our hostess crash our romantic dinner; and the old-fashioned countryside joy of being woken by a hundred thousand squawking chickens.'

'You beast,' she said. 'Don't even—'

Another shudder of lightning, even brighter and more prolonged. Samantha barely made it to the dogs before the thunder came crashing in. Their distress was painful to hear, even before a loud click from the utility room heralded the electricity going out, the lights and the washing machine. 'Hell,' said Samantha. She grabbed a candle from the island and went next door to check the fusebox. Then she came back in and went to the window, cupping her hands around her eyes, the better to see outside. 'The stables are on a different system,' she explained. 'If their lights are off too, it means it's a proper power cut, not just me.'

'And?'

'Looks like it. Though they'll all be in here soon to have a moan at me anyway, if experience is anything to go by.'

As if to validate her words, the kitchen door opened slightly just after she'd returned to her seat, and Orlando Wren came sidling in, using his body as a barrier to make sure the dogs couldn't escape. 'My lights went out,' he said.

'Yes,' said Samantha. 'It's a power cut.'

'How long will it last?'

'Come on, Orlando,' she sighed. 'How on earth am I supposed to know that?'

'Are there any more candles?'

'Of course.' She passed him a lit one from the table, then found a couple more fresh ones from a drawer, along with a box of matches. 'Be careful, though. Open flames are fine down here, but upstairs with all that carpeting and curtains…'

'I'm not a child.' He sniffed the air. 'That smells good.'

'It *is* good,' Samantha assured him.

'Ah. Glad to hear it.' He stood there uncertainly for a few seconds longer. 'Well, I guess it's cheese and pickle for me again, then.'

'My writer lodger,' murmured Samantha, once he'd left. 'As I'm sure you guessed. Though I confess I checked him out on Amazon and I think I can safely say that Stephen King isn't in any immediate danger. I shouldn't mock people for their reviews, not after what I just told you how I feel about mine, but…'

'Maybe he's just ahead of his time,' said Anna.

'Aren't you the sweet one,' said Samantha, taking away their bowls then fetching the cheesecake from the fridge. 'It's possible, I suppose. And maybe this will be his great breakthrough. I mean he did have a front-row view earlier this afternoon when you found that… that… What did you say it was again? A sword in a stone? A huge round table? The holy grail?'

Anna laughed and held her glass up to the candlelight. 'I'm loving this wine, but it'll take at least another bottle before I fall for that. Though we'll not be finding anything from that list. That much I can assure you.'

'You can't know that. Not for certain.'

'We can, I'm afraid,' said Anna. 'This could well be where the Battle of Mount Badon took place, as your friend Quentin believes. Maybe the British forces were even led by Arthur. But even assuming both those to be true, *that* Arthur wasn't the Arthur of Camelot and the Round Table. He wasn't given Excalibur by the Lady in the Lake. He never drew a sword from a stone. Those Arthurs never existed. They were made up by storytellers and bards who weren't even born for another six hundred years after the real Arthur was dead and buried. They concocted all those stories about the holy grail too, I'm sorry to say; and how his queen betrayed him with his most valiant knight.'

'Stop it right there!' cried Samantha. 'Now you've gone too far. I won't have you taking Guinevere and Lancelot away from me. I just won't.'

Anna laughed, but then she nodded. 'Actually,' she admitted, 'there may just be a tiny seed of truth to that one. Though not in the way you'd think. You won't know this, but I've just written a book about a man called William Marshal.'

'Of course I know it,' protested Samantha. 'I googled you the moment you booked in. I even promised myself a copy for my birthday.'

'No need,' said Anna. 'I've got a metric ton of them upstairs. I'll sign one for you before we—'

The lights suddenly sprang back on. The washing machine began again to churn. 'Thank god,' said Samantha. 'Let's hope that's it for the night.' She turned back to Anna. 'You were saying about your book?'

'Yes. Though not about my book so much as the subject of it. Because the Arthurian stories we're so familiar with today are all about chivalry and gallantry and courtly love, even though those concepts didn't exist back in Arthur's day. They were very much twelfth century innovations. And William Marshal was pretty much their embodiment. The Greatest Knight, as he was known – though to be fair that was largely thanks to the biography commissioned by his sons. Anyway, right around the time Marshal was in his prime, a Breton poet called Chrétien de Troyes published a piece of Arthurian fan-fiction about a knight called Lancelot. It's the first ever mention of him, which is how we can be so sure that he wasn't a real historical figure. And what does de Troyes tell us about him? He was a peerless warrior, a model of chivalry, and King Arthur's right hand – at least until he had an affair with Arthur's queen, leading to their violent rupture. And what do we know about William Marshal in the early 1180s, when de Troyes was composing his poem? He was a peerless warrior, a model of chivalry, and Young King Henry's right hand – at least until he had an affair with Henry's queen, leading to their violent rupture.'

Samantha gazed wide-eyed at Anna. 'Are you saying that my Lancelot was really your William Marshal?'

'People have certainly suggested it, yes. I even thought about putting it in my book, though I chickened out in the end. It was too speculative for that, not least because the timing is so iffy. It's hard to be sure about publication dates from eight hundred and fifty years ago, but it seems the poem came out *before* the Young King broke with Marshall.'

'Then surely that makes it nonsense?' frowned Elias.

'Not necessarily. Henry and Margaret had been married for almost ten years by then, and Marshal had been Henry's closest friend that whole time. Is it so implausible that he and Margaret had been at it for a fair few years? She only ever had one child, and she named him William, so you can see how tongues might have started wagging – certainly enough for a poet to use as inspiration for his next work, only for its publication to get people laughing openly. Kings can survive pretty much anything but ridicule. But it's all speculation, at the end of the day. And, if speculation is allowed, there's another possibility I prefer, though it's completely scurrilous and based on nothing whatsoever.'

'Excellent!' cried Samantha, with a gleeful clap of her hands. 'There's no gossip quite like scurrilous and baseless gossip. Out with it.'

'Okay,' said Anna, 'so this is a few years further back, in the mid 1160s. Marshal was an unheralded young knight in his early twenties, working for his uncle Patrick, in service to King Henry II and his wife Queen Eleanor of Aquitaine. They were escorting

Eleanor through the countryside one day when they were set upon by a party of Poitevin knights seeking to kidnap her for ransom. Marshal managed to hold them off pretty much all by himself, buying Eleanor and the rest of her escort enough time to escape. He got wounded in the process, and was held captive for months, until Eleanor secured his release. She brought him to court as a reward for his courage, and had him made mentor to her son the Young King.'

'You're suggesting *she* was Guinevere?' asked Samantha.

'Why not? She was twenty years older than Marshal, but famously charismatic, strong-willed and beautiful. As for him, he was handsome, brave and ambitious, and he'd risked his life to save hers. Frankly, it would have been surprising if she hadn't developed a special kind of fondness for him – certainly enough for a mischievous poet to have his fun with.'

'And who could blame her?' asked Samantha rhetorically, covering Elias's hand with her own and throwing him a wildly flirtatious glance. 'There's just something so *delicious* about younger men.'

'Is there?' said Anna, rather more tartly than she'd intended. 'I wouldn't know.'

SIXTEEN

Anna apologised and excused herself with tiredness before making her way up to her room, feeling both mortified and bewildered by her sudden cattiness. Even Samantha's delighted shriek of laughter hadn't much helped, nor the triumphant look she'd thrown Elias, suggesting that she'd been set up in some way.

She did her teeth, prepared for bed. The storm had finally passed its peak, the thunder sounding ever further away, and the rain not hammering quite so fiercely upon her window. There were more and deeper lulls now too, in which she could hear Samantha and Elias chatting away downstairs, though she couldn't make out what they were saying. It brought back that ugly feeling from earlier, the one that had been building inside her all evening, watching Samantha as she'd flirted away with Elias, touching his arm, leaning forwards to show off her cleavage, laughing a little too loudly at his jokes. And how he'd seemed to enjoy it too.

Elias liked Anna. He liked her a very great deal. She knew that. What was more, she liked him too. What she'd never been quite sure about, though, was the precise nature of her liking for him. Was he simply a very good friend? Her best friend, if she was being honest, and that by a country mile. Or was he something more? Her trouble was that she'd been so bruised in the past that she'd come to mistrust men as a class. Being stuffed into a car boot to be raped and murdered would do that to you. Yet every time she saw the scarring on Elias's hand, she'd remember how he'd risked his life to save hers, the mad way in which he'd jumped up onto the wing of a light aircraft after it had already started its take-off run. She'd remember it and suffer a sweet little pinch of the heart. And they added up, those sweet little pinches of the heart. They came to feel an awful lot like something more.

Seventeen days she'd stayed at his Ingatestone cottage. It had come to feel like home, like how she'd dreamed a home could be. She'd been so happy there that her pride had started to revolt. She'd insisted on leaving while she'd still been able. He'd driven her up to York then had taken her in a long hug before he'd left. He hadn't said anything, not even then, though she could tell he'd wanted to. It had trembled on his tongue. She'd watched him from her window as he'd returned to his car, remonstrating furiously with himself. He hadn't said anything, but only because he'd respected her too much, what she'd been through. He hadn't dared jeopardise their friendship. But there'd been nothing to stop her from speaking, from giving it a chance. Nothing but cowardice. Because how could you ever know if a man was the right one, if you never opened your door to him, not even a crack?

Footsteps on the back stairs. She recognised his heaviness of tread. He went briefly into his room, then into their shared bathroom. She heard a tap running, the low buzz of his electric toothbrush followed by the flush of the loo and the creak and groan of the old plumbing. She found herself stiffening as she listened for the click of his door as he returned to his own room. But she didn't hear a thing, which she wouldn't have done had he slipped instead through the fire-door on his way to see Samantha. She was an attractive woman, after all, and she'd been making her interest in Elias clear all evening. Why wouldn't he want to spend the night with her? It wasn't as if he owed Anna anything. The opposite, in truth. With a sickening lurch, she remembered all the texts and emails she'd sent him over the months, teasing him about how he needed to get himself a girlfriend. She'd only done so because she'd never really believed he'd do it, not in her heart, let alone that she'd be there to witness it. Yet suddenly the possibility made her feel quite ill.

She couldn't leave it be. She had to know. She threw back her duvet and went to her door, then stood there uncertainly for a moment before stepping quietly out into the passage, lit by a tabletop lamp, so that she couldn't even see beneath Elias's door whether his light was still on or not. She padded through to the bathroom, ran a tap, flushed the loo, then waited for the plumbing to complete its cycle before going back out again and standing by his door, listening for any kind of noise. But she couldn't hear a thing, save for the wind and rain outside. *So this is what jealousy feels like*, she thought abstractly. *How horrible it is.* She was about to return to her room when she heard the creak of bedsprings and the click of a bedside light being turned off, and an immense wave of relief washed all over her. Yet it was quickly gone, leaving her feeling sick again, sick and foolish and ashamed. She returned quietly to her room, climbed back into bed, then hugged a pillow to her chest as she tried her best not to think about what it all might mean, let alone what to do about it.

SEVENTEEN

Most mornings, Quentin Parkes woke a minute or two before his alarm could go off. Not today. Drained from yesterday's excitements and a lack of sleep, he groaned, rolled over and slapped his clock quiet before lying there for a minute more, longing to remain in the comforting warm clasp of his duvet. But he'd made Vic a solemn promise, when asking him to serve as Grove Farm's nightwatchman, that he'd be in on the dot to relieve him every morning without fail.

He yawned and stretched and sat up. He allowed himself another moment before pushing himself to his feet and making his way through to his bathroom for a brisk shower. He breakfasted standing up on muesli and an apple, washed down by a large mug of milky sweet tea. He made sure he had everything he needed then locked up and went out to his car. It was still dark, even though a glow or two of moonlight showed in places through the cloud. Yet it was still raining in patches, though so thinly that he barely even needed to give his wipers a flick.

The storm had left detritus everywhere, turning the road into an obstacle course of fat puddles and fallen branches, of toppled bins and strewn rubbish. The council still hadn't cleared the drains at the end of his road, so that the dip had turned into a lake, deep enough that he feared for his engine. But he took it slowly and came through unscathed. He normally liked silence when he drove, but today he felt the need for company. The news was depressing, though. He put on music instead.

The roads were quiet, even for a bank holiday. He only saw one other set of headlights. But he still indicated well before turning onto Liddington Lane and then into Grove Farm, because it was his nature. The drive was still so badly puddled that he couldn't see all the potholes. He winced every time he hit one. He pulled up by the gate. First in, as always. He grumbled about it, but actually it was a point of pride. And, to be fair, he also enjoyed these moments with Vic, sharing a joke, putting the kettle on, opening a fresh pack of biscuits and generally making the place welcoming for when the others arrived.

Vic was usually waiting for him by the gate. But not always. Quentin had his own set of keys, of course, but one time when he'd let himself in, he'd found Vic fast asleep in his armchair with his book open upon his lap; and he'd been so embarrassed for him that he'd reversed back out, relocked the gate, then had tooted until Vic had finally appeared, apologising and claiming he'd been off doing a round. So Quentin had taken to tooting ever since, rather than risk a repeat.

He did so now, but Vic still didn't appear. He gave a longer, louder toot. Still nothing. He got out, unlocked and opened the gate for himself, drove on through. Vic's Fiat 500 was where he'd parked it last night. Nothing looked out of place. Yet the silence and the darkness were unnerving enough that he left his engine running and his headlights on, laying comforting yellow stripes over the muddy courtyard.

He slammed his car door deliberately loudly then shouted fruitlessly for Vic once more. He looked in through the sash window next to the front door. The standard lamp was on, and Vic's book was lying face down on the floor beside the armchair. But he could see no other trace of the man himself. The front door was locked on the latch. He let himself in, gave another shout. All he got was echo. He took out his phone for his torch, because not all the rooms had working lights. He checked the basement and then upstairs. Still nothing. He was taking a second, slower tour of the ground floor when he felt a whisper of fresh air coming from the sash windows, even though they were supposed to be closed and bolted. He went over to them. The left hand one was up an inch or two, its jamb splintered, as though it had been jemmied up from outside. And there were some spatters and smears on the outside windowsill, so dark red they were almost black.

'Vic!' he shouted. This too died away to silence.

He made his way out the back door and to the opened window. The light was improving all the time, yet he could still see no trace of Vic. He made a full circuit of the house, shouting out every few moments, though half-heartedly now. He crossed the courtyard to Vic's car. He tried the door but it was locked, so he cupped his hands around his eyes to look inside. Nothing. He went over to the open-sided barn. Sacks of cement powder were piled high on a row of wooden pallets by the mixer, while a huge mound of building sand was covered by a tattered tarpaulin. The rain that had swept in overnight had eroded this mound at its base, spreading sand out across the barn's concrete floor, thick and wet and plastic enough to take and hold footprints. He knew this for sure because he could see two sets of them in front of him. The set going deeper into the barn were partially obscured by drag marks. But not the one coming back out again.

His heart in his mouth, he stepped carefully forwards. A dark bundle on the floor at the back of the barn disaggregated as he advanced, turning from a shapeless dark mass into the unmistakeable form of a man lying on his front with his hands thrown up over his head, as though in the act of surrender. Quentin's stomach gave a lurch at the sight of the heavy black boots caked in mud, the old khaki trousers and the familiar dark blue waterproofs with the hood peeled back so that he could see the back of his old friend's head and the mess of clotted blood on his thin grey hair.

He fell to his knees beside him, indifferent to the moisture soaking through his trousers. He rolled him onto his back. His face was covered in gore from the gash on his crown where his skull had been caved in. His skin was cold; his eyes obviously vacant. He checked for a pulse anyway, futile though it was. He got back to his feet and turned away, bending double and gagging several times, but managing to hold back the vomit. He stepped carefully away from the body, not wanting to disturb the scene any further. Then, with shaking hands, he opened the phone app on his mobile and tapped in the number for the police.

EIGHTEEN

Anna had never been the soundest of sleepers. But last night had been unusually bad, thanks to the combination of an unfamiliar bed, an electric storm and the general creaking and groaning of an old house, all on top of the general roiling of her thoughts. And when she did finally fall asleep, it seemed as though she was woken again almost at once by a loud knocking at her door. 'What is it?' she groaned, turning on her phone to confirm it really was as early as she thought.

'It's me,' said Elias. 'May I come in?'

'Of course,' she said. But then, puzzled, she added: 'Why?'

He didn't answer that, but rather opened her door just wide enough to slip inside. She turned on her bedside light, sat up. He was wearing jeans and a sweatshirt, she noticed, yet neither shoes nor socks, suggesting he'd only just got up himself. 'What is it?' she asked again, holding her duvet shyly up in front of her chest, even though it made her feel slightly ridiculous, what with the T-shirt she had on.

'Something's happened,' he told her. 'Up at Grove Farm. There are police cars everywhere. They've got their siren lights on too.'

'Christ. Why?'

'I don't know. But it's far too big a response for a simple break-in. I'm going to go over there myself to take a look, see if it's anything to do with us. You want to come?'

'Of course. Yes. Can I have five minutes?'

'Take ten. I'll be in the kitchen.'

She arrived downstairs to find a hot buttered croissant and a cup of coffee waiting for her. She wolfed them down greedily and they were good to go. The courtyard was covered in shallow wide puddles, including one so close to the Leaf's passenger door that Elias bid her wait until he'd reversed clear of it. She climbed in, fighting a yawn. They set off up the drive, turned left along the lane. A squad car was blocking the mouth of Grove Farm's drive, its siren lights turning the dawn a fluttery blue. A burly young uniformed constable waved them on. Elias pulled into the lay-by opposite instead, buzzing down his window to ask what was going on. The constable refused to answer, other than to shake his head and turn his back. Quentin Parkes had clearly seen them arrive, however, for he came hurrying down the drive and crossed the lane to climb into the back of the Leaf, his eyes so red and raw that Anna knew instantly. 'What is it?' she asked. 'Is it Vic?'

He nodded miserably. 'I found him myself. Some arse had jemmied open a window round the back. He must have heard them breaking in and gone to check. Only they clobbered him and hid his body in the barn. Though god knows why. He was certain to be found.' He shook his head in disbelief. 'I've just given my statement. I had to tell them everything, including about you two. So I'm afraid they'll probably want to speak to you at some point.'

'No problem,' said Anna. 'However we can help.'

'I just don't understand it. You saw Vic. He was almost eighty, with arthritis in his hands and feet, heart problems and a bad hip. Even if he did catch someone, what was he going to do? All they'd have had to do was walk away, and not even very fast.'

'Maybe he saw their face,' suggested Anna.

'I suppose.'

'What about your security cameras?' asked Elias. 'Did they catch anything?'

'I don't know. I told the police about them. And gave them my photographs too.'

'Photographs?'

'They left footprints in the sand when they dragged Vic into the barn.' He took out his phone to show them. 'I took these before they got washed away.'

'Good work,' said Elias. He took the phone from him to have a quick look before handing it back. 'Anna told me you made some finds last night. Worth breaking in for?'

'God, yes. But that's precisely why we packed them all off to the museum. There was nothing of any real intrinsic value left in the house. And everyone knew it.'

'I didn't know it,' said Elias. 'I mean I knew something good had been found, because Sam told me; but not that it had been moved. And anyone who saw you guys digging away in that filthy weather must have had some kind of clue. Plus everyone they told.'

A thirty-something woman in gumboots and worn blue waterproofs came trudging down the drive, pausing to look both ways before crossing the lane, motioning for Elias to lower his window as she came. She had messy short dark hair and bleary eyes, as though woken early after a heavy night. She held out her warrant card for them to read. Detective Inspector Vanessa Ransome. 'And you two are?' she asked.

'Ben Elias,' Elias told her. 'And Anna Warne.'

'The detective and the archaeologist, yeah? The ones this bright spark called in?'

'Ex-detective,' said Elias. 'And he called us in because you and your colleagues couldn't be arsed to find out who'd pissed through Ms Ward's letterbox.'

'That investigation is still very much ongoing, I assure you.'

'Not really, no. I solved it myself last night. Took me all of twenty minutes.'

'You know who it was?' She didn't look altogether happy. 'Who?'

'What?' he scoffed. 'And undermine your ongoing investigation?'

'If you know anything material, you have a—'

That was as far as she got, however, for a silver Audi A5 came racing up the lane at that moment, and travelling so fast that Ransome had to step aside, only for it to come screeching to a halt alongside them. 'Please tell me it's not true,' said Melissa Ward, buzzing down her window. 'Not poor Vic.'

'How do you even know about that?' asked Ransome.

'Quentin told me.'

Ransome scowled at him in the back seat. 'I thought I told you not to.'

'This is my site,' retorted Melissa. 'Vic was my employee. Of course he had to notify me.'

'So you're Ms Ward, are you?'

'Yes. Yes, I am. And I'll tell you exactly who did this.' She undid her belt the better to turn around in her seat and jab a finger back down the lane. 'Wynn bloody Grant, that's who. I've been telling you and your colleagues for weeks how dangerous he is. I've been begging and begging you to take him seriously. If you'd dealt with him back then—'

'This wasn't Wynn,' muttered Quentin. 'He's not that kind of man.'

'He *is* that kind of man,' insisted Melissa. 'First he killed his brother and now he's killed Vic too, the kindest, gentlest person you could ever hope to meet, and supposedly your friend.' She turned back to Ransome. 'I drove past his house just now. Not a single bloody police car in sight. He could be destroying evidence, for all you know, while you lot just stand around here doing nothing.'

'Why would Mr Grant do something like this?' asked Ransome.

'Because he's *evil* and he *hates* us,' said Melissa. 'He squats out here every other day, glaring at us. He smeared shit on Quentin's windscreen and he pissed through my letterbox and he sabotaged our equipment and he painted horrible messages on our walls.'

'Sorry,' said Elias. 'He didn't do any of those.'

'He did. I'm telling you, he did.'

'And I'm telling you he didn't,' said Elias. 'I spoke to one of the people responsible last night. They admitted to it all. For what it's worth, they say they never meant you or your children any harm. And I believe them.'

'Who was it?' asked Ransome.

'Sorry,' said Elias. 'I don't work for you.'

'No,' said Melissa. 'You work for me. So? Who was it?'

'Perhaps in private?'

'No. Now. I'll only tell her anyway. Who was it?'

Elias sighed. He'd liked Archie and didn't want him caught up in this unholy mess, if he could possibly avoid it. But murder was murder. 'The Miller boy. Just like Mr Parkes said.'

'That little brat?' said Melissa.

'Him and his King's Head crew, drunk after a big night out. He felt pretty sick about it, to be fair. He promised to come here this morning to apologise personally to you for it. So I can't see him being involved in whatever happened here last night. Apart from anything else, Vic was his friend.'

'Or so he told you,' said Ransome.

'I worked Major Crimes for ten years,' Elias said irritably. 'I'm not easy to bullshit.'

'Okay,' said Melissa. 'Maybe those other incidents weren't Grant. But that hardly clears him of killing Vic, does it? He's already murdered one man here. Why not another?' She must have realised how vengeful she sounded, for she took a calming breath and made an effort to make her case in a more reasonable tone. 'He was here all yesterday afternoon, remember? He was even here when I left. That means he saw us digging up those artefacts last night – artefacts that he no doubt thinks of as rightfully belonging to him. You think he'd just let them go? Of course not. Especially not with a full bottle of gin inside him. He'd have come for them, for sure. Only Vic caught him at it.' She turned back to Ransome again. 'I'm telling you, send a car over there right now or all the evidence will be gone. And I'll make sure the world knows how you let him slip through your fingers.'

'Please leave the investigating to us,' said Ransome. But she was already reaching for her radio as she turned on her heel and headed back up the drive.

NINETEEN

'Archie bloody Miller,' said Melissa, once Ransome had left. 'That little shit. But you're sure we won't have any more trouble from him?'

'I was until a minute ago,' said Elias. 'Not so much now.'

'How do you mean?'

'Archie won't do anything himself, I'm sure of that. But the crew he hangs out with...' He gave a shrug. 'If the police go in too hard on them, and they decide that we're to blame...'

'Oh, hell,' she said. 'That's just great.'

'Yeah. Sorry.'

'Fat lot of use "sorry" does me now,' scowled Melissa, conveniently forgetting that she was the one who'd insisted he name Miller in front of Ransome. 'But at least it means our business is concluded, I suppose. Send me your invoice. I'll see you get paid.' She buzzed up her window then sped off down the road, spattering their bonnet and windscreen with gobbets of watery mud, leaving them alone with Quentin, sitting shrunken and miserable in the back seat, clearly lost for what to do, what with his car still in Grove Farm's courtyard, sealed off by Scene of Crime.

Elias turned around to him. 'Can we drop you somewhere?' he asked.

'Home, if you wouldn't mind?' he sighed. 'It's not too far. Just the other side of Badbury.'

'You can give me directions?'

'Of course. Though it's best to turn back the other way.'

'What about your volunteers?' asked Anna, as Elias pulled a three-point turn in the lane. 'Are they on their way in?'

'No,' said Quentin. 'Dave texted me earlier, before he even knew about Vic. He's called the dig off for the day because yesterday's finds come first. He even asked if I'd go into the museum to help.'

'You should,' Anna told him.

'No car,' he said simply. 'And I don't have the heart for it either, to be honest.'

'It'd do you good,' said Elias. 'You'll feel a lot better for keeping busy, believe me. As for getting there...' He raised an eyebrow at Anna.

'Absolutely,' she said. 'I'd love to see it all again, especially without a monsoon going on. And if they're in need of help, maybe I could be of use?'

'They are very short-handed,' admitted Quentin.

'Good,' said Anna. 'That's settled, then. Let's do it.'

The drive south proved a brute. The road was straight but rolling, with several of its dips still badly flooded from the storm, forcing traffic to slow right down before carefully splashing through. But this, of course, was leading to long and dangerously hidden tailbacks, vehicles slamming on their brakes as they crested the hills behind only to see traffic at a standstill ahead. One driver hadn't been quick enough, sitting by the side of the road with a police blanket around his shoulders, staring disconsolately at his crumpled bonnet, and the back of the van he'd run into.

Further on, a lightning strike had riven a tree in two. Its blackened trunk was still smouldering, while its sheared-off part had come to rest precariously against a power cable, forcing the police to close off one of the two lanes, leading to long tailbacks in both directions as people waited to be waved through. And Marlborough, when finally they reached it, was little better, its high street congested by day-trippers playing musical chairs over the handful of free parking spaces. But congestion finally cleared a little as they made their way out the town's other side, passing as they did so a sign that caused Anna to turn and point it out to Quentin. 'The Wansdyke,' she said. 'It really came this far east?'

'Oh yes,' he nodded. 'All the way from Savernake Forest behind us to just shy of Devizes. Then again around Bath and Bristol.'

'The Wansdyke?' asked Elias.

'It's a corruption of Wodan's dyke,' said Quentin. 'That was its Anglo-Saxon name. Though it wasn't them that built it. Or even Wodan.' He gave a thin smile, less at the joke itself than in acknowledgement of its feebleness. 'They had to call it something, I suppose, and they didn't know who to credit it to, so Wodan it was. We're still not entirely sure who built it, but most likely it was the Britons, perhaps even in the aftermath of the Battle of Badon, to mark the border, or even as a way to hold back the Saxons.'

'How do you know it wasn't the Saxons trying to hold back the Britons?' asked Elias.

'A very good question,' said Quentin, sitting forwards a little, the lecturer in him taking over from the bereaved friend. 'It's partly because the Saxons were the more aggressive of the two, and so needed defending against. But it's more from the way the dyke was built. The way they did it was, they dug out a ditch and put all the spoil from it on just one side, creating a high bank to run alongside it. So you can deduce which side built it because they made sure to have the bank on their side, and the ditch on the other. It's much easier to defend that way.'

'And the ditch is on the Saxon side?'

'Exactly. Yes.'

'Still,' said Elias. 'A ditch and a bank. It's not exactly Hadrian's Wall, is it?'

'No,' agreed Quentin. 'And it runs for thirty miles or so, too, which was way too long for it to have been kept properly manned. So maybe its real purpose was to stop cattle raids.'

'A thirty mile embankment to protect a few cows?'

'It's not as absurd as it sounds. Livestock was real wealth back then, particularly during famines – of which they suffered more than their fair share, for one reason or another. It's easier to steal than grain, and it sits better in the stomach than gold. So cattle raids were a big deal. In fact, there's reason to think that a good number of the battles we hear of from that era were really cattle raids gone wrong. And dykes were a surprisingly effective defence against them. Not so much for keeping the raiders out, but rather for keeping the cattle in. Driving a herd of cows over a steep drop is hard. They'll panic and scatter and you'll be back at square one. Try it yourself sometime.'

'Thanks,' laughed Elias. 'But I think I'll take your word for it.'

TWENTY

The traffic eased a little before thickening again as they approached Avebury, whose great henge and sacred landscape were always popular draws on a bank holiday. They passed the haunting cone of Silbury Hill, turned south towards Devizes. The Leaf's battery was edging towards the red by this time, so Elias had Anna search her phone for a charging station near the museum. It left them with a good ten minute walk, so Quentin texted Dave to alert him to their imminent arrival; yet it was another of the curators who came out to meet them and sign them in.

Pamela Pearce, as she introduced herself, was a short, round woman in her mid to late sixties whose grey hair had at some point yesterday been tied up in a bun, only for most of it to have escaped since, leaving it as frazzled as she looked, out on her feet after an all-nighter, constantly fighting back yawns and shaking her head to clear it. Yet, every so often, she'd remember the reason for her exhaustion, and her face would light up with an enchanting teenage delight. 'Dave told me about your nightwatchman friend,' she told Quentin, giving him a hug. 'I'm so sorry.'

'Thank you.'

She turned next to Anna and then Elias, clasping their hands warmly between both of hers. 'And Ms Warne and Detective Elias. You certainly have the touch, you two. You must come stay with me when all this is over. I'll give you a spade each and send you out into my back garden.'

'If only it were that easy.'

'Ha. Yes.' She handed them each a visitor's pass then led them across the lobby to a door marked Authorised Personnel Only that she unlocked and held open for them, pausing to make sure it clicked shut behind them again before walking on. 'We're not really set up for this kind of thing,' she said. 'We have some lovely pieces here, but nothing that would tempt me to pull on a balaclava and saw down my husband's shotgun. But what you found last night... My god!'

'It was quite a haul, wasn't it?' said Anna.

'Amazing. Just amazing. Which makes it rather stressful, to be honest. All those coins are one thing. They were made to be robust, and we've dealt with plenty of them before. But those brooches and rings, the goblet and the saucer and my god your bowl...' She shook her head. 'You only get one first shot at pieces like these, and who knows what damage we might cause by getting it wrong? *Striving to better*, as the great man put it.' The overhead lights kept flickering on as she led them along a gloomy corridor with shabby worn red carpeting, only to turn off again once they'd passed by. There were storerooms with partially glassed doors on either side, offering glimpses of dusty artefacts on metal shelves, broken statues and great slabs of monumental stone. 'So I'm afraid I made an executive decision earlier. I called an old colleague of mine who now works at the British Museum. She's terribly good. She flies all over the world, advising museums on best practice. I rather downplayed what we'd found, because I didn't want word getting out. But she got so snotty about it, telling me how frightfully busy she was, and how she might be able to spare me an afternoon the week after next, that I'm afraid it got under my skin a little. So I sent her some of our photographs. From the squealing and yelping that came down the line, I rather think she now has a very nice litter of kittens to look after.'

Anna laughed. 'How very satisfying.'

'Indeed. But of course it only made her go the other way,

demanding I ship it all up to her. As if! Honestly, once that place gets its hands on a piece, you'll never get it back. Just ask the Greeks.' Her jaw trembled as she fought off another yawn. 'But I did promise to lock everything away until she and her team get here first thing in the morning. It's probably for the best, to be fair, seeing how knackered we all are. I had to send Dave home after he walked into a wall. And Anish and I will both be off home ourselves, the moment we've seen you lot off.'

'Oh god, of course,' said Quentin. 'We're keeping you up.'

'No, no, no, no,' she said hurriedly. 'I absolutely didn't mean it like that. It's wonderful to have you here. Truly. A privilege. Besides, strictly between you and me, I managed to shut my eyes for a couple of hours while Anish was beavering away on his computer; but I don't think he noticed, so please not a word. The little wretch does like to rag me about my age. I let him have his fun, because frankly there's no way I could do what he does. Old dog, new tricks, all that. But he's done marvellous things, I must say.' She pushed open a door and turned on the lights to reveal something between an office, an IT suite and a sitting room, with a line of darkened computer monitors and audiovisual equipment to their left, and a pair of armchairs and a sofa around a coffee table to their right. 'You can tie a rock to your social media and digital currencies and all the rest of it. Toss them in the deepest ocean, see if I care. Just leave me all this wonderful new imaging technology. When I think of the photographic equipment we had to work with in my own student days...!'

'They had cameras back then?' muttered an unshaven young man curled up on one of the armchairs.

'And hand-axes,' retorted Pam. 'We knew how to use them, too, believe me.' She nodded in his direction. 'Anish, in case you couldn't guess. I'm cutting him some slack this morning, because of his magnificent efforts overnight. But at some point that will end, and I'll have him fired.' She went to sit at the workstation, invited them to pull up chairs alongside. 'So, then, yes. What can one even say? The hoard as a whole, wonderful, just wonderful. We've cleaned it as much as we trusted ourselves to, and we've taken scans and photographs too. I'll email you a selection of the latter, if you leave me your details. But that's where we left it, I'm afraid. As I say, we didn't dare risk doing any damage, particularly to your bowl, if it even is a bowl... Dave thinks we should call it a cauldron, thanks to its size; but I always imagine cauldrons as being used for stewing soup and the like over open fires, and I can't imagine anyone ever hanging *this* over an open fire. It's far too precious and too beautiful. Besides, there's no sign of a handle, or of any scorching. No. The gemstones strongly suggest it was a mixing bowl of some kind. Most likely for wine, what with all those amethysts.'

Elias frowned. 'How does that follow?'

'Forgive me, detective. I keep forgetting you're not one of us. Amethysts were the stone of Dionysus and of Bacchus, gods of booze. They were supposed to prevent excessive drunkenness, though I road-tested that theory myself at university, and I can assure you it doesn't work. Yet they studded their goblets with them nonetheless. Your bowl or cauldron too. A masterpiece, of course. That goes without saying. Anyone who'd commission a piece this grand would only ever use the very best artists. And virtually unique too. The closest parallel is clearly Gundestrup, which is why I suspect Dave is right that it will end up being called a cauldron, even though that was double-walled and had a separate silver band around its top that was crimped into a rim to hold it together. Whereas with yours they folded the top of each leaf back upon itself instead, making a rim that way, while also creating a hollow tube into which they inserted a series of short iron pins between the neighbouring leaves to provide extra structural support that way. I tell you that because it's significant for a reason I'll come back to. What else? Yes. The Gundestrup cauldron was seventeen inches tall. We think yours was probably a little taller, though that depends on exactly how it fitted together. Also, Gundestrup was first century BCE, whereas yours looks like early fourth century CE, give or take a hundred years. And Gundestrup was repoussé too, of course.'

'Repoussé?' asked Elias.

'It means the designs on it were created by hammering the metal from the inside, to make them bulge out, like a sculpture in relief. Yours is engraved instead, both around the top of each leaf and on its base plate too.' She paused to pour herself a glass of sparkling water, took a long and grateful swallow. 'You wouldn't have been able to make the engravings out last night, not beneath all that mud and dirt, but we cleaned them up enough for Anish to work his magic.' She tapped a key to bring up a photograph of the torn, crumpled and filthy mess they'd recovered from the ground last night. 'This is what Dave brought us,' she said. 'And now here is Anish's first attempt at recreating how it might have looked fresh out of the workshop.' She tapped another key and a new image appeared, of a golden cauldron that swelled out from its base before contracting again towards its rim, its lower parts studded with brilliant gemstones topped by a double band of pearls, while the upper part was decorated with a series of etchings or engravings.

'Dear god,' said Anna. 'That's our bowl?'

'It's *kind of* your bowl,' said Anish, yawning massively as he wandered over, not bothering to fight or hide it. He took the mouse from Pam to rotate the bowl 360 degrees, then he tipped it forwards and back again to show them the insides and underneath. 'A crude first pass, let's call it. What I did was, I photographed it from different angles under different lights and using multiple filters. Then – to get all technical – I splodged the photos together with my image processing software.' He paused for another gigantic yawn, then slapped himself across the cheek to stir himself back awake. 'After that, it was just a matter of playing around with it, smoothing out the leaves, rejoining them along their seams, generally tarting it up. A lot of guesswork involved, as I'm sure you can imagine, and a fair bit of cheating too. This double band of pearls, for example. There was a double band of something, we're sure of that, but we've had to guess that they were pearls, because they were completely eaten away, which of course can happen to pearls in acidic soil.

I've made the gemstones larger and more colourful than they really are, so that they're easier to tell apart. I've thickened and deepened the engravings too, for the same reason. So a working model, like I say, not a replica.'

'You've made it gold,' protested Quentin.

'It *was* gold,' said Pam. 'Or gilded, at least, though only on the outside. Most of it has rubbed off, but we've found enough traces to put it beyond doubt. The only oddity is that you'd expect a piece this splendid to be mercury-gilded. The Romans were masters of the art, after all, and it gave off such a wonderful gleam. But I'm not sure that mercury-gilding was even possible with items like this. No doubt Rebecca and her British Museum chums will know. Anyway, whatever the reason, they went for gold leaf or cold gilding instead, which is why it's almost all rubbed off. I suspect it was mostly gone even before it was buried, in fact, simply from all the polishing it would have got. It still would have looked amazing, though. Silver and gold together have a way of playing off each other that makes them all the more dazzling.'

'Those engravings?' asked Anna, squinting at the screen. 'Are they buildings?'

'Some are,' said Pam. 'Most notably the one on the base plate, which looks to be a rather substantial Roman villa. If so, of course, it ties it even more closely to the one you've found nearby.'

'And the others?'

Pam nodded. 'The bowl originally consisted of a base plate and eight separate leaves, of which we've only recovered seven so far. Each of those seven is engraved with a different landmark of some kind. Two are stone circles. Two look like hill-forts. And three appear to be towns or small cities. Our best guess right now is that it was kind of a statement of domain by the lord of the villa.'

'Like a cat marking out its territory,' suggested Elias.

'A touch less pungent, but yes, essentially.'

'You said there was something significant about its rim,'

prompted Anna.

'I did, yes. Well remembered. We think it may explain the missing leaf, you see, because the lack of corrosion where it was joined to the base plate suggests it only became detached quite recently. Years or decades, I mean, rather than centuries – though of course we'll need to do proper testing to be sure. From what Dave told us, the top of the missing leaf would have been only a foot to eighteen inches beneath the surface of the field, yet above the battlefield layer, which obviously is an oddity in itself. So our current best guess is that it wasn't buried at all.'

'Aren't hoards buried by definition?' asked Elias.

'*Almost* by definition,' said Pamela. 'But not invariably. Imagine it's midwinter, say, and the ground is frozen solid. You get word that the enemy is barely a dozen miles away, and approaching fast. You don't have time to bury all your valuables, not with the ground so rock hard. You don't have time to flee with them either. So what do you do?'

Elias shook his head. 'Well?'

'This is obviously only an hypothesis, you understand? But wouldn't one option be to gather everything up in your cauldron then tie it up in a sack and take it out to one of your farm buildings, to hide it in the thatch, meaning to recover it once the danger's passed. But something goes wrong, of course. It always does, with such hoards. Maybe you're driven off for good. Maybe the only people who know where it is get killed. So there it remains, in the roof of an abandoned and then derelict outbuilding, until finally it collapses. Wouldn't that explain why it was above the battlefield layer? And wouldn't it explain how, if the field was deep-ploughed at some point, the tip of one of the blades might have snagged upon the rim of its topmost leaf, ripping it away and dragging it a foot or so underground before dropping it off again.'

Quentin frowned. 'You're saying it's still somewhere nearby?'

'I'm saying it's certainly worth a look.'

'My god. We need to get back there. Before anyone else finds it.'

'It should be safe enough for the moment,' said Elias. 'What with all the police around.'

'Oh hell,' said Quentin, mortified that he'd forgotten his friend so quickly.

Pam took the mouse back from Anish, set the bowl slowly rotating. 'It's going to be world famous once word gets out, of course,' she said, shaking her head. 'The Badbury cauldron from the Badbury hoard. More to the point, though, it would have been famous back then too. Pieces this spectacular acquired a tremendous mystique, all the more so because it would undoubtedly have had an important social and ceremonial purpose. Sharing was a key part of Celtic culture, as you know, and this is exactly the kind of vessel that kings and chiefs would have served their peers out of at the sort of tribal gatherings where they'd have given their oaths and formed their bonds. Can't you just picture it, the high priest or the king of kings holding it up in front of a great assembly, late at night, so that it glittered with the light of a hundred bonfires. No doubt there'd have been bards and storytellers there too, both to entertain the guests and to memorialise the event. And little doubt, either, surely, that those bards and storytellers would have been inspired by the sight to use the cauldron in the new songs and poems they went on to compose.'

'Dear god,' muttered Quentin.

'You can't be serious,' said Anna.

'What am I missing?' said Elias, noticing the stunned looks on both their faces. 'What do you all know that I don't?'

Pam gave a mischievous little quirk of her lips. 'A cauldron or mixing bowl like this… It was what the French came to talk of as a *gra'al*.'

TWENTY-ONE

There were too many people in the museum foyer and on the street outside to make conversation wise, so Elias waited until they were safely back in the Leaf and on their way north out of Devizes before turning to Anna and Quentin. 'Are you guys seriously telling me that you've found the holy grail?'

'No,' said Anna firmly. 'And even if we have, we haven't.'

'What's *that* supposed to mean?'

'Well, what was the holy grail?' she asked. 'According to legend, it was either the cup from the Last Supper or the one that caught the blood that flowed from Jesus's side after he was stabbed with a spear. The story goes that Joseph of Arimathea or maybe his followers brought it to Glastonbury at the end of the first century CE when they established Britain's first church there. And whatever else our cauldron might be, it has nothing to do with that. It was made at least two hundred years too late, for a start. More likely three. And those two stone circles on it are surely Avebury and Stonehenge, which makes it a very Romano-British artefact, not a Levantine one.'

'Then why all the excitement?'

It was Quentin who answered this time. 'Because the Joseph of Arimathea holy grail was only added to the Arthurian canon late on, by a Breton poet called Robert de Boron. But there's a different kind of grail in early Arthurian lore. Not holy, exactly, and with zero connection to Jesus or even Christianity, but with quite a potent aura all the same. I don't know how you'd describe it exactly. The mystic grail, maybe. The revered grail. The sacred grail.' He pulled a face, unhappy at each of these descriptors. 'Help me out here, Anna. What's the word I'm looking for?'

'Hallowed?' she suggested.

'Yes. Perfect!' He rolled the words around his mouth. 'The *hallowed* grail. It appears first in a poem called *Preiddeu Annwfn* that's attributed to a Welsh bard called Taliesin who lived in or around the sixth century. It's a deliberately obscure piece of work, very hard to understand. It has rather the flavour of a masonic ritual, if you're familiar with those. Essentially it tells how Arthur led three ships of men into the Celtic otherworld in pursuit of a magical cauldron.'

'Ah,' said Elias.

'Exactly,' said Quentin. 'This same cauldron also appears in another early Welsh poem, only now it's able to heal serious injuries, even bring people back from the dead. Unfortunately, we have what you detectives might call a break in the chain of evidence at that point. So the question is, can we make a plausible link between a seventh century Welsh cauldron and a French holy *gra'al*.'

'And? Can we?'

'Yes. I believe we can. Though we have to go back a little, to Arthur's defeat at the Battle of Camlann. It led to a dark period for the Britons, during which the Saxons pushed them further and further back, ultimately penning them into Wales and Cornwall, while also driving a great many others overseas instead, primarily to Brittany – which is how the province got its name, of course, and why the people there came to be known as Bretons. These three populations all essentially started out the same, with a shared history, language and culture, only separated by geography, allowing them to evolve in different ways. Now let's skip forwards a few centuries to when William the Conqueror set about earning himself his nickname. A Norman, yes, but with a disproportionate number of Bretons in his army, not least because they believed they were reclaiming their rightful home. And more Bretons followed the conquest, too, very possibly including a husband and wife who settled in Monmouth with their son, who grew up to become a monk and write a book called *The History of the Kings of Britain*.'

'Ah,' said Elias. 'Geoffrey of Monmouth.'

'Exactly so. His book, of course, included a very extensive section on Arthur, for which there's precious little corroborating evidence, and which he claims was largely based on a source that has conveniently disappeared. It reads as immensely fanciful too, which has naturally led most of my colleagues to dismiss it as largely the product of his imagination. But I don't see it that way. I don't see it that way at all. I believe instead that Geoffrey did the very best he could with the materials he had to hand. You can tell from all the nonsense in it.'

Elias laughed. 'That's a bit back to front, isn't it?'

'No. No, it isn't. It sounds strange, but nonsense can sometimes be a sign of integrity. Take his claim that the Britons got their name from Brutus, a refugee from the Trojan War. Rubbish, right? Except that it was a common belief among fourth century Romans like Juvenal. So it seems likely that that's where Geoffrey got it from. Which isn't a strike *against* Geoffrey's honesty. It's a strike *for* it. Or how about the way he describes Caesar invading Britain three times, when we know he only did so twice. A close reading of Geoffrey makes it clear that he has two separate sources for Caesar's first invasion, only written from such different perspectives that he assumed they were describing separate events. A similar thing happens with that merry old soul King Cole, who appears twice in Geoffrey's book, though under slightly different names. It's the same thing with King Lear of Shakespeare fame. Every time something like this happens, it shows that Geoffrey was working from multiple sources, and that he was doing his level best to make sense of them all. There's a particularly infamous passage about Britain being invaded by an army of one hundred and sixty thousand Africans. Surely *that,* at least, was fantasy on Geoffrey's part. Except Britain was constantly being harassed at that time by a marauding Irish tribe called the *Attacotti*, who vanished long before Geoffrey was born. Now put yourself in his shoes. You've got an ancient document to interpret, written in a script whose lettering you have difficulty making out. *Attacotti* would have meant nothing to you. But *Affricani* would.'

'A mistake in transcription?'

'Why not? They happened all the time. We have very few original documents, just copies of copies of copies. And which is more likely, do you think? That Geoffrey made up this mysterious army of Africans, or that there was an error in transcription somewhere along the line, to render *Attacotti* as *Affricani*? I know where I'd put my money. Because you see this same dynamic again and again in Geoffrey's history; and the more it happens, the more certain I am that his book is based on real but conflicting sources. That's before you even look at all his sudden changes of style, how he switches from long dry lists of names to vivid descriptions of battles or first-hand accounts of conversations he couldn't possibly have witnessed, which surely suggests that he was stitching together wildly different types of sources. And then finally we come to Arthur. Now you tell me, which is the more likely: that Geoffrey suddenly started inventing great chunks of history out of whole cloth, or that he carried on as he'd done before, only with an even greater quantity and variety of material to work with – material that came not only from his mysterious book and other records, but also from his Breton brethren too, whose ancestors had taken their Arthurian lore with them when they'd fled to France, and which had then evolved in its own particular way, as stories will, so that the same incident was remembered in multiple different ways. Which is why so many Arthurian stories were composed by Breton poets, of course. By Chrétien de Troyes and Béroul. By Raoul de Houdenc and Robert de Boron and all the rest, who had their whole cultural hinterland to mine for inspiration. And it's why Geoffrey's account of Arthur is both so extensive and so confused. Because he had this insanely large heap of material to make sense of somehow, so he splodged it all together as best he could, much as Anish did to get that picture of the cauldron. A working model, not an exact replica.'

'If Arthur was so real,' said Elias, 'how come he doesn't appear in the historical record, then?'

'Because there *is* no historical record,' said Quentin irritably. 'All we have is a single sermon by that wretch Gildas. And who's to say he doesn't appear in that?'

'Ah,' said Anna. 'So you think he was Ambrosius Aurelianus.'

Quentin hesitated, a touch annoyed with himself for giving so much away. 'You'll have to wait for my book, won't you?' he said. 'But that's not the point I'm trying to make. The point I'm trying to make is that to dismiss Geoffrey as a fantasist is to do him a grotesque injustice. And it's not just the historical record that says so. The archaeological record does too. Take Stonehenge for example. Geoffrey tells us that Arthur sent Merlin to Ireland to bring back the stones from there. That never happened, of course. All the stones were in place long before Arthur was born. Yet recent excavations have shown that Stonehenge's blue stones were indeed stolen from their original beds in the Welsh hills. Coincidence? Maybe. But also maybe another tick for Geoffrey. Or, again, he tells us of a great gathering of tribal chiefs there. Recent excavations have provided evidence to support that. He claimed an Arthurian link to Tintagel, even though none existed when he was writing. Yet we now know there was something to that too. Then there's Cadbury Castle, just south of here, which folklore has claimed forever was the real Camelot, only to be dismissed out of hand by academics on the basis that no such forts existed in the post-Roman world. Except excavations have now shown that there was a massive and thriving community there at exactly the time Arthur would have lived. So Geoffrey was proved right once again, and the sceptics wrong.'

'What about all the European campaigns Geoffrey talks of?' asked Anna. 'How do you account for those?'

Elias's phone rang before Quentin could reply, however. Elias held up his finger to beg silence as he answered it. 'You arsehole,' said a young man, without even waiting for Elias to speak. 'You absolute bloody arsehole.'

'Hard to argue with that,' said Elias equably. 'But who is this?'

'Who do you think? Me. Archie Miller. From last night.'

'Ah,' said Elias. 'Yes. Of course. What do you want?'

'I've just had the police around, you dick. We all have. In front of my parents too.' His voice took on a whine. 'You said you wouldn't tell.'

'That was before Vic got murdered.'

'That wasn't me, for god's sake. He was my mate, like I told you. I'd never have done anything to hurt him. Never.'

'Which is what I told the police,' said Elias. 'Because they were thinking that whoever pulled the shit you pulled on Ms Ward was most likely responsible for killing Vic too. Which meant I had a duty to tell them otherwise, or they'd have wasted god knows how much time chasing the wrong people. And they'd have found you for sure in the end anyway, only having missed their best chance of catching the real culprit. Is that what you'd have preferred?'

'You arse,' said Archie. 'Everyone thinks I'm a grass now.'

'I'm sorry about that,' sighed Elias. 'Seriously.'

'You will be, believe me.'

'What's that supposed to mean?'

'You'll see,' he said darkly. 'If you think my mates are the kind to take shit like this lying down…' But then the line went dead.

'Another friend made,' murmured Anna. 'How do you do it?'

'It's a gift,' he told her. 'You either have it or you don't.'

TWENTY-TWO

It was two minutes to the hour. Anna turned on the radio and found a local station for the news. No surprise that Vic's murder was top story. What was unexpected, though, was that the police were due to hold a press conference shortly at Grove Farm, although the headline news was already out: A man had been arrested on suspicion of murder, named locally as Wynn Grant.

Quentin gave a heartfelt sigh. 'Oh god. Not this rubbish again.'

'They must have something solid on him,' said Elias. 'They wouldn't have arrested him otherwise.'

The bulletin ended. Anna turned the radio back off. What with all the disruptions on the Marlborough road, Elias opted for a different route back north, this one taking them through Avebury and its famous stones, surely one of the landmarks depicted on the cauldron. It was enough to stir Quentin from his gloom. 'You mentioned Ambrosius Aurelianus earlier,' he murmured to Anna. 'Did you know there's a chance he and his brother Uther Pendragon were buried here?'

'I thought that was Stonehenge.'

'Stonehenge is what Geoffrey said,' admitted Quentin. 'But it's pretty clear he doesn't know one stone circle from another. They're all Stonehenge to him. Accept that and Avebury becomes the far more promising candidate. Apart from anything else, Stonehenge has been investigated as thoroughly as any patch of turf in the country, and there are no burials from the right period. And then there's what this place is called.'

'How so?'

'Well, Gildas implies strongly that Ambrosius Aurelianus was related to a Roman emperor. Who more likely, then, than Aurelian, the man whose name he bore? If so, wouldn't this whole area have become associated with the Aurelians. And Avebury wasn't originally called Avebury, did you know? Our earliest mention of it is in the Domesday Book, where it's written Aureburie.' He spelled it out for them. 'Doesn't that have the ring of Aurelius burgh, the Aurelian place of fortification. Or even Aurelius barrow, the place where the Aurelians were buried. Not just Ambrosius Aurelianus and his brother Uther. Maybe even Arthur too.'

'I always thought Arthur was taken to Avalon,' said Elias.

'Avalon is what Geoffrey calls it, yes. Except it wasn't originally called that either, did you know? Or not exactly. Geoffrey actually calls it *Insularis Auelonis*. With a "U" rather than a "V", I mean. A subtle difference, I admit, but a telling one – especially as the first word probably wouldn't originally have been *Insuralis*, but rather *Ynys*. *Ynys Auelonis* that is. And *Ynys* can refer to a realm or piece of land, not just to an island. Which is to say, *Ynys Auelonis* could just as easily mean "Realm of the Aurelians" as "Island of Apples".'

'Are you being serious?' asked Anna.

'Why not?' said Quentin. 'Think about it. Where was Arthur killed, after all?'

'I haven't a clue. No one does.'

'Not true. We have all kinds of clues. According to Geoffrey, Arthur was campaigning in France when his nephew Mordred seized the throne, forcing him to return in a hurry. Ask yourself this: where would that throne have been, the one that Mordred seized? Where else but Camelot? And where else, then, would the battle for the throne have taken place, if not there? So where was Camelot? Well, tradition and archaeology both agree that Cadbury Castle is by far our best candidate. And do we have anything else to suggest that the Battle of Camlann took place there? I'm glad you asked. Let's start with the place names. A River Cam runs right by it. West Camel and Camel Hill are both within a stone's throw. There's even a place called Queen Camel there, which is one interpretation of what Camlann actually means. And an ancient mass grave was even once dug up there, much like our body-pit here. Are those not clues? And if Arthur was indeed mortally wounded in it, where else would his men have taken him to bury, except back home to his family plot? The realm of the Aurelians. The Aurelian Barrow. A place where Arthur, Uther and Aurelianus could finally be reunited.'

'My god,' said Anna, turning to Quentin with a delighted smile. 'That's it, isn't it? The thesis of your book. You think Aurelianus *was* Arthur. And not just Aurelianus either, but Uther too, only called different names in different sources, leading Geoffrey to believe they were different people, forcing him to fit them together as best he could.'

Quentin looked set to deny it for a moment or two, but then enthusiasm for his project took over. 'It seems so obvious to me,' he said, spreading his hands wide for emphasis. 'I mean Uther and Arthur – could they be easier to confuse? And did you know that Arthur and Pendragon can anyway both mean "Great King". Then there's Riothamus. Remarkably, that can mean "Great King" too. Everyone was a great king back then, it would seem. Unless, of course, there's a simpler explanation. Because if you add Riothamus's campaigns in France to what Gildas tells us about Ambrosius Aurelianus, you have Geoffrey's King Arthur right there. You don't need to do another thing. So why can't that be the answer? That there was really only the one Great King, only given different names and different titles in the various sources poor Geoffrey had to work from, leaving him so bamboozled that he made much the same mistake he'd made with his two King Coles and his two King Lears, and thought them different people.'

'That's all very well,' said Anna. 'Except the dates don't work, do they? No man could have lived long enough to be them all.'

'Not if Gildas wrote his piece in the mid sixth century, as most of my colleagues believe. It would make a Methuselah of the man. But that's all based on a couple of lines in a chronicle written long after the event, which they'd dismiss in a heartbeat if they had anything more solid to go on. And there is something more solid, that's the point. Though appreciating it takes a proper understanding of the style of Latin Gildas wrote in. The formality of it. It's unmistakeably late fifth century. I'd stake my reputation on it. Even if you push it back to the first decade of the sixth century, it would put the Battle of Badon at somewhere around 460 CE. Accept that and everything else snaps sweetly into place. Aurelianus was Uther was Riothamus was Arthur. The mystery is solved.'

They'd reached the Ridgeway while Quentin had still been talking, and now took the right-hander onto Liddington Lane. They passed by Sam's B&B and carried on to Grove Farm, curious to see if the press conference was still in progress. The squad car had gone from the end of its drive, but only to be replaced by a police van. The gate across the way had however been opened wide to give the media a place to park, their heavy trucks scoring deep ruts in the waterlogged earth and churning it into such an ugly slurry that Elias feared the Leaf would get stuck. But they made it through okay, and found some relatively solid ground on which to park, before walking along the verge of the field to avoid the worst of the mud, their shoes licked to a shine by the long wet grass. But, when they tried to cross the lane, they were blocked once more by a uniformed constable, this one tall and narrow shouldered. 'You're too late,' he told them, nodding up the drive at the pack of reporters and their crews coming through the gate. 'It's all over.'

'We're not here for that,' Quentin told him. 'My car's in there. I need it back.'

'Name?'

'Quentin Parkes. I was the one who called this in this morning.'

'Wait here. I'll ask.' He walked off a few paces then turned his back to make a call on his radio before wandering back over again. 'They're not done with it yet,' he said. 'They've got your number, though. They'll text you when they're through.'

'How long will that be?'

'They said an hour.' But then he gave a sympathetic shrug. 'Don't hold your breath, though. Honestly, with that lot, you never know.'

The press pack was almost upon them. They didn't much want to appear on tonight's news, so they turned and made their way back across the lane, only to be chased down by a local TV news reporter in her early thirties and her balding cameraman. 'I know you, don't I?' said the woman to Quentin, perhaps sensing a fresh angle for the story. 'You're Parkes, right? Quentin Parkes. You were his friend.'

'I was indeed,' said Quentin, turning to face her.

'Perhaps you'd care to say a few words about him?'

'Of course,' said Quentin. He turned to the camera, waited until he'd been given the signal. 'Victor Unwin was a wonderful man and a very dear friend of mine for many, many years. Everyone around here loved him. It's impossible to believe this has happened.'

'I wasn't talking about Mr Unwin,' said the reporter. 'I was talking about Wynn Grant, the man they've arrested for his murder.'

'Oh,' said Quentin irritably. 'I have nothing to say about that.'

'You think he's guilty, then?'

'That's not what I said.'

'It kind of is. I mean you were quick enough to defend him last time. After he murdered his brother, I mean.'

'You people,' said Quentin angrily. 'He never murdered anyone. The police needed a scalp, that's all.'

'So they planted all that evidence, did they?'

'What evidence?' demanded Quentin, shaking off Elias as he tried to draw him away. 'A coerced confession and an anonymous phone call. I'll bet they don't have anything better this time either.'

'You'd lose that bet, from what I hear,' returned the woman happily. 'Word is, they've found the murder weapon in his house, and his boots all spattered with blood – boots that just happen to be a perfect match for the prints left at the scene.' Then she added, with barely concealed relish: 'And they're saying it was you who took the photographs to prove it.'

TWENTY-THREE

They drove the Leaf back to Hillview Manor where they found Samantha in the courtyard, sweeping up the debris from last night's storm with a stiff-bristled broom. She marched straight over as Elias parked, rapped angrily on his window. 'I had those bloody Millers over here earlier,' she said, jabbing a finger in the rough direction of their house as he got out. 'They accused me of harbouring spies. Spies! They said you're not here to do a programme at all. They said those horrible Aston Farms people had hired you to trick their son into confessing to some teenage prank.'

'Yeah,' said Elias. 'Pretty much.'

'Yeah?' said Samantha, taken aback. 'That's all I get?'

'We have had talks with the BBC,' said Anna hurriedly, getting out the other side. 'And we will need more material if we're to make our programmes. But yes, I'm afraid it's essentially true. Some horrible, horrible stuff was done to Ms Ward. She was scared for her daughters. They thought we might be able to help.'

'But why you two? Why would they even think to...' Then she caught sight of Quentin, still in the back, looking so guilty it was almost a confession in itself. 'Don't tell me this was your idea.'

'Sam,' he said. 'You have to understand...'

'I don't believe this!' she cried. 'I thought I could at least have trusted you.'

'They poured two bottles of urine through Ms Ward's

letterbox,' said Elias coolly, having had enough of being attacked. 'Then they waited until she was on her way downstairs before dropping in a match, to make her think she and her two girls were about to burn. Are you really okay with that?'

'Of course I'm not bloody okay with it,' said Samantha furiously. 'How dare you even suggest such a thing? But I'm not okay with being lied to either.' She pointed her broomstick at Quentin. 'Especially not by *him*. He's supposed to be my friend.'

'I am your friend,' said Quentin miserably. 'How could you possibly think otherwise?'

'A funny way of showing it.'

'I never thought you'd find out,' he said, before realising that this might not be the wisest line to take. 'You were always telling me you didn't have enough guests to cover your bills, and I saw you had those two rooms free... Honestly, I thought I'd be doing you a favour.'

'Then tell me about it. Don't do it behind my back. Making me look like an idiot in front of those horrible Miller people. Or was that the point? To make me look like an idiot?'

'Come on, Sam,' he pleaded. 'You know perfectly well I'd never want to hurt or upset you. But you're not exactly discreet, are you? Even you must admit that. If I'd told you what was—'

'So I can't keep a secret now? Is that what you're saying?'

'Don't be mad at me, Sam. I beg you. Not after the day I've already had. I can't bear it.'

Her expression flickered. Vic had been her friend too. She bit her teeth together in an effort to keep her scowl, but she couldn't quite manage it. Her expression softened, perhaps at some shared memory. She shook her head. 'Was it really you who found him?'

'And who got him the job in the first place.'

'You can't blame yourself for that.'

'I know. But still.'

She nodded a couple of times, buying herself a few more moments to decide whether the time had come to open the doghouse door. Then she made a little beckoning gesture to him and opened up her arms. He gazed at her for a second or two, not quite trusting his eyes. Then he got out of the Leaf before she could change her mind, stumbling over a loose seatbelt in his hurry. 'Oh god,' said Sam, as they hugged. 'I should be so angry with you, but I can't seem to manage it somehow. Come in. We'll have tea. You need to say hi to the dogs too. They've been missing you terribly.'

They had indeed, it quickly transpired. They went into raptures when they saw him, jumping up on him and turning circles in their excitement. Samantha put the kettle on and produced a freshly-baked chocolate cake from the pantry, handing the knife to Elias to do the honours. He was cutting them a slice each and passing them out when Orlando Wren came in. 'Ah,' he said. 'Tea and cake.'

'Well spotted,' said Samantha. But then she softened. 'Would you like some?'

'That would be wonderful. Yes. Thanks.' She poured him a cup then added a dab of sugar and plenty of milk, evidently familiar with how he took it. She handed it to him along with a slice of cake and a smile that somehow managed to convey both warmth and the wish for him to go. 'I'll leave you to it, then,' he said.

Samantha watched him across the passage into the conservatory before closing the kitchen door on him and pouring tea for everyone else. 'They were saying earlier that they've arrested poor Wynn,' she said, taking care not to look at Quentin. 'Any idea why?'

'One of the reporters told us that his boots were a match for the prints at the scene,' said Elias. 'Apparently they had blood on them too. But you shouldn't take that as gospel. There's nothing quite like a murder investigation for breeding false rumours.'

'They hinted he was after whatever you guys dug up last night,' said Samantha, fishing for more. No one took her bait, however, so she tried again. 'Did you recover it all, do you think? Or might there still be more out there? Only it was so close to me, and if there are thieves after it, and they think it might be on my land...'

'We're pretty confident we've got it all,' Quentin assured her. 'Except for one small piece. But that's almost certainly still somewhere in that field.'

'I wonder,' said Anna.

'How so?' asked Quentin.

'Maybe I'm just imagining it,' she told him. 'But wasn't there something slightly off about Vic's reaction when he saw it last night? I mean he looked stunned, of course he did. But didn't you get the sense that it was because he was puzzled as much as amazed? As if he'd maybe seen something like it before?'

Quentin slowly shook his head. 'I can't say that I did. But then I was looking at the bowl rather than at his face. How confident of this are you?'

'Not at all. There was a monsoon going on. And it didn't strike me at the time, only when Pam suggested that that piece had maybe got snagged by a plough-blade and dragged along a little way. Because what if it had got pulled to the surface instead? What if some random local had spotted it there while out for a walk, and had taken it home?'

'Those fields are certainly a great place to take the dogs,' admitted Quentin.

'Exactly,' said Anna. 'And Vic sounds like the kind of man who'd have been in and out of half the homes around here, at one time or another. What if he saw it in one of them and recognised it when he saw the rest?'

'Wouldn't he have said something?' asked Quentin.

'Maybe he wasn't sure. Maybe he didn't want to get a friend into trouble.'

'We could put the word out,' suggested Samantha. 'See if anyone comes forward.'

'I'd hold off on that,' advised Elias. 'At least for a bit. No one's going to come forward while there's a murder investigation still going on.'

'They seemed pretty confident on the news that they've got the right man,' said Samantha.

'Yeah,' said Elias. 'Even so.'

'But surely if his boots match, and there's blood on them too... How else would you explain it?'

'It's not so hard,' said Elias. 'I mean how about this for a scenario? Someone from around here knows about the hoard, but not yet that it's been moved. Vic's on duty, sure, but he's a doddery old man and they reckon they can break in round the back without him hearing. Only he *does* hear. He catches them at it, giving them such a shock that they thwack him with their crowbar. Now what? Someone's going to spend the rest of their life in jail for this, and they'd rather it wasn't them. So they need a scapegoat. And who better than the brother down the road, the one out on parole for another killing, and who's sure to be blackout drunk right now, leaving them free to go borrow his boots.'

'Are you serious?' asked Anna.

'It would explain why they dragged Vic's body over to the barn, wouldn't it? To leave those footprints in that wet sand. In fact...' He frowned at a further thought, turned to Quentin. 'You still have your photos from this morning?'

'Of course,' said Quentin, fishing his phone from his pocket and opening his gallery before passing it over. 'Why?'

'Let me have a gander first,' said Elias. 'Maybe I'm remembering wrong.' He zoomed in on one of the photos, then nodded and turned it around for Quentin to see. 'Anything strike you?' he asked.

Quentin shook his head. 'Like what?'

'While I was chatting to Wynn yesterday afternoon, he went off to fetch a fresh bottle of gin. He had a pretty severe limp, as you'll know, going up onto the ball of his right foot. Now look at these prints. Both feet planted equally. No hint of a limp. Fair enough while he was dragging Vic's body behind him. But it's the same with these other ones coming back out again.'

'My god,' said Quentin. 'You're right.'

'Let's not get ahead of ourselves,' cautioned Elias. 'It's an anomaly, that's all. A blip. They happen in investigations. Maybe your mate exaggerates his limp for sympathy when he's got an audience, or when his leg's particularly stiff. Maybe dragging Vic affected his gait even after he'd let him go. Maybe he was carrying something else when he came back out. There are all kinds of possibilities.'

'Maybe,' acknowledged Quentin. 'But we still need to let the police know, don't we? How about I tell them when I go back for my car?'

'Sure. Why not? Though for god's sake don't push it too hard. You'll do your mate more harm than good. If there's one thing sure to get on a detective's tits, it's civilians playing at Miss Marple.'

TWENTY-FOUR

Samantha was brewing up a second pot of tea when Scene of Crime finally texted Quentin to let him know they were finished with his car, and he was welcome to go collect it. Elias offered to drive him over, but the sun was out again, it had turned into a fine afternoon, and he chose to walk. They went outside with him, waved him off. The courtyard was still a mess from the storm, so Anna helped Samantha sweep up and bag the worst of the debris while Elias strapped on the power sprayer and finished clearing the grass and moss from between the cobbles, cleaning them of their winter muck.

The spirit of spring was still on them once that was done. They moved to the house instead. Sam and Anna washed its downstairs windows with soapy warm water, sponges and a squeegee, while Elias hosed down the conservatory, clearing it of the moss that the storm had brought down from the Manor's roof. It was growing dark by the time they'd finished. They returned inside the kitchen, glowing with the pleasant tiredness of chores well done. But it wasn't in Samantha's nature to stay still for long, and she soon stirred herself once more. 'So,' she said. 'Dinner.'

'We could always order in,' suggested Anna.

'Nonsense. I'll cook. I enjoy it, and as a thank you for last night. But it'll have to be quick and easy, okay? I picked some lovely mushrooms while I was walking the dogs earlier. So how about a cream fettuccine, maybe with a tomato and onion salad?

Then what's left of your cheesecake to follow. If Orlando hasn't already snaffled it.'

'Sounds wonderful,' said Anna.

'Do you need a hand?' asked Elias. 'People travel from all over the world to watch me salt and stir.'

'I think I can manage,' said Samantha. 'But the company would be nice.'

The grandfather clock in the hallway struck the hour. Samantha took it as her cue to turn on the TV for the local news. Grove Farm was top story, of course. The woman reporter who'd approached them earlier gave a brisk summary of the situation, confirming that a man named locally as Wynn Grant had been arrested, and that the police weren't currently looking for anyone else. But then, with a mischievous smile, she added that not everyone was so sure of Mr Grant's guilt. She cut to a clip of Quentin – taken not from their earlier encounter, but rather on his return to Grove Farm to fetch his car. The reporter had clearly got under his skin somehow, for he was already scowling before he spoke. 'Yes,' he insisted, 'Wynn *is* innocent. They screwed him once before, but we're not going to let that happen again, believe me.'

'We?' asked the woman.

Quentin jabbed a finger back down the road. 'I have a Major Crimes detective working on it right now. And, let me tell you, he's already made one significant breakthrough.'

'Good Christ,' muttered Elias.

'He's only standing up for his friend,' said Samantha, leaping to his defence.

'You've changed your tune,' smiled Elias.

The reporter handed back to the studio, only to be asked whether there was any word yet on motive. Nothing from the police, she said, but it was well known locally that a dig was underway on Grove Farm, and there were widespread rumours of an extraordinary find made just hours before the tragedy. The segment ended. Samantha turned the TV back off. 'An extraordinary find,' she said. 'And everyone knows about it but me. I'm going to have the whole bloody world digging up my lawns, aren't I? And I don't even have a clue what they'll be looking for. Come on, Anna. Spill. It's only fair.'

'I can't,' said Anna. 'I gave my word. Ask Quentin. It's really his decision. Though that woman was right, I can tell you that much. It is extraordinary. So much so that you're almost certain to get some form of heritage park next door, whether you want it or not. And you can probably expect a visit from Historic England too.'

'Who?'

'Historic England. The people responsible for sites of national importance.'

'Responsible for?' squinted Samantha. 'What does *that* mean? Would they buy this place from me? Or will they just slap me with restrictions?'

'I honestly don't know. They do provide some grants, I know that much. But there's not a huge amount of money floating around for new projects right now, I'm afraid.'

'Bloody hell,' she said. 'That's all I need.'

The fettuccine was delicious, but conversation lagged even so, all of them drained by their long and taxing days. They finished off the lemon cheesecake, put the dishes in the washer then by mutual consent bid each other goodnight and retired to their various rooms. Anna checked her messages on her laptop. Pamela Pearce had finally done as promised, emailing her a selection of images of the hoard. She went through them each in turn, spending most time upon the cauldron, zooming in on the engravings to see if she could place them – but there simply wasn't enough detail in them to make that kind of identification. The hill-forts looked like hill-forts; the towns like towns. Even the henges looked so alike that it was impossible to know which was Avebury and which was Stonehenge – assuming those were the two depicted.

The gemstones were little more helpful, a random scattering of brilliant colours. There were more amethysts than any other stone – some two dozen of them. Anna also counted sixteen rubies, eleven turquoises, ten emeralds and sapphires, five beads of what looked like amber and three of carnelian. She puzzled over this for a while, for surely the default choice would have been roughly equal numbers of each, especially as no one who could afford a piece like this was going to skimp on the stones. Presumably, then, this had been a deliberate choice. But why? She tried to think it through, but her long day had turned her brain to sludge. She'd tackled such problems in the past by going to sleep on them and waking to the solution, so she put away her laptop and got ready for bed, early though it still was. Then she lay there in the dark, pondering on it some more, until her tiredness finally overwhelmed her curiosity, and she dropped off.

TWENTY-FIVE

It was ever a risk of going to sleep early that you'd wake in the small hours with the edge taken off your tiredness so that you'd never quite manage to drop off again. So it was with Anna, disturbed by an odd yet disconcerting noise that was gone before she was even properly aware of it, yet which had spoken to her somehow, though for the life of her she couldn't think why. She listened out for it again, but a minute passed without her hearing anything further, so she put it from her mind, turned over and was doing her best to get back to sleep when she heard it for a second time. A single tap with a metallic note to it, like a shutter banging against a window. Except her window had no shutter and there was no wind to speak of.

Her mind was fully alert now. She couldn't help it. It was how she was. It went unbidden to work again, fretting on the problem she'd taken to bed with her, of whether the cauldron gemstones had been randomly scattered, as first appeared, or whether they followed some kind of pattern. And suddenly she was struck by a thought. There were only three carnelians on the entire cauldron, yet two of them had been on the same leaf, she was sure of it. Not only that, but they'd been, respectively, the topmost and bottommost stones on that leaf.

Her laptop was on her bedside table. She opened it up to check. Yes, she was right. The stones were all so higgledy-piggledy that it was easy to miss, especially as the two carnelians were only a fraction higher or lower than the others on that leaf.

Perhaps it was coincidence, then, except that the neighbouring leaf also had the same stones top and bottom, only turquoises this time. Then came rubies, emeralds and amethysts. In fact, each leaf was the same, with matching stones at top and bottom, and only the ones in between still seemingly scattered at random.

Her eyes were dry and sore. She blinked some moisture into them, gave them a rub. It didn't much help. She felt a tickle in her throat too, so she coughed into her hand to clear it. Then she did it again, with more force. Still it did no good. Only then did she become aware of a hint of something acrid in the air, like catching a whiff of a distant bonfire on Guy Fawkes night. She sat up and turned on her bedside light, only now realising what that tapping noise earlier had reminded her of. It had reminded her of the sound Melissa Ward's letterbox had made when Archie Miller and his mates had been pouring their bottles of urine through it.

She threw back her duvet and was on her way to her bedroom door to make sure that all was well when everything kicked off in earnest. First, she heard one of the horses whinnying in the paddock. Then Tristan, Gertie or both started barking furiously downstairs, despite being the friendliest dogs a burglar could ever hope to meet. Barely a second later, the smoke alarms went off, filling the house with their hideous blackboard screeching. Even so, when she opened her bedroom door, she still didn't entirely believe it could be serious, only for a great orange fireball to come roaring up the staircase at her, as though it had been bellowed by a dragon standing guard at its foot.

She leapt back and slammed shut her door before it could reach her, yet still she felt the scorch of it on her face. She counted to five, took another look. The passage was a furnace, flames licking up its walls and a thundercloud of smoke already trapped beneath its ceiling. She closed her door once more, lost for what to do. The alarm was so loud and so intrusive that it must have woken all the others. There was no way across the passage, let alone down the back stairs. It was everyone for themselves, then. For sure it was what Elias would have told her to do. She hurried to her sash window, undid its catch, lifted it high. Smoke leaking out of the downstairs windows came pouring in, so thick and toxic that she had to turn away and clear her eyes before putting her head back out and squinting down. The flames had already taken such firm hold downstairs that they were making the back lawn flicker. She looked both left and right. The nearest drainpipe was out of reach. The ivy, then. It certainly looked sturdy enough, ropes of it as fat as her forearm having burrowed into the paintwork.

Her light went out. The fuses had blown. She pulled on her shoes, jeans, a blouse and a jacket, then packed her laptop, purse and phone into her overnight bag before wadding the rest of her clothes around them. She zipped it up then reached it down as far as she could before dropping it onto the grass beneath. She climbed out onto her sill then turned around and grabbed a fistful of ivy, and was about to commit herself to it only to stop and think again. Elias would indeed have told her to save herself. Anna had not the slightest doubt of it. But she was equally certain that he wouldn't have followed that advice himself. He'd have come to make sure she was safe, however fierce the inferno, whatever burns it would have meant taking. And the fact that he hadn't come for her could only mean one thing: the smoke had got to him before the dogs and the alarms had managed to wake him.

She climbed back into her room. With the fuses blown and her phone in her bag on the grass beneath, she had no light to work by. She felt her way over to her bedside table and the heavy earthenware jug of water that Samantha had left on it. She splashed it out over her duvet then wrapped herself in it like a cloak. She returned to her door, opened it just long enough to peek out. The fire had abated somewhat, and the flames licking up the walls offered enough light to see by, reflected off the underbelly of trapped smoke. The fitted passage carpet had burned away in patches, revealing some old wooden floorboards beneath, already so badly charred that she feared she'd put her foot straight through them. But thankfully Elias's door was still closed and looked to have held.

The heat was extraordinary. Even wrapped inside her duvet, it roasted her face and set tears running down her cheeks. She couldn't stop coughing. She fumbled her way back to her window for a breath of relatively clear air, only for the crash of something tumbling over somewhere in the house to tell her she had no more time to waste. She hurried back to her bedroom door, narrowed her eyes into a slit, then threw it open and leapt without hesitation across the narrow passage to Elias's door, using her jacket sleeve to turn its handle before slamming it closed behind her. Too fast, though, for she caught the skirts of her duvet in it, forcing her to open it again to snatch it all the way inside, only for it to catch fire in that brief instant, so that she had to stamp out the smoulder on the carpet before it could spread.

The smoke was even thicker in here than it had been in her own bedroom. She couldn't see a thing. She sank down onto hands and knees and felt her way over to the bed. As she'd feared, Elias was still lying there, unconscious. She slapped him across his cheek. He gave a kind of grunt, but that was all. She slapped him again, as hard as she could. This time she got nothing. She went to his window, drew back the curtains. A little moonlight filtered in, enough that she could see. The window was a sash, like her own, but it got stuck fast a few inches up when she tried to lift it, and then she couldn't push it either up or down. Her head was spinning by now. It was an effort even to think. But Samantha would surely have left another of her jugs of water on Elias's bedside table. She felt her way over to it, tipped it out over Elias's face, then returned to the window with the empty jug and used it to smash the glass, only for some perverse trick of ventilation to pull the bedroom door open, sucking in flames and more of the toxic black smoke.

She got back down onto hands and knees and felt her way to the bed, so woozy by now that it took an effort of pure will not to keel over. She stripped back Elias's duvet. He was wearing only a plain white T-shirt and a pair of reindeer boxer shorts, no doubt a Christmas present from the twins. He was too heavy for her to lift, so she pulled him from his bed instead. He thudded to the carpet but still didn't wake. She dragged him to the window then rested him against the wall beneath while she stuck her head outside for some relatively clear air and to work out what next.

The conservatory was directly below. The frame of its pitched glass roof was already badly warped, allowing clouds of black smoke to pour out, like from a landscape of industrial chimneys. She doubted it would hold Elias's weight, but what choice did she have? She smashed away the remaining shards of glass from the window frame with the jar, covered the rest of it with her duvet. She reached down to grab Elias around the chest and tried to lift him, but he was so heavy that he kept slipping from her grasp. She squatted instead, to lift him with her legs, heaving him up onto the sill then taking a moment's rest before grabbing him around the thighs and simply tipping him out head-first so that he tumbled onto the conservatory below. Its frame bent but somehow held and thankfully he rolled down its pitched roof to fall off it into the rose bed alongside.

The fire was now raging behind her. She had no time left. She leaned forwards out of the broken window and let herself fall onto the glass roof beneath, hoping to follow Elias in rolling off it to the ground. But Elias had buckled its frame so badly that her leg plunged through the gap between two panes; and when she tried to draw it back out they came together again to clamp around her ankle. The harder she tried to pull herself free, the tighter the two panes bit. Smoke was pouring up through the gap, making the air unbreathable – except that she had no choice. Her brain fogged. She couldn't think. Her strength left her; she grew feeble. It was almost over. Only the fierceness of the heat itself kept her awake for one final thought: *The harder she tried to pull herself free, the tighter the panes bit around her ankle. A Chinese finger puzzle! It was a Chinese finger puzzle!* She pushed her foot down instead, releasing her ankle and pulling it free before the trap could close again. Then she went tumbling down the slope of the roof to land flush on top of Elias in the rose bed beneath.

She rolled off him onto the dewy grass of the lawn, kicking off her smouldering boots before they could burn her. A terracotta tile came crashing down from the roof to land close by, shattering into pieces and spattering them both with its shrapnel. She laboured back to her feet, grabbed Elias beneath his arms and dragged him away across the lawn. His boxer shorts kept catching on the grass and pulling down. She had to stop three times to pull them back up again, despite knowing how heartily he'd have laughed at her over such concern for his dignity.

They were far enough back now to be safe. She let go of him and was about to go check on the others when he gave a groan, opened his eyes and gazed groggily up at the flames and smoke pouring out of the Manor's windows, even as a section of its roof caved in, sending up a vast fireworks display of sparks and flaming ash. 'What the hell?' he muttered.

'There was a fire,' she said.

'I got that far all by myself,' he told her. 'I used to be a detective, you know.' He laboured up onto an elbow. 'But I don't remember the first damned thing about it. How did I even get out?'

Anna hesitated. 'We made it out together,' she told him.

He looked back up at the house, taking in his broken bedroom window and the smouldering duvet half hanging out of it, the buckled conservatory roof and the drag marks on the grass. 'You came for me,' he stated flatly.

'Someone had to.'

'You idiot.'

'You'd have come for me.'

'Yeah,' he said. 'But there's a reason for that.'

Samantha came hurrying around the side of the house at that moment, saving Anna from having to answer. She gave a piercing shriek when she saw them and ran over to them. 'Thank god!' she cried, throwing her arms around them both. 'I saw your bag beneath your window. I thought you were still in there.'

'Is Orlando okay?' asked Anna. 'The dogs?'

'They're fine. Everyone's fine. All my guests too. It was you two who had me freaking out.' Another crash from the house as more of the roof caved in, launching a hot-air balloon high up into the sky, turning the whole night orange, blazing so hot that they could all feel it on their faces, even at this distance. 'I can't think how it could have started,' wailed Samantha. 'I had the wiring checked just last year. Or not that long ago, anyway. And I did my rounds, like always.' She gazed up at her house with a mix of awe and horror. 'Oh god, my insurance. The money those bastards take off me every month. Yet they always find some way to make it your fault.'

'Not this time,' said Anna. 'Someone did this. Deliberately.'

Samantha turned to stare at her. 'How do you mean?'

'I heard a slapping noise right before it started,' she said. 'Exactly as Melissa Ward described hearing when Archie Miller and his idiot mates poured urine through her letterbox.'

'Archie Miller?' said Samantha, bewildered. 'But why? I've never done anything to him.'

'It wouldn't have been for you,' Elias told her wearily. 'It would have been for me. And it wouldn't have been Archie either. Not something this big.'

'He did threaten us pretty bluntly yesterday,' said Anna.

'That wasn't a threat,' said Elias. 'It was a warning. A warning that his mates might try something. There were a couple of them in the pub the other night...' He was clearly too drained to say any more, however. He stretched back out on the grass instead, arms above his head, even as the wail of a distant siren announced the approach of the first fire engine.

TWENTY-SIX

It took until well after sunrise for the blaze to be brought fully under control – and then mostly because it ran out of fresh fuel. A pair of ambulances arrived, though thankfully it was only Anna and Elias in real need of attention, having suffered a variety of cuts, bruises and burns during their escape from the house. The paramedics treated and dressed these as was necessary, then checked them both for shock and smoke inhalation before releasing them to give their statements to the police.

Elias had lost all his clothes in the fire. Luckily, Orlando Wren had been roused in good time to save his own belongings before getting out, and he was generous enough to lend him a pair of trousers, a shirt, a jacket, socks and trainers, all of which fit reasonably well, even if they were a bit on the large side, so that he had to roll up the bottom of the trousers and secure them with a belt. More problematically, Elias had also lost his phone, keys, laptop and wallet, so he borrowed Anna's phone to call his ex-wife, with whom he'd left his spare debit card and a full set of keys for emergencies just like this. She clucked her tongue at him when he told her that he needed them couriered down, though her manner transformed into an appalled and affectionate concern once he'd explained about the fire. She promised to take care of it all as soon as possible, only they were in Paris for the weekend. She could come back early if it was important enough, but would first thing tomorrow do? It would, he assured her.

Everything stank of smoke. Wet smoke. No surprise, then, that the guests in the converted stables headed off as soon as the police allowed, for this was hardly the weekend break they'd signed up for, and the bank holiday was almost over anyway. At least that freed up the three apartments, allowing Samantha and Orlando Wren to take one each, leaving the third for Elias and Anna to share.

Anna took her bag over to it. It was compact but charming, with twin beds in the only bedroom, a bathroom and a sitting room area with a sofa-bed that the previous guests had left out and made up. She stripped it of its rumpled sheets, pillowcases and duvet cover, intending to run them through the wash, only to remember that the machine had been another casualty of the fire. She made a bundle of them, instead, that she stowed out of sight in a cupboard. The stables' electricity supply was still working, and they shared a router too. With nothing better to do, Anna hooked her laptop up to it then sat on the sofa to pick up where she'd left off before the fire, bringing up Anish's working model of the cauldron to see if she could crack its secret.

Word of the disaster had meanwhile spread through Badbury and the surrounding area. Some neighbours came to gawp; others came with sympathy and offers of support. Quentin was among these latter, arriving with a pair of large jute shopping bags filled to bursting with bread, butter, cheese, ham, biscuits, crisps, milk and the like that he and Samantha then doled out among the stables. Anna caught his eye while he was at it and gestured for him to come back alone when he had a moment. He reappeared a couple of minutes later, standing uncertainly in the doorway. 'Did you want me for something?'

'Yes, please.' She patted the sofa cushion to invite him alongside, then showed him the image of the cauldron on her screen. 'I realised something last night,' she told him. 'Not about the cauldron itself so much as about all its gemstones. It's that the bottom and top stone on each leaf always match.'

'How do you mean?' frowned Quentin.

She zoomed in on a particular leaf, the better to show him.

'See here, for example. This lowest stone is an amethyst. So is the top one. What's more, there's no third amethyst on this leaf either, despite there being lots of other gemstones on it, as you can see, and plenty of amethysts elsewhere on the other leaves. It's the same with this leaf next door too, only with amber beads at top and bottom this time, and nowhere else upon it – though again there are several of them elsewhere. And it's the same with all five of the other leaves we have too, which surely means it isn't random but rather a deliberate pattern.'

'Signifying what?'

'Well, yes,' agreed Anna. 'That's the question. And I'm pretty sure I've got at least some of the answer. The first bit is that the top and bottom stones provide a kind of link between the villa engraved on the base plate – which let's assume for the moment represents the one you've found next door – and the landmark engraved on the top of that particular leaf. And also that the distance between them is very broadly proportional to the total number of that particular gemstone.'

'Oh,' said Quentin. 'Yes. That makes sense.'

'That's not all,' said Anna. 'I think the leaves are arranged with relative orientation in mind. So let's take these two stone circles as an example, because they're what helped me work it out. They surely represent Avebury and Stonehenge, right? Let's plug that into our model and see how well it fits. Avebury is about a third of the distance from here as Stonehenge is, give or take, and roughly in the same direction too, only a little bit to one side. Which is to say that, if you were to stand on your villa mosaic facing south, and you could somehow see them both, Stonehenge would be a touch to the left of Avebury, only three times as far away. Now look at our two leaves with the stone circles. They're bang next door to each other on the cauldron, as our theory would predict; and the one to the left has nearly three times as many emeralds as the one to the right has beads of amber – once you've subtracted the top and bottom stones, at least.'

'But that's brilliant!' said Quentin.

'It is rather, isn't it?' grinned Anna. 'Which means we should be able to work out what each of these other engravings represent by counting up the number of their particular gemstone and checking their relative placement upon the cauldron. Which is what I was working on just now, when you came in.'

'And?'

'Let's start with the three towns or cities. They're quite tricky, because there are so many plausible candidates, and we can't be sure of the exact number of gemstones, not without the missing eighth leaf. But, as it happens, Bath, Winchester and Exeter are approximately the right distances and directions, and they certainly all existed at the time, and were important. So let's go with those for the moment.'

'And the hill-forts?' asked Quentin.

'Well, quite,' nodded Anna. 'Those are the only two remaining – except for whatever was on the eighth leaf, of course. The first has rubies at top and bottom, and there are plenty of rubies elsewhere on the cauldron too. In fact, the orientation and number of stones is an almost perfect match for Cadbury Castle.'

'Camelot!' exulted Quentin. 'What did I tell you? And the other?'

'It looks to be pretty much due north of here, as best I can tell. And it's on the leaf with the carnelian beads, of which there are only three. Which implies it's really close, right? Surely, then, the hill behind us, whether Mount Badon or not.'

'But this is amazing, Anna,' said Quentin. 'God, but we need that eighth leaf!'

'I know. Though I'm not sure that...' But then she drifted to a halt.

'You're not sure that what?' asked Quentin.

Anna didn't reply at once, too concentrated on her own thoughts. 'I was about to say, I'm not sure that it will follow the same pattern as the others, because there is no eighth gemstone on the cauldron – if you discount the double band of pearls, at least.'

'How do you mean?'

'I mean exactly that,' said Anna. She held up her hands to tick them off on her fingers. 'We've got sapphires, emeralds, ambers, rubies, amethysts, turquoises and carnelians. But that's it. There is no eighth stone. So what was the stone on the eighth leaf?'

'How are we supposed to know that?'

'Well, that's what I realised just a moment ago. Maybe it doesn't matter. Not for this. What matters is that it doesn't appear on any of the other leaves. Think about it. If we're right about how the pattern works, as we surely are, and if it continues onto the eighth leaf, as it most likely does, then the eighth stone – whatever it might be – can only appear twice in total on the whole cauldron. Once at the top and once at the bottom. Which means that the landmark inscribed upon it has to be the closest of all; even closer than the hill behind us, I mean. And it should be roughly in the same direction too, only a little to its left. Now imagine that you're standing on your mosaic next door, looking towards Liddington Hill. What do you see, only a bit closer and a little to the left?'

'Samantha's paddock,' murmured Quentin.

'Exactly,' said Anna. 'And you know those aerial photographs that you guys took of this whole area? Would they have her paddock on them, do you think? And, if so, would you have access to them here?'

TWENTY-SEVEN

Samantha was wearing holes in the carpet of the end stable, engaged in what was clearly a stressful phone call with her insurers, judging from the way she kept rubbing the nape of her neck. She beckoned Anna and Quentin in anyway, gestured them at the sofa, where Tristan and Gertie gave them a far more effusive welcome, wagging their tails and licking their hands, showing no signs whatsoever of last night's trauma.

Samantha jotted down a name and a number on a pad, someone else for her to speak to. 'Bloody woman,' she said, ending the call. 'She thinks I set the fire myself, I know she does.'

'Don't let them get to you,' said Quentin. 'Suspicion is their default position. It has to be. They'll come around.'

'If I can prove it wasn't me. But how do I do that?'

'That's what the fire investigation team is working on right now. They'll prove it for you.'

'And in the meantime? This place is going to be a building site for years. Where will I even live?'

'You'll find something. If the worst comes to the worst, I have a whole half of my house that I never even use. You could stay there as long as you liked. You'd never even have to see me, not if you didn't want to.'

She came over to give his shoulder a grateful squeeze. Only then did she notice how Anna was sitting, perched forward with her laptop on her knees, clearly poised to show her something on its screen. 'What?' she asked.

It was Quentin who answered. 'Forgive us in advance,' he said. 'We know absolutely that this is going to sound ridiculous, given all the circumstances. But we have a weird question to ask, and we don't want you getting upset or offended.'

'And? Am I supposed to guess?'

'Okay. It's this. Do you know if there was ever some kind of building at the far left-hand corner of your paddock? A small one, it would have been. A shed or hut, maybe. About three yards wide by four yards long.'

Samantha shook her head, though more to give herself time to think than in denial. 'There wasn't when we bought the place, I'm sure of that. I've seen photos of it going back a good hundred years, too, and I can't recall there ever being anything like that. Though it was just another field back then, of course. It was the people before us who bought it from the Grants to turn it into a paddock. Why?'

Anna turned her laptop around to show her the photograph already up on its screen. 'The Aston Farms people took a lot of aerial photos as part of their survey. This is one of them, as you can probably tell. It shows the back left-hand corner of your paddock, right where it meets the foot of Liddington Hill.'

'Okay,' said Samantha. 'So?'

'So do you see this patch of grass here, where it runs up to the rear railing. See how much paler it is than the grass around it?'

'And that means something, does it?'

'It can do, yes,' said Quentin. 'Especially when the sides are as straight as this. It means there was likely a building there at some point.'

'And you think it was part of your Roman villa?'

'Not part of it, exactly,' said Quentin. 'It's too far distant for that.' He put his finger on the screen, tracing for her a faint line that ran from the patch of pale grass all the way across her paddock and then part of the way across the Grove Farm field to the mosaic they'd found in it. 'But see this? It looks like there may have been some kind of path between the two. And of course Roman villas weren't just villas, any more than a modern farm is just a house. They had multiple outbuildings too. The bit we've found next door is what they called the *pars urbana*, where the main family and their guests would have lived. It had mosaic floors, marble colonnades and stone walls, pretty much everything people think of when they think of Roman villas. But they think that in large part because those bits have survived so much better than the so-called *pars rustica*, even though those would likely have been far more extensive, only built from perishable materials like mud and wood and thatch. Quarters for the servants. Stabling for the horses. Storage for farm equipment. Barns for the harvest.'

'You couldn't store much of a harvest in *that*,' said Samantha.

'No,' agreed Quentin. 'Nor sleep many staff neither. Which is one of the reasons we think it was likely something else. Something far more intriguing.'

Samantha looked sharply at him. '*One* of the reasons? There are others?'

'Ah,' said Quentin, regretting his slip. 'There is one, yes. It was in the hoard we found last night. But I can't be more explicit than that, I'm afraid. I truly can't. Not just yet. But please believe me when I say that it gave us good reason to think that we'd find something significant in that general area. It's what made us check the aerial photographs in the first place. We don't know what it is, not for certain, only that it must have mattered a great deal to the owners of the villa. So it's surely worth taking a look at. But we wouldn't want to do that behind your back, of course. So here we are.'

'You want to carry out a survey of my paddock?'

'Not a survey, exactly. Not for the moment. Just to take a look.'

'Okay,' nodded Samantha. 'Let's do it.'

TWENTY-EIGHT

The fire was out, but the house was still far too dangerous to approach, its surviving walls unstable and burnt tiles falling sporadically from what little was left of its roof. Yet it held Elias rapt even so. He paced around and around the safety cordon set by the fire crews, brooding on what had taken place. Specifically, he brooded on the purpose behind the fire – whether it had been a warning that had got out of hand, or a serious attempt at murder. And, if the latter, would they try again?

Ransome arrived in the back of a squad car. She buzzed down her window to beckon Elias over, then invited him to climb in alongside her. She was wearing jeans, heavy army boots and long green waterproofs, as if she'd been about to set off on a hike with the family and the dogs when the call had come in. And she didn't seem altogether thrilled about it either. 'So,' she said. 'They tell me you think it was set deliberately.'

'It *was* set deliberately. Anna heard the letterbox go bang before it started. Twice.'

'It was the early hours,' pointed out Ransome. 'She'd have been half asleep at best.'

'She said she heard it. That means she heard it.'

'Fine,' said Ransome, with an amused twitch of her lips. 'So what are you thinking? Archie Miller and his mates, I presume? I understand he threatened you yesterday afternoon.'

Elias gave a sigh. 'Yeah, kind of. Though honestly I think it was a warning more than a threat. And I can't see him having the meanness or the stupidity for something this big. Or the balls, frankly. More likely his mates. There were a couple in the pub the other night I wouldn't want to find myself at the mercy of. A tall, red-headed bodybuilder type with a broken nose and bad teeth. And a shorter, thinner, more athletic one with a pair of hoop earrings, a high-top fade, and a scar just here on his upper lip.'

'You know how to spot them, I'll give you that,' said Ransome. 'Keegan Inwood and Billy Scott. A right pair of charmers. And yes, we pulled them both in yesterday over the letterbox thing, so they'd have had cause too. But how would they have known where you were staying?'

'Archie may have told them that much,' admitted Elias. 'Though not if he'd known what they had planned.'

'I don't get it. Why are you so strong for him? He may have almost killed you.'

'I don't know. I liked him. He struck me as a good kid with bad friends. Could have been me ten years ago.'

Ransome slid him a look. 'Ten?' she asked.

'Oi,' he laughed. 'Okay. Go round them up, if you think they're good for it.'

'Thanks for the permission,' she said dryly. 'We already have.'

'Ah. Okay. I was about to add: just keep an open mind.'

'I intend to. Because you know what my first thought always is, with arson?'

Elias shook his head. 'I don't see it as an insurance job, if that's where you're going. Sam's not the type.'

'Sam, is it now?' asked Ransome.

'Samantha, if you prefer. Ms Forrest, even. And no, I've not succumbed to her charms, if that's what you're wondering. Someone tried to kill me and Anna last night, so I'm not in any kind of mood for being beguiled. It would be out of character, is all I'm saying. Maybe if the house had been empty. But with guests upstairs? No way.'

'She had smoke alarms, yes? She'd have figured they'd wake

you and you'd get out in time. And the word is that she's struggling pretty badly for money. I'm told she's been making noises about selling up for a while now, only having a chicken farm next door has really affected what she'd get for it.'

'Yeah,' said Elias. 'She told me and Anna that herself the other night. Which she'd hardly have done if she was thinking about torching the place.'

'Maybe she acted on impulse,' said Ransome. 'She gets the letterbox idea from Miller and his mates, thinks they'll get the blame if she goes copycat. And she may be more ruthless than she looks. Her husband died from Covid, did you know? She admitted herself that he could only have caught it from her. There were whispers at the time that she'd exposed herself deliberately in order to pass it on, before they went completely bankrupt.'

'Yeah. We heard a few whispers like that up in Lincolnshire too. I even checked out a couple of cases. Malicious neighbours, both times.'

'Fine,' sighed Ransome. 'Then who?'

'Well, it's not my job any more. But, back when it was, if a man got murdered one night, and the house next door went up in flames twenty-four hours later, I wouldn't be wondering *if* they were connected, I'd be wondering *how*.'

Ransome nodded. 'Your mate Quentin was on the news last night. Did you see? Said you were on the case and that you'd already made some kind of major breakthrough. Anything to it?'

'Not really, no. I had a thought, is all. About why Vic's killer bothered to drag his body behind that mound of sand.'

'To hide him, surely?'

'From what? From whom? How long would it have taken for him to be found?'

'Okay, then, smartarse. Why?'

'To leave those footprints behind, of course,' said Elias. 'Footprints that, sooner or later, were bound to lead you to Wynn and the murder weapon, which I'll bet you found hidden behind the sofa or on top of a cupboard or some equally dumb place like that. Yet still with Vic's blood and hair on it. Go on. Tell me I'm wrong.'

'I'm not about to discuss confidential details of the investigation with you,' said Ransome irritably. 'Anyway, Occam's razor.'

'Occam's razor!' snorted Elias. 'You must have seen the way Grant walks by now. How he goes up onto the tiptoes of his right foot. Now look at your footprint photos again. Would he really have left ones with both feet level like that? But someone trying to implicate him would, if they weren't thinking clearly. And who thinks clearly after killing a man?'

'Yet they were thinking clearly enough to frame Grant for it?'

'Yes,' agreed Elias. 'Clearly enough for that.'

Ransome fell silent again as she gave it thought. 'You honestly believe that's how it happened?'

'Not a clue,' shrugged Elias. 'But I'm open to the idea. And I reckon you should be too.'

TWENTY-NINE

The back lawn was still spongy from the storm, and covered by such a thick snowfall of dirty grey ash that Samantha, Anna and Quentin left clear trails of prints as they trudged across it. 'You'll never guess what else happened earlier,' said Samantha with a kind of weary bitterness as she lifted up the paddock gate latch then gestured the others through ahead of her. 'My barn people came to see me. They've moved their horses out, as you can see. Which, you know, fair enough. They were pretty badly spooked by the fire. But they wanted their month's rent back too. I mean, come on. I lost my bloody house five hours ago. At least give me the day.'

They wended their way between the showjump fences to the paddock's far left corner. The patch of grass they'd identified was indeed a swatch paler, though the effect was so slight that it was no surprise it hadn't been spotted before. Samantha dug an unimpressed heel into the soft turf. 'It doesn't look like much.'

'It never does,' said Anna. 'Not from ground level. That's what makes aerial photography such a godsend.'

'So what do we do now?'

'We organise a proper survey,' said Quentin. 'A non-invasive one, to start. I'll see if I can't bring back that ground penetrating radar we used next door. That should let us know if there really is something down there. If so, it should give us a general idea of its size and shape and depth. If it looks promising enough, we'll put together an excavation plan. It's just about possible we could organise it for after we finish next door, but frankly it's far more likely to be later in the year or even early next. Assuming you give us permission, of course.'

'And if I were to give you permission right now?'

'I'm sorry?'

Samantha nodded across the width of the paddock at the hedge that separated her property from Grove Farm, over the top of which they could see the digger's raised yellow bucket. 'I've seen you working that thing when your other driver isn't around. I'll bet you even have your own keys to it, don't you?'

Quentin's hand moved guiltily to his pocket. 'That's hardly the point, Sam,' he said. 'You can't just dig up a site of such potential importance without—'

'Why not?' she asked. 'Why can't we?'

'Because excavation is a highly sensitive and delicate process. You can't just drive over a machine like that and—'

'Delicate process, my arse,' said Samantha. 'I've seen you at it, remember? You bring that bloody digger over to your next spot then claw off great mounds of earth until you hit whatever's down there.'

'That may be how it looks from the outside,' said Quentin. 'But honestly a lot of work has gone into it before we even think of—'

'Bollocks,' she said.

'It has. I swear. I've spent days studying the data from our survey. That means we have a very good idea of what might or might not be down there, and how deep it is, before we even think about bringing in the digger.'

'I don't care,' she said. 'I'm not waiting until next year. I want to know now. I *need* to know now.' She gestured back at her house. 'My life is falling apart, in case you couldn't tell. I'm going to have to make some major decisions over the next few days, and this could make a huge difference. So I'm going to check it out, with or without your help. If you won't do it yourself, I'll bring in a crew of my own first thing tomorrow, and have them dig up this whole damned area. And I'll make sure there aren't any archaeologists around to supervise them either, or to take over from them if we hit something important.'

'Come on, Sam,' pleaded Quentin. 'You don't mean that.'

'I *do* mean that.'

'What about your tenants? Their horses?'

'They gave up their rights when they asked for their rent back. So this is your chance. Your one and only chance. Either you go fetch that digger now, or I'll have all this dug up first thing tomorrow morning. And you'll never even get to see what's down there.'

THIRTY

Ransome didn't reply to Elias for a few moments. But then she sighed and shook her head. 'For the record, I still fancy Wynn Grant for Vic's murder. But – and this is for your personal information only – I spent a good hour with him last night, and another again this morning. It's why I was so late getting here. He's not talking yet, which wouldn't worry me in the slightest, except that there's a particular flavour of injured righteousness that these arseholes give off when they're actually innocent for once. I'm sure you know it.'

'Like they deserve a medal,' said Elias.

'Exactly. Yes. So let's say for the moment that you're right. Let's say it was someone else who broke into Grove Farm the other night. They killed Vic when he caught them at it, then framed Grant for it. And last night's fire was a pre-emptive strike to prevent you from taking on the case and clearing him. So where does that get us? We're still looking for someone who knew about the hoard, right? But not that it had already been moved to Devizes.'

'Maybe.'

'Only maybe? Why else would they break in?'

'I was noodling around with exactly that question when you arrived. And what I got to wondering is, what if the break-in wasn't about stealing the hoard at all? What if the point of it was simply to get Wynn Grant back into trouble?'

'Are you being serious with this?'

'Sure. Why not? He's hardly Badbury's most popular man, is he? And he's only out on parole. Imagine you wanted him back in prison for some reason or other that we can come back to. You find out somehow about the hoard being discovered. It gives you the idea. If you can nick a few pieces and plant them around his house for you guys to find, not only will that get his parole revoked, he'll likely be looking at a good few years on top too.'

'It's one thing to dislike the man. But that…?'

'Yeah, but what if it's not just dislike? What if it's fear?'

She looked shrewdly at him. 'You have someone in mind, don't you?'

'Maybe. Though it means going back a few years, to the death of Wynn's brother Caleb. Were you involved in that investigation yourself?'

'A bit of door knocking, that's all. Too junior for anything more.'

'Okay, so as I understand it, Wynn would have inherited his brother's estate, except that he was automatically barred from it after being convicted of his manslaughter, so that it went to some cousins instead. Now imagine you're one of those cousins. You hear on the family grapevine that your cousin Caleb has just died, and that the police are looking at your other cousin Wynn for it; and you already know that neither of them have kids, so you'll be next in line if he gets convicted. Pretty tempting to put a finger on the scale, no? Say by making an anonymous phone call claiming to have seen him coming out of the farmhouse at the key moment, looking all flustered.'

'It's possible, I guess.'

'Wynn swore blind he'd never been there that day. He's a liar, so a pinch of salt and all that. But the way he tells it, that phone call was a deliberate act to get him convicted. Let's say he's right. He may be an addict, but I don't think he's dumb. He'll have figured out the *cui bono* by now. I only spoke to him for ten minutes or so, but he made it pretty clear that he had someone particular in mind, and that he intended to make them pay for it too. So I'd be very surprised if I was the only person he's mouthed off to.'

'You think he meant it?'

'Probably not. Too much to lose, and too much like hard work. But my opinion isn't the one that matters. The one that matters is that of whoever made that phone call. And you know those idiot criminals who keep coming back to the scene of their crime. It's not to gloat, not in my experience. It's because they're *scared*. They're scared that they've left some telling piece of evidence behind that'll lead straight back to them, or that the police have made some new breakthrough. So they can't sleep, they can't eat, they can't sit still. They have to know. They follow the investigation obsessively on TV and the internet. They visit the site to be on hand in case there's something that needs dealing with. It only ever increases their chance of getting caught, and they know it too. They just can't help themselves.'

'Is this going somewhere?'

'Imagine it was you who'd made that phone call, and that it's been eating away at you ever since. That fear of being found out. So you've been tracking Wynn ever since his conviction, his various appeals and hearings. Finally the dreaded day arrives when Wynn gets released. Wouldn't you be feeling sick about it, wondering what he was up to, and whether he'd be coming after you? Wouldn't you be praying that he'd slip up somehow and get his parole revoked? At one blow, all that weight would be off your shoulders for another five or even ten years. But only if it gets reported. So you decide to make sure it *does* get reported, even if you have to do it yourself. Unfortunately for you, Wynn knows where the lines are, and he stays well behind them too. But then a hoard is discovered in a field that Wynn clearly believes should rightly belong to him. Wouldn't you be tempted to put your finger back on that scale?'

'Do you have *any* evidence to back this up?' asked Ransome.

'Not a scrap, no,' admitted Elias cheerfully. 'But I'd still want to find out more about those cousins, if this was my case. I'd want to know what they were up to back then, and what they're up to now, and whether any of them have been down this way recently.' Then he turned and nodded across the courtyard at Orlando Wren, standing outside his stable, pretending to check something on his phone, only glancing anxiously every few seconds at the squad car in the back of which Ransome and Elias were sitting. 'And, while I was at it, I might just want to ask him if he was one of them.'

THIRTY-ONE

The five-barred gate that separated Samantha's paddock from Grove Farm's back field looked to be secured with a chain and padlock. But only looked to be. The padlock had actually rusted shut years ago, but had been left draped over the junction of gate and post in the hope of fooling anyone who didn't check too closely. The real security was the gate itself, for it dated back to when the paddock had been part of the farm, and was so old and heavy that it had sagged on its hinges and dug deep into the sodden earth, forcing Anna and Samantha to heave it up and shuffle back with it in baby steps until it was open wide enough for the digger to make it through.

'You think I'm nuts, don't you,' said Samantha, rubbing her sore palms on her trousers after setting it back down.

'Not nuts, no. I might well do the same, in your position. And I can't deny that I'm dying to know what's down there. Plus we archaeologists can get a bit precious sometimes about our methods. But there's a good reason for that. Excavation is inherently destructive, you see. You only get one first go, and if you mess it up...'

'Oh god. I'm not going to get Quentin into trouble, am I?'

'I don't think so. He's good at this. Let him take it at his own pace and it should be fine. But please bear in mind that it wouldn't only be heartbreaking if we were to damage something historic, it could prove extremely costly too. To you personally, I mean. Anything found on your land legally belongs to you. How would you feel if you broke it?'

'Ah. Yes. I see what you mean. And you think that's possible? That there's something valuable down there?'

'It's possible, yes. Though I wouldn't get your hopes up too much. If we're right about this, the owners of the villa weren't just proud of what was here, they rather showed it off too. Everyone who lived around here back then would have been certain to know about it, as would any invading armies too. That's a recipe for getting robbed, frankly. So the chances of finding anything of intrinsic value are pretty small. But you never know.'

Quentin came lumbering through the gate on the digger, its caterpillar treads churning a pair of muddy tracks in the paddock's wet grass. He arrived at where they were standing then jumped down from the cab before reaching back inside for the metal detectors that had been stowed in there during the storm. 'At least let us check it first,' he begged Samantha.

'Don't worry,' she told him. 'Anna's talked me down. Slowly slowly it is. But you two obviously know far more than you're letting on. Isn't it time to tell me? Come on. It's only fair.'

Quentin glanced at Anna. Anna nodded. 'Very well,' he said. 'But this has to stay between us, okay?' He waited until Samantha had agreed before carrying on. 'Right, then. So we found a large bowl or cauldron the other night with some intriguing markings on it – markings that suggest that there was something right around here that was very important to the owners of the villa. They were Christians, so maybe it was a shrine or chapel. But both Anna and I think it's more likely to have been the family mausoleum. Probably not the whole thing. It's too small for that. But what the Romans often did was, they built their mausoleums underground, then covered the access to it with some kind of grand superstructure. And this would be exactly the right size for that.'

'What do you mean by access? Do you mean some kind of staircase?'

'We think that's most likely, yes. And what makes it even

more exciting is that we think there's a real chance that the villa – and indeed everything else around here – might have belonged to members of the Aurelian family.'

'The Aurelians?' She looked a little dizzily from Quentin to Anna and then back again. 'But wasn't King Arthur an Aurelian? The man you always thought to be King Arthur?'

'Ambrosius Aurelianus,' said Quentin. 'Yes. Exactly.'

'And you think this is his family tomb?' she said, sounding almost indignant. 'Are you seriously telling me that I may have King bloody Arthur buried beneath my paddock? But what about Avalon? Wasn't he buried there? And isn't that Glastonbury. And didn't they already find his body there, hundreds of years ago?'

'The monks there claimed that, yes,' said Anna. 'But it was almost certainly a hoax.'

'Though not necessarily in the way most people think,' added Quentin.

Anna glanced curiously at him. 'How do you mean?' she asked.

Quentin hesitated a moment, long enough for her to sense that this was another nugget that he'd wanted to hold back for his book. But then he went ahead anyway. 'Okay,' he said. 'So the hoax theory runs something like this. Glastonbury was ravaged by a terrible fire back in 1184. Many of its buildings were destroyed or badly damaged, and repairing them was going to cost far more than the monks could afford. One of the best ways for such places to raise significant funds back then was by attracting pilgrims. But pilgrims didn't go just anywhere. You needed to give them a reason to visit. This was right around the first peak of Arthurmania. Possession of his relics would therefore have been immensely valuable. That obviously gave the monks there every incentive to make it up, as Anna rightly says. I certainly can't prove otherwise. All I'll say is that it may not be quite so cut and dried as that. For a start, precisely because relics were so valuable, abbeys and monasteries were constantly bickering over who had whose bones. Yet no one ever challenged Glastonbury's claim to having Arthur, which strongly implies there was a pre-existing tradition of some kind to connect him to the place. And it wasn't even their own idea to look for him. It was Henry II's. Why would he have thought of it, if no such tradition had existed? Then there's the grave itself. It included a headstone claiming it as the grave of Arthur and Guinevere.'

'Yes,' countered Anna. 'But in the wrong script.'

'It wasn't a sixth century script, if that's what you mean. But it wasn't a twelfth century one either. That's the point. The headstone itself is lost, but we have a drawing of it that suggests a likely tenth century creation. Which is telling, because the tenth century was when St Dunstan became abbot of Glastonbury, rescuing the place from an earlier malaise.'

'So?' asked Anna.

'So pilgrimages didn't start in the twelfth century. They'd already been a major source of income for religious institutions for hundreds of years by then. And St Dunstan is a fascinating character. Highly spiritual, yet worldly wise enough to become a key advisor to a succession of Anglo-Saxon kings. But he's *especially* fascinating to proponents of a West Country Arthur like myself, because he was born and raised in a village called Baltonsborough that claimed to have supplied a disproportionate number of men for Arthur's army. So you'd expect him to have had a special affinity for the man.'

Anna shook her head. 'I still don't follow.'

'Of course not,' said Quentin. 'I haven't got there yet. You just need the background for it all to make sense. So then. Baltonsborough is maybe three or four miles south east of Glastonbury, close enough for Dunstan to have studied there as a boy, despite it having largely fallen into ruin. It's why he was so attached to the place, and why he became its abbot while still a very young man. An extremely well-connected and wealthy young man, true, but not so wealthy that he could afford to rebuild the place himself. He'd therefore have needed to raise funds somehow, and – as I say – pilgrimages were a great way of doing that. We think Arthur was already becoming a major folk hero by then, and he had strong links to the area, so it would have made perfect sense for Dunstan to want to associate Glastonbury with the man.'

'You think it was Dunstan who was behind the hoax?'

'I think it was Dunstan who was behind the *claim*. Not necessarily that it was a hoax. Because there's something else you need to know. One of the parts of Glastonbury that had fallen into disrepair when he took over was its cemetery. The same cemetery in which Arthur and Guinevere were to be found two and a half centuries later. So here you have Dunstan, a devotee of Arthur and with a pressing need to raise funds, at a time when the best way to do that was by attracting pilgrims. And what do you suppose he did, while in favour with the king?'

'What?'

'He had him grant the village of Badbury here – and all these surrounding lands – to Glastonbury, even though it was the best part of a day's ride away. And why would he have done that, do you think, unless there was something here of great value to him?' He looked down at the pale grass beneath his feet. 'Something, perhaps, that he coveted for his abbey.'

THIRTY-TWO

Ransome followed Elias's gaze across the cobbles to Orlando Wren, even as he turned away from them and made his way back inside his converted stable. 'You seriously think he's one of the cousins?'

'I seriously think it's worth asking him the question,' said Elias. 'He came here at around the time Wynn was released on parole. He took a room overlooking Grove Farm. He hides his face behind a baseball cap and that bushy great beard. And he spends his days out on long walks, doing god knows what.'

'One hell of a risk. What if Grant recognised his name?'

'Yeah. Except doesn't Orlando Wren have the ring of a pseudonym to you? Samantha told me he's paying cash. Maybe there's a reason for that. I heard him giving his statement earlier. He sounded pretty edgy when your people asked him for his name and address. Plus he managed to get all his clothes out of his room last night, yet apparently he somehow left his wallet behind, with all his cards and other ID. So yes, I'd say it's definitely worth asking the question.'

'Okay,' said Ransome. 'But you're coming with me.'

'So you can blame me if it turns to shit?'

'Exactly,' she said. 'Well done.'

They got out of the squad car, made their way across the courtyard together. Ransome knocked loudly but then went in without waiting for an answer, even as Wren came out of the bedroom carrying his overnight bag. 'Off somewhere?' she asked.

'I'm a writer,' he said. 'How can I be expected to write with all this going on?'

'Fair enough. Are you okay to get home, though? They tell me you don't have a car here, and I understand you lost your wallet in the fire.'

'I'll be fine, thanks. I found some cash in one of my pockets.'

'How about a lift? I could have you taken to the station.'

'That's okay. You have far more important things to do.' He gave them a polite yet cool smile, the kind designed to declare the conversation over. Unfortunately for him, it was also the kind of smile that had the opposite effect on experienced detectives like Ransome and Elias.

'What was your name again?' asked Ransome.

'Wren,' he told her. 'Orlando Wren.' But his swallow was visible even beneath his beard, and despite his effort to hide it.

'That's your real name, is it? Not your pen name?'

'What is this?' he asked. 'Why would I give you a pen name?'

'That's not an answer, though, is it, sir? Well?'

'Yes,' he said. 'Wren is my real name.' But he couldn't hold her gaze. He turned his back on her instead, made his way stiffly over to the kitchen area where he ran some hot water into the sink, scrubbing the dirty mugs and plates that the previous occupants had left to soak. 'Is that all?'

'Not quite,' said Ransome. 'One last question. Are you a cousin of the Grants, by any chance?'

'I'm sorry? The who?'

'Caleb and Wynn Grant. Surely you've heard of them. We arrested Wynn yesterday on suspicion of the murder next door. It was all over the news.'

'Ah. Yes.' He rinsed out a mug and teaspoon, dried them both vigorously with a sheet of kitchen paper. 'So that was his name, was it? Why would you think me his cousin?'

'She doesn't, as it happens,' said Elias. 'It's my idea. Specifically, I thought you were maybe one of the cousins who got to inherit Grove Farm after Wynn was convicted of killing

Caleb.'

'This is ridiculous,' said Wren. 'This is slander.'

'How on earth is it slander?' asked Ransome. 'It's just a question.'

'Yes. But I've already answered it. I've answered all your questions.'

'Not this one, you haven't,' said Elias. 'And it's a pretty straightforward one, I'd have thought. Eight billion people on the planet, and all but a handful can answer no without a blink. So why do you have a problem with it?'

Wren hung the mug up on a hook, put the teaspoon away in a drawer. 'I have a problem with it because why are you even asking? Am I suspected of something?'

'Yes,' said Ransome. 'I'd have thought that was obvious by now.' She turned to Elias. 'Wouldn't you have thought it obvious?'

'It's obvious to me.'

'Suspected of what, exactly?'

'Of making the phone call that placed Wynn Grant at Grove Farm at the time of his brother's death,' said Elias. 'And a word of warning: don't even bother trying to lie. You wouldn't believe how good voice analysis software is these days. They tried it on me last year, before I quit. Nailed me every time, even when I was putting on my best Scottish accent. Even when I was speaking French. Don't ask me how they do it, exactly. Apparently there's some combination of timbre, pitch and cadence that's impossible to disguise, no matter how you try. Better than fingerprints, they tell me.' He held up his phone to show him that he'd been recording the conversation. 'So I'm going to take a wild guess here. I'm going to take a wild guess that when we test your voice against that phone call, it's going to come up cherries.'

'You're bluffing,' said Wren, but the croak in his voice was so pronounced that it might as well have been a confession. And all three of them knew it.

THIRTY-THREE

The wooden rail fence at the back of the paddock ran slantwise across the patch of paler grass, cropping off its far left corner, which was given over anyway to much longer grass, some thick bushes and then the steep foot of Liddington Hill. Anna and Quentin swept the remaining area briskly with the two metal detectors, netting themselves some rusted nails, an old 10p coin and a buckle with a length of frayed brown leather still attached, likely torn from some piece of horse-tack. But that was all. 'Are you still sure about this?' Quentin asked Samantha, before climbing back up into the digger's cab.

'I'm sure,' she told him.

He turned the engine back on, brought it close, reached out its long hydraulic arm. The turf was still so wet from the storm that the bucket's bladed edge easily bit six inches deep into it. He drew it back in a strip, ruffling it up like so much loose carpeting, before dumping it off to the side for Samantha and Anna to check with the metal detectors. He cleared an area some six feet square this way before reversing a safe distance off, allowing Anna and Samantha to step down into the shallow pit he'd created and sweep their detectors over the newly-exposed earth. But all they harvested this time was a bottle cap and a rusted horseshoe.

Forward came Quentin once more, scooping off another six inches of soil, then a third and a fourth, until the pit was deep enough that Anna and Samantha had to take care when stepping down into it. Their detectors were now turning up more interesting pieces too, or at least older and more obscure ones: a rusted toy fire-truck; the broken blade of a farm implement; a George III token. But still nothing more substantial. In went Quentin for a fifth time, the blade of his bucket biting yet deeper into the earth then dragging it back so that—

It happened so quickly that it gave Anna a proper fright. A sudden grating, grinding noise and the digger's rear tracks momentarily lifting up off the grass before thudding back down again, even as the ground before her simply collapsed and fell away, landing a second later with such a thump that it sent shivers through her feet and threw up a cloud of dust that wasn't quite thick enough to hide the great sinkhole that had opened up right in front of her.

Quentin immediately raised his bucket and reversed away. He turned off his engine, jumped down and came to join them as they all edged closer, wary of more ground giving way. The collapse seemed to be over for the moment, however, save for a few trickles of earth and the odd clatter of a loosened stone. The dust began to settle too, so that Anna could now see that the sinkhole wasn't a sinkhole exactly, but rather the ancient staircase that they'd all surmised, its mortared drystone walls covered by a row of monumental limestone slabs to serve as its roof. The digger had caught the far edge of one of these with its bucket, dragging it back far enough that it had come off one of its supporting walls, allowing it to tip into the space beneath like a stage trapdoor swinging open on its hinges, before coming to rest at an awkward angle on the steps beneath – steps that, as the dust settled some more, she could see led even further down to an arched stone doorway that headed away from Samantha's paddock directly beneath the hill.

'My god,' muttered Samantha. 'It's your mausoleum. I don't believe it.' And, before either Anna or Quentin could stop her, she sat on the edge of the sinkhole, reached her feet down for the slanted surface of the fallen slab, then twisted around to place her hands against the drystone wall. She shuffled her way carefully down the slab to its bottom edge, then sat once more to drop herself down onto the staircase beneath. Then, ignoring Quentin's increasingly desperate pleas for her to stop and come back, she took out her phone for its flashlight, ducked her head beneath the doorway's stone lintel, and passed boldly into the velvet darkness beyond.

THIRTY-FOUR

Quentin gave a groan of dismay as Samantha disappeared from view, taking her torchlight with her. 'My god,' he muttered. 'What have I done?'

'It's done already, whatever it is,' said Anna, sitting down upon the edge of the pit, just as Samantha had done. 'All we can do now is make sure it doesn't get any worse.'

'You can't be serious.'

'Why not? What else would you suggest?'

He had no answer for that, so she placed her feet upon the slab. It was more steeply angled than she'd expected, and she wasn't sure her soles would have enough grip. But they held well enough for her to slide her feet down it, much as Samantha had done, keeping her balance with her hands against the drystone wall. She sat upon the slab's lower edge then dropped herself down onto the staircase beneath, her shoes squishing into the fallen earth. Then she made her way down the last few steps to the arched doorway, into whose limestone lintel a dove had once been neatly chiselled, only for it to have been crudely hacked at and scored through.

She photographed it with her phone then turned on its torch and went inside, reaching a short flight of steps down into a large circular domed atrium with five more open archways leading off it, two on either side and one straight ahead. There were stone benches between the arches on either side, iron beckets on the walls for holding torches, and a mosaic that seemed to cover its entire floor, though it was so covered in dust that she could only see how gorgeously coloured and well preserved it was in the places where Samantha had already stepped, leaving a clear trail into the nearer of the two left-hand chambers.

'Is he very mad at me?' asked Samantha, when Anna joined her in there.

'He'll be fine,' Anna assured her. 'He'll be down here himself in a minute, I expect.' They shone their torches this way and that. It was an impressive looking space, maybe seven or eight good strides across, with a barrel-vaulted ceiling, a flagstone floor and frescoes of what appeared to be rural scenes on the walls – though the plaster was so cracked and the paint so faded that it was hard to be sure. Besides, they weren't the main points of interest. The main points of interest were the matching high-sided sarcophagi that sat side by side on a wide low plinth that ran from the centre of the chamber all the way to its far wall, and over to which they now both made their way, taking care where they trod. For while the two sarcophagi and their lids had been beautifully sculpted out of limestone, they'd subsequently been hacked at and defaced, much like the dove on the doorway lintel. Both lids had been hauled off and smashed, leaving chips and fragments scattered all over the floor. There were scraps of cloth, bone and teeth mixed in with them too, strongly suggesting that both bodies inside had been dragged from their resting places, presumably the better to strip them of their rings and necklaces and other grave goods. Bizarrely, however, both had subsequently been returned to the sarcophagi, yet so carelessly that their long-bones, ribs and skulls were in impossible relation to one another, with each sarcophagus having one long leg and one short, and one of the heads being turned upside down. Several of the larger pieces from the broken lids had also been rested back on top of the sarcophagi again, to give the remains a little cover.

Samantha shook her head. 'What the hell happened here?'

'Grave robbers, I imagine,' said Anna. 'Then others came

along afterwards to tidy up.'

'Ah, well. So much for finding Arthur and all his treasure.'

'Isn't this enough for you?' asked Anna, a touch more sharply than she'd intended. 'These sarcophagi and those frescoes. The mosaic outside. They're magnificent.'

They photographed everything on their phones, went back out to check the next chamber along. This too had charming frescoes on its walls, but four sarcophagi rather than the two in the previous chamber – all so small, though, that they clearly belonged to children of various ages, the youngest only an infant. That had cut no ice with the robbers, however, for these had been desecrated too, their lids thrown off and shattered, the little bodies dragged out and torn apart, only subsequently to be replaced, as before. Across the atrium now, into the third and fourth chambers, each containing more of the wall paintings as well as two more vandalised adult sarcophagi each, suggesting that at least three generations had been interred here.

Scuffing noises reached them from outside after they returned once more into the atrium. Quentin was finally on his way down to join them, it seemed, though the amount of puffing and grunting suggested he wasn't finding it easy. 'I'd better go make sure he's okay,' murmured Samantha. 'He's not as young as he was.'

Anna left her to it, heading alone through the fifth and final arch, the one directly opposite the entrance. It proved to be a passage, flanked by two more pairs of tomb chambers, though these were in a very different style to the ones off the atrium. There were no sarcophagi here. Instead, the end walls had been cut into columns of burial niches or loculi of varying sizes and grandeur, perhaps for lesser members of the family, for friends or senior staff. And, in place of frescoes, each niche had been closed with a plaster seal that had then been painted with a likeness of the deceased, only for them all to have since been torn open so that the remains inside could be hauled out and despoiled. Again, though, they'd been restored to their niches – though even more haphazardly here than elsewhere, for there were multiple skulls in at least three of the loculi, and none at all in others; while large numbers of surplus bones, teeth and locks of hair had been swept into the corners, along with dust and broken seals.

Onwards she went. She reached what had clearly been the original end of the mausoleum, except that a hole had been smashed in its end wall so that an extension could be put in, marked by an abrupt switch from the smoothly finished walls in the earlier chambers to rough mortared drystone topped by monumental limestone slabs, much like the staircase down into this place, making Anna realise something that should perhaps have been obvious – that the atrium and the first few chambers had been built from Rome's famous concrete, whose astonishing strength and longevity had been one of the marvels of the ancient world, and whose secrets were still not fully understood, but which had owed much to the self-healing properties of the materials they'd used, especially the volcanic ash mined from around the Bay of Naples and shipped across the empire. The withdrawal of the legions had however put an end to that particular trade, in Britain at least, forcing a reversion to earlier, cruder methods like this, allowing her to assign a provisional third or fourth century date to the atrium and the first few chambers, but a fifth century date to this extension.

Some strands of gossamer caught in her hair. She saw the scuttle of a tiny pale insect. Life always found a way, it seemed, no doubt nourished and refreshed by the moisture she could see weeping on these walls, having seeped through the cracks in the mortar and between the slabs, laying a thicker carpet of dust and earth upon the floor here, bringing with it spores and pollen, seeds and grain from the field above, and no doubt larvae too.

There were more chambers on either side, all small and built in the same way, and all empty. The passage then came to its end in what – despite the passing of the Roman age – proved to be the grandest space of all. Like the atrium, it was circular, domed, spacious and tall, with a vaulted coffered ceiling of sunken panels held up by sculpted marble ribs patterned like a cobweb, putting her in mind of the rotunda of Rome's Pantheon – though with a plain circle at its peak, instead of the famous aperture to let the sunlight in. For there was no sunlight here, deep under Liddington Hill as it was. Its walls were made from courses of the same limestone blocks she'd seen in the villa next door, making her think that this was where at least some of the plundered materials had ended up. Its floor was made from smoothed and polished slabs of all different shapes and colours and types of stone, cunningly fitted together into a kind of crazy paving around a white marble dais some three paces square, which looked as if it should be the final resting place for a person of extreme importance, yet without anything upon it.

She made her way carefully inside, though there was little enough here for her to damage. Apart from a patch of dark scuffing or staining on the end wall, the place looked pristine, as if decades rather than centuries old. Closer to the dais now, she could see that three separate outlines were thinly encrusted upon it, suggesting that there had indeed once been objects here – matching square ones on each of the two front corners, and a much larger one between them, in the familiar shape of a coffin or sarcophagus. She crouched down low and held her torch out to the side to exaggerate the shadows, helping her to spot a long thin splinter of dark wood lying upon the marble. She picked it up and turned it around, wondering what it meant.

Quentin cleared his throat behind her. 'What's that you've found?'

'Wood,' she told him.

He came to join her, squatting down to take it from her. 'Are you thinking what I'm thinking?' he asked.

'Which is what?' asked Samantha, joining them inside the chamber.

'A grand burial vault,' he said. 'Likely fifth century, fit for a king and maybe his queen. Yet neither king nor queen in sight. Could this not be where St Dunstan got his coffin and his bodies from?' He raised a wry eyebrow even as he touched one of the crusted outlines with his forefinger. 'A man called Gerald of

Wales was at Glastonbury when Arthur's grave was discovered. He claimed they'd found it deep underground, between a pair of pyramids. He didn't know what these pyramids were, and they're long-since lost, so all we've been able to do is guess. But how about a pair of stone crosses or the like.'

'Taken from here?'

'Why not? Why ever not?' He shook his head, spinning with possibilities. 'I do know one thing, though. We need to leave. We need to leave right now. We have to report this and get it secured as soon as possible.'

They returned in silence to the staircase. Quentin cupped his hands into a stirrup to help Samantha back up onto the slab, from which she scrambled out. He did the same for Anna, who sat upon the stone then reached back down to give him a hand. Even with her help, however, it was a struggle for him to make it out, causing the pair of them to be the best part of a minute behind Samantha. And none of them, of course, had the slightest idea of how consequential that minute was about to prove.

THIRTY-FIVE

Over his many years in the police, Elias had seen guilt manifest itself in any number of ways. Right now, standing by his kitchen counter, Orlando Wren seemed to be running through the lot. He gulped and trembled and turned pale. His breathing grew faster and more shallow. A shimmer of sweat even appeared upon his brow. 'Yeah,' grinned Elias. 'Thought so. It was you who rang up that tip line, wasn't it? It was you who claimed to have seen Wynn coming out of the farm.'

'No.'

'Sure it was. A little nudge to help the police nail their man so that you could get your hands on all that lovely loot – enough to give up your day job and make a go of it as a writer instead. He was surely guilty anyway. You were only helping to bring a villain to justice. But the fierceness with which he protested his innocence at his trial and ever since made you feel a little queasy. You tried to put it from your mind, but never quite managed it. The years ticked by. Finally he got released. He, of all people, knew that phone call was a lie. And who else but you cousins would have had the motive? You were terrified he'd be coming after you, so you took a room here under a false name, intending to watch him as closely as you dared, hoping he'd slip up badly enough for you to get him carted back inside. But that didn't happen, so you decided to give him a nudge instead. You saw them digging up the hoard next door, so you went over there that night, planning to nick some pieces to plant around his house. Only Vic caught you at it, didn't he? And you realised the whole shitty story was bound to come out, how you'd framed Wynn for his brother's death, and all the years in prison he'd wrongly served. So you smashed your crowbar down on Vic's head. You murdered him in cold blood, and then you planted all the evidence on Wynn.'

'No,' said Wren. 'You're crazy! This is crazy!'

'Even that wasn't enough for you, though, was it? Because yesterday afternoon you overheard me talking about how those footprints had been deliberately planted in the sand. You couldn't risk me telling the police that, could you? So you came downstairs in the small hours. Maybe you covered up the smoke alarms, to make sure they didn't go off too soon. Then you slipped out the back door, siphoned petrol from one of the cars and poured it through the letterbox to make it seem like an outside job.'

'No!' he cried again, but there was a note in his voice now that was less denial than a plea for understanding. He must have realised it himself too, for a wild look entered his eyes. There was a kitchen knife drying on the rack. It wasn't that he sought it, exactly. It just happened to be close to hand. Even after he'd picked it up, he seemed uncertain what to do with it. But then a uniformed constable appeared in the doorway, and Wren turned towards him with the knife held out, giving it a little twitch to warn him to keep his distance. And so was the decision made.

'Don't be an idiot,' said Elias. 'What good will that do you?'

'Stay back,' said Wren. He gestured for the constable to move aside, then he edged his way to the door and out, turning this way and that with the knife held out, making sure no one could get the jump on him. More and more police officers and fire-crew came across to see what the commotion was, forming a ring around him. The mood was strange, for while the knife warranted a certain respect, there was no great alarm. As long as they all stayed a safe distance back and kept their concentration, there was little harm he could do. He looked towards the cars, but a pair of fire-engines were blocking the drive, meaning there was no escape that way. No escape *any* way, in truth. He simply hadn't accepted it yet. But he surely would soon. So they kept him penned inside their circle, backing off whenever he moved towards them, yet never offering him a way out.

He headed around the stables into the back garden. Perhaps he saw the yellow digger sitting there in the paddock, and thought it offered him some kind of chance. Or perhaps he thought that escape might still be possible if he could only reach the foot of Liddington Hill. Whatever his reasoning, he began to move with more purpose than before, still holding out the knife and jabbing it theatrically towards anyone who drew too close. He passed through the latched gate into the paddock, while the members of the cordon climbed over the wooden rails on either side, making sure to keep their distance. Then he turned circles as he crossed the paddock, weaving between the showjump fences, his mouth moving as if in speech, but no sound coming out.

He must have realised, then, that it was hopeless, for he slowed and came to a stop. His face scrunched up in self-pity and he looked so on the verge of tears that Elias was sure he was about to drop the knife and give himself up. But then Samantha rose like a magician's assistant up out of a pit in the ground behind him, and a look of utter bewilderment appeared on her face at the sight of Wren standing there with a knife in his hand, surrounded by all these uniforms.

'Get back,' yelled Elias. But all he achieved with that was to jolt Wren from his stupor. He turned and saw her standing there behind him and strode over to her before she even properly realised the danger she was in. He grabbed her around the chest with one arm then pressed the tip of his knife to her throat with his free hand before turning back to Elias and Ransome with a look of wild triumph in his eyes, as though he truly believed he'd turned the tables on them, and had found himself a path out.

THIRTY-SIX

Anna clambered up the slab and out of the sinkhole into the pit scooped out by the digger. Then she turned back to help Quentin as he laboured up after her, wheezing and muttering to himself. She took his hand once more and almost had him out when she heard Elias shouting warning to Samantha, followed a moment or two later by her strangled cry of alarm.

Anna motioned for Quentin to stay where he was, then crept over to the edge of the pit to see what was going on. Wren was just three or four paces away from her with his back turned, clearly having no idea that she was there, all his attention on the cordon of police officers and fire-crew gathered in a semicircle around him. 'Keep back,' he yelled. 'Keep back or I'll do her. I swear to god I will.'

'No, you won't,' said Elias, in his most soothing voice. 'You're not that kind of man.'

'Screw you, not that kind of man!' said Wren. 'You just accused me of murder.'

'Maybe I was wrong. Maybe it wasn't you. Put down the knife and we can talk.'

'What kind of idiot do you take me for?'

'No one thinks you're an idiot. You're in an impossible sit—'

'Stay back, damn you. Stay back or she gets it. I mean it. You know I'm capable.'

'She's your friend,' said Elias. 'She's never been anything but kind to you.'

'Kind!' he scoffed. 'Like the other night, you mean? When I asked her for a bit of fish stew, and she told me to piss off and go eat my sandwiches.'

'That was my doing,' said Elias. 'Not Samantha.'

'Bullshit. I know what she thinks of me. All that "Lovely Orlando" guff, then mocking me behind my back. Snickering about my reviews. Bitch.' And he pressed the tip of his knife so hard into her throat that it drew a trickle of blood.

'Don't,' begged Elias. 'She's never done anything to you. Let her go and we'll talk this through. Or at least tell us what you want.'

'I want a car,' said Wren. 'I want a car and money. Money and a car and a new identity, that's what I want. And immunity. Immunity and a written guarantee that no one will ever come after me.'

Samantha was sobbing helplessly by now, her resilience already depleted by her other ordeals, her house in ruins and her life falling apart. The sound touched Anna to her heart. Little wonder, then, that it touched Quentin too, as he arrived alongside her. His expression turned cold and hard. He left her for a moment, going back to the drystone wall to wrest free a flint the size of a grapefruit. And there was a look of such furious intent on his face when he came back that Anna shook her head and grabbed hold of his sleeve to stop him. But he simply shook her off.

'A car we can maybe manage,' Ransome was saying. 'But money? A new identity? What planet are you on? And what would you do with it, anyway? Where would you go? If you think there's anywhere safe for you—'

'I don't care,' shouted Wren. 'Just do it or she dies.'

It was the final straw. Before Anna could stop him, Quentin jumped up out of the pit and ran forwards, turning almost sideways on, a javelin thrower about to launch. All eyes turned automatically to him, allowing Wren to sense the danger and swing Samantha around to serve as his shield. Too late. Quentin smashed his flint into the side of Wren's head with an ugly low clumping noise and all the force he had. Wren grunted and staggered sideways, striving to keep his feet even as he scratched a thin red line along the side of Samantha's throat with his knife. But then his legs crumpled beneath him and he went down onto his knees before toppling unconscious onto his face, dropping the knife as he went.

THIRTY-SEVEN

The police and the fire crews were between them well enough versed in trauma management to keep Orlando Wren alive until the first ambulance arrived. But his pulse was still down to a flutter by then, while the blood from the gash in his scalp and his badly splintered skull had reduced to an ominously thin trickle. The paramedics took over, working to stabilise him as best they could. They gave him antibiotics, plasma, morphine and fluids before stretchering him into the back of their vehicle and setting off for the Great Western Hospital with their siren blaring. But no one held out much hope for his survival – or for what condition he'd be in, should he make it.

The rest of the afternoon passed in a blur. The police were everywhere, collecting evidence, taping off sites of interest, taking statements. Not that statements were much needed, the whole sad episode having been witnessed by so many officers of one kind or another. Even so, Quentin was still in such a clear state of shock when he gave his that Samantha insisted on staying with him, holding his hand as they sat together on the sofa. And the moment it was done, she booted the police from her stable and closed the door on them, on the basis that the therapy they both most needed was an afternoon alone together with a pair of loving dogs.

With Quentin indisposed, it fell to Anna to call Pamela Pearce at the museum to let her know about the mausoleum beneath Samantha's paddock, explaining how they'd found it, that its entrance was currently wide open, and that it therefore needed securing as soon as possible. Word of it, after all, was sure to spread around the local community, not least because it was clearly visible to their neighbours and to anyone who'd come to gawk at the fire, as well as to the hikers on Liddington Hill. But it was mid afternoon on a bank holiday Monday, and there was little that could reasonably be done before morning.

It grew colder, darker. It looked sure to rain. The fire crews left first, after delivering stern warnings to stay well clear of the Manor, whose surviving walls and roof could collapse at any moment. Then the police left too, with Ransome promising to return first thing to update them on the state of the investigation. Samantha and Quentin reappeared a minute or two later, suggesting they'd been waiting for her and her team to leave. And maybe they weren't the only ones, for three motorbikes with pillion passengers came slowly by, revving their engines aggressively as they passed, led by a man in black leathers with red flashes on his helmet. Then they turned around a little further up the lane and came rolling back past again, their visors now up, gazing menacingly into the courtyard.

'Bollocks,' muttered Elias.

'Archie Miller?' asked Anna.

'His mates, for sure.'

'What *is* their problem with us?' sighed Samantha.

'It's not with "us",' Elias told her. 'It's only with me, I think.'

'Phew,' said Anna. 'That's okay, then.'

Elias laughed. 'Don't get too complacent. They're not the kind to fret about collateral damage. Besides...'

'Besides?'

He didn't answer for a moment, thinking it through. 'They're born vandals, I reckon. They get a kick out of breaking stuff. Which wouldn't matter much except what if they know about your mausoleum, or at least that you've found something beneath the paddock? The fire crews and all those police earlier drew quite an audience, remember? And I'll bet the paddock is visible from the Miller's place too. Once they've sunk a few pints down the pub and worked up a bit of a grievance, I wouldn't put it past them to come back in the small hours with a sledgehammer or two, meaning to trash the place.'

'Hell,' said Anna.

'It's okay,' said Elias. 'I'll camp out in the paddock tonight with a tyre iron or something. I can't see them trying anything, not if they find me waiting. At least, they'll regret it if they do.'

'Except it's going to tip it down again tonight,' pointed out Anna.

'Then I'll kip inside.'

'With all those dead bodies?' asked Samantha, giving a theatrical shudder. 'Won't they freak you out?'

'Only if they start moving.'

'Ben's right,' said Anna. 'We need to keep an eye on the place. But he shouldn't have to do it alone. I'll go down there with him.'

'And leave me up here by myself with a gang of arsehole bikers?' said Samantha. 'No way. I'm coming too.' She seemed almost to brighten at the prospect. 'We'll take down lots of duvets and pillows, make a proper night of it. Hold torches beneath our chins and tell each other ghost stories. It's got the right atmosphere, you can't deny that.'

'You're all mad,' said Quentin. 'It was hard enough getting in and out of that place when it was light and dry. You'll break a leg for sure once it gets dark and starts to rain.'

'Nonsense,' said Samantha. 'We'll use my ladder.' But then she looked around at the shell of her house and remembered that it too had been lost to the fire. She gave Quentin's arm a squeeze. 'Come on. You must have one at home.'

'You can't be serious.'

'Would you really rather leave it at the mercy of those hooligans?'

'No. Of course not.'

'Well, then. What are you quibbling about? You should come with us.' She took his hand and gave him one of her best sunshine smiles, too dazzling for him to resist. 'Tell you what. You go fetch your ladder, I'll rustle up some bedclothes, and we'll spend our first ever night together.'

THIRTY-EIGHT

Quentin had only been gone some ten minutes or so when two sets of car headlights approached up Liddington Lane, slowing in unison before turning into Samantha's drive. A royal blue Rolls Royce Phantom arrived first, followed closely by a silver Audi A5 convertible. Ravindra Pandey and Melissa Ward. They parked side by side on the cobbles and got out as Anna, Elias and Samantha went over to greet them.

They popped their boots in unison, revealing obscene quantities of leftovers from the Pandeys' annual barbecue all safely sealed in kitchen wrap: a huge platter of chicken wings, two racks of ribs slathered in sauce, sausages on sticks and a plate of king prawns, their shells a little charred from the firepit, and glistening with oil and garlic. There were baked potatoes wrapped in foil; half a pound of butter and an unopened pack of buns; a bowl of mixed salad, another of tomato and onion. There were tubs of coleslaw, potato salad and chopped beetroot; squeezy bottles of ketchup, mayo and brown sauce, and a jar of Dijon mustard. And, on their back seats, two crates of wine, beer, cola and sparkling water, along with a cardboard box of napkins, plastic plates, cups and cutlery.

'Heard about your fire on the news,' explained Ravi, in his characteristic no-nonsense manner. 'Thought you'd have more use for all this than us.'

'That's so kind,' said Samantha, taken aback, more

accustomed to seeing him and Melissa as adversaries rather than friends. 'I'm not sure where we'll put it all, though.'

'Just have to eat it quick, then, won't you? No-one ever made a disaster better by going hungry.' He gazed at the ruined farmhouse for a few moments, shaking his head in disbelief. 'What a mess. I'm so sorry. If there's anything I can do… Seriously. Anything at all…' Then he added with a wry smile: 'I have fairly substantial resources. You may have heard.'

'Thank you. That's so generous, and I do appreciate it. But I'm sure I'll make it through somehow.'

'Good on you,' he said approvingly, taking his card from his wallet. 'Even so. If things ever get on top of you… That's my private number on the back. No one else will ever need to know.'

'Thank you,' she said again.

'Do they know how it started yet?' asked Melissa.

'Orlando Wren, my bloody lodger,' scowled Samantha. 'Not that that's even his real name. I should have guessed it was a pseudonym. I mean who the hell goes through life called Orlando Wren? He's actually Peter Moorcock, it turns out. No wonder he changed it for his books.' She touched a finger to her throat, to show where he'd scratched her with his knife. 'The little shit nearly killed me, would you believe? After sleeping under my roof for all this time, and the dozens of meals I'd cooked him.'

'Do they know why?' asked Ravi. 'They didn't say on the news.'

'Ask him,' she said, nodding at Elias. 'He's the one who worked it out.'

'They're still putting it together,' said Elias. 'But they've confirmed the key point, which is that he was one of the cousins who got to inherit Grove Farm after Wynn was jailed for his brother's death.' He talked them through it all, from Vic's murder to the fire and how they'd challenged Wren only for him to take Samantha hostage before Quentin had managed to save her.

Ravi looked around. 'So where's Quentin now?' he asked.

'Surprised he's not here, to be honest. Getting his due rewards, so to speak.'

'He'll be back in a minute or two,' said Samantha. 'He's just gone to fetch his ladder. Because we've had even more excitements here today, would you believe? That Roman villa of yours – it turns out that the owners had a mausoleum, and it's right beneath my paddock. We opened it up this morning. Robbed ages ago, sadly, but still. There's a lovely mosaic in the atrium, and some wonderful frescos too. As good as anything ever found in England, or so Quentin and Anna tell me. And who am I to argue? We're actually going to go back down in a minute, if you'd like to see?'

'Absolutely we would,' said Melissa, only to check her watch and give a wince. 'It'll have to be lightning, though. My parents are already about to disinherit me for all the babysitting I've been having them do this weekend. If I'm late picking up the girls again…'

'We'll have to wait at least a little bit, I'm afraid,' Samantha told her. 'It's really tricky getting in and out. That's why we need the ladder.'

'And it's no bother?' asked Ravi.

'None at all. We're going to spend the night down there anyway. That wretched Miller boy and his idiot mates keep riding past. Apparently they're mad at Elias for telling the police about that horrible letterbox stunt they pulled on you, Melissa. Though how they have the nerve to blame anyone but themselves… Anyway, we think they may know about the mausoleum, and they're just the kind of louts who'd rip the place apart out of spite.'

As if to underline her point, they heard again the distinctive rumble of motorbike engines rapidly drawing closer. The lane lit up and the three bikes from earlier came fizzing by, so close together that they blurred almost into one. A fourth set of headlights appeared maybe thirty seconds later, heralding Quentin's return. He pulled up alongside Melissa's Audi and got out, his hands trembling. 'Did you see them?' he asked, pointing angrily off down the lane. 'I swear to god they tried to make me crash, the little shits.' Then he noticed Melissa and Ravi standing there and shook himself from his funk. 'What are you two doing here?'

'Heard about the fire,' said Ravi, gesturing at the open boots. 'Thought this would be a better home for all our leftovers. But now we hear there's a mausoleum for us to look at. Only we need your ladder, apparently?'

Quentin nodded and lifted up his hatchback. He'd put his back seats down to accommodate his ladder, an aluminium two-piece extension job. He tossed aside an overnight bag then pulled it out and passed it to Elias, standing behind him. Then he gathered up his other supplies: a battery lamp, a heavy-duty torch, a pair of sleeping bags and a double-barrelled shotgun that he slung casually over his shoulder, as though it were barely worthy of comment. But Elias commented anyway. 'What the hell's that?' he demanded.

'Don't worry,' Quentin told him, patting his jacket pocket. 'It's not loaded. I'm not a complete idiot.'

'Then what's the point of it?'

Quentin jabbed a finger out at the lane. 'Those little arses won't know that, will they? Not for sure. You didn't see what they got up to just now. They followed me all the way home then they hung around outside while I was getting this stuff together, shouting and throwing stones and clods of mud. Then they rode alongside me all the way back here again, revving their engines and spurting their bikes at me, trying to run me off the road. They might not scare you, what with your boxing and all that, but I don't mind telling you that they scare the hell out of me. There are six of them, at the end of the day, and only the one of you. So, I'm sorry, but this makes me feel better. It'll make them think twice when they see it, that's for sure.'

Ravi went back over to his own boot. 'So what about all this food? Where do you want it?'

'We'll take it down with us,' said Samantha. 'We'll have ourselves a midnight feast.'

'No!' protested Quentin. 'I'm sorry, but there has to be a limit. What if one of us were to get barbecue sauce on the walls?'

'Oi,' said Elias. 'Why's everyone looking at me?'

They carried it all into the stables, divided the perishables between the fridges, then locked up and set off across the back lawn with their arms full of duvets, pillows and other supplies. It began to drizzle as they went, putting some lacy glitter in their hair, making the grass slick underfoot. Melissa's mobile started to play *Für Elise* as she was passing through the paddock gate. 'Mum,' she muttered. 'I knew it.' She walked off a few paces to give herself some space, but they could still all hear her as she tried to justify her lateness, explaining to little avail how a friend's house had burned down, and how she'd had to take her some food, but that she was setting off absolutely this minute.

'You really need to go?' asked Samantha, once she'd rejoined them.

'I should, I truly should. But I have to see your mausoleum first. Literally in and out though.'

They passed the digger and the police tape, clambered down into the larger pit. While Quentin provided light with his heavy-duty torch, Elias extended the ladder to its full length and lowered it into the sinkhole, working its feet into the bed of fallen earth below then resting it at a manageable angle against the drystone wall. Just as well, for the rain now started coming down more heavily, turning the earth to mud and running in rivulets down the sloped surface of the toppled slab, making it look dangerously slick.

Melissa went down first, followed by Anna, to give her the one-minute tour while the others busied themselves with the supplies. Elias stood halfway up the ladder to take them from Ravi then pass them on down to Samantha and Quentin at the foot, who carried them through to the atrium. They'd barely finished when Melissa returned from her tour, exhilarated by what she'd seen but still set on leaving. Ravi insisted on going with her. He borrowed Quentin's large torch for the purpose, and promised to be back in a minute or two for a tour of his own.

Elias offered to accompany them, conscious of the bikers still being around, but Ravi assured him there was no need. 'If they're the bastards who pulled that letterbox stunt,' he said darkly, 'they're the ones that'll need protecting, not me.'

Elias was less confident, however. 'I don't think he realises how dangerous those kids could be,' he said, once they were out of earshot. 'I just want to make sure they're safe, okay?' He set off after them, hanging well back so that they wouldn't see him and be offended. Not that there was any need to get too close, for the way Ravi was swinging the torch back and forth as they hustled through the rain made them easy to follow. And there was no cause for concern, it turned out, for the courtyard was quiet and empty. Elias waited anyway, just in case, watching Melissa as she unlocked her car then turned to Ravi and took him in a hug, resting her head against his chest for a good half minute before ending it in the kind of kiss that would have sent the jitters through Aston Farms' Human Resources department, had they seen it. But the nature of their relationship was hardly Elias's concern, so he turned and hurried back across the lawn to the paddock, making sure he was down the ladder and inside the mausoleum before he could be spotted.

THIRTY-NINE

They'd spread the duvets, sleeping bags and pillows out over the atrium floor by the time Elias made it back. Ravi appeared a minute later, rubbing his hands together and looking uncommonly pleased with himself. 'So, then,' he said. 'My turn for the grand tour. Though not too grand. I've got to be off myself in a bit. And be gentle with me, please. None of your long archaeologist words. I left school at sixteen, remember.'

They followed the same route Samantha and Anna had taken earlier, starting with the chamber to the left of the entrance. 'My god,' muttered Ravi, as they stood by the doorway and played their torches over the sarcophagi and the wall paintings, which already looked distinctly brighter and fresher, thanks to all the new moisture in the air. He turned to Samantha. 'I knew I should have bought your damn paddock when I had the chance.'

'Maybe we could do a trade,' she said dryly. 'My mausoleum for your hoard.'

'You heard about that, then?' grinned Ravi. 'The holy bloody grail on my land. Who'd ever have believed it?'

'The *what*?' Samantha turned indignantly on Anna. 'But I asked you about it! I asked you specifically. You said it wasn't even possible.'

'It isn't,' Anna assured her. 'Whatever it is we've found, it isn't the holy grail, I swear. It's a bowl, yes, a kind of cauldron.

And it's just about possible that it *inspired* the holy grail. But it isn't the thing itself, I promise you. It can't be. It's at least three centuries too late.'

'Even so,' scowled Samantha. But it wasn't in her nature to stay angry long, and she burst out laughing instead. 'The holy bloody grail!' she said. 'My god. This gets crazier and crazier.'

'How did you even find out about it?' Quentin asked Ravi, striving unsuccessfully to keep the note of censure from his voice. 'It's meant to be a secret.'

'My land, remember,' Ravi told him. 'My hoard. Just because you guys nicked it the other night – without clearing it with me first, may I add – doesn't mean I don't still have rights. One of which is being able to ring up your curator friend and have her tell me exactly what she's got, unless she wants me doorstepping her first thing in the morning with a bus full of lawyers, demanding it all back.'

They entered the next chamber, the one with the child-sized sarcophagi. The mood grew more sombre. Then they made their way through the rest of the mausoleum, while Quentin explained to Ravi and Elias his thinking behind what they were seeing, its Romano-British provenance and how the scoring out of all the Christian imagery strongly suggested the place had been robbed and despoiled by pagans of one kind or another, most likely the Saxons during their advance across the country, a good century before their own conversion. And how, if this really was Badon Hill, where the Britons finally turned the tide, this whole area would likely have become a kind of no man's land for a while – a buffer zone between the two forces, possibly explaining why the reburials had been so hastily done, in and out before they could be seen.

'Tell him what you told us about Arthur and Guinevere,' urged Samantha.

'What about them?' asked Ravi.

'He thinks they were buried here. In this actual chamber, I mean. He thinks St Dunstan stole their coffin and their bodies, then reburied them at Glastonbury.'

'For real?'

'Thinks is putting it far, far too strongly,' said Quentin. 'It's possible, that's all. This chamber certainly looks fit for a king, and it's post-Roman too. If this is indeed the Aurelian family mausoleum, which obviously still needs to be confirmed, where else would they have brought Arthur after Camlann? And you can see for yourself that a great coffin did once sit here.'

Anna left them to it, drawn instead back to the curious scuff-marks on the end wall. She couldn't think how they'd been made, or why they'd been left that way. Yet she sensed they were important. They were anomalies, to put it simply, and her antennae were always set twitching by anomalies. She ran her finger across the different courses of limestone blocks. The mortar between them was in noticeably worse condition here than elsewhere, with numerous small fragments dislodged and lying on the floor below.

She crouched to examine these more closely. That was when she noticed a faint outline of grit and dust on the floor, trapezoid in shape, some three feet across at its widest point, before narrowing to two. And its edges, like the patch of pale grass in the aerial photographs, were too straight to have been made by chance. She was still puzzling over it when Elias came to join her. 'So what's that that's caught your eye?' he asked.

Anna didn't answer at once. She looked up from the floor at the scuff-marks on the wall and then at the coffered ceiling, with all its sunken panels, one of which was directly above the outline in the floor. Not just above it, indeed, but of the exact same size and shape, so that grit falling from around it in the perfect stillness of a sealed tomb would have landed just like this. 'These old West Country forts weren't always just enclosed spaces on the tops of hills,' she said slowly, still thinking it through. 'Quentin will know this better than me, but some of them had fairly extensive underground networks beneath them called fogous, for storing supplies and housing refugees and protecting their water supplies from all the diseased carcasses that besieging forces liked to sling in with their engines.'

'So?'

'So picture this: It's the fifth century CE, and you're a Briton. The Saxons defeat you every time you take them on in the field, pushing you further and further back until finally they're here. You can't stop them. They're too strong. But you can *prepare*. You've had years to do it in, after all. What's more, you've seen how the Romans turned hill-forts into deathtraps after making the first breach. So why not create an emergency escape route for when all else fails? An escape route that might also serve as a way to launch a counterattack, enabling you to sneak out in the dead of night to take the enemy by surprise, destroying their army and halting their advance for the next twenty to thirty years.'

'Where are you headed with this?' frowned Elias.

'Maybe I'm just going crazy,' she replied. 'But doesn't this outline on the floor match that panel in the ceiling? Now imagine you could open that up somehow, and sling a rope down from it. Wouldn't all this scuffing on the wall then look like it could have been made by feet?'

FORTY

Elias and Ravi went together to fetch the ladder, collapsing it first before taking one end each to avoid banging the walls as they carried it through the mausoleum. They extended it back out again and rested it at an angle against the end wall. Elias insisted on being the one to go up and check. The coffered panels were recessed maybe three or four inches behind the cobweb ribbing. There was nothing obviously different about the one Anna had identified, not even when he ran his fingernail around its edges. If it were indeed some kind of secret hatch, it had been exceedingly well crafted. He set his feet upon the rung anyway, placed both palms upon the underside of the panel, and pushed. Nothing. He pushed again. Still nothing. He dropped his hands, rubbed them against his trousers.

'Let me have a crack,' said Ravi.

'I'm fine, thanks,' said Elias; but the implicit challenge needled him enough that he stepped up another rung, so that his head was almost touching the panel. He spread his feet wide, for maximum stability, then gave it a final heave with everything he had, so much so that he feared that the rung might even buckle beneath him. But the rung held fine. It was the panel that popped, springing up from its centuries-long bed with such force that it leapt out of Elias's control up into the empty space above before tipping onto its side as it came back down again, so that it almost slipped past him to smash to the floor below. But he grabbed it against his leg before it fell, then passed it down to

Ravi in exchange for Anna's phone.

He stepped up another two rungs to poke his head and shoulders through the open hatchway and look around. It proved to be one end of a narrow passage that went further than the flashlight on Anna's phone could reach. It looked to be maybe six feet tall, though lower in places, built as it was from the familiar drystone walls topped with the uneven monumental slabs. There was also a space to one side in which two sets of heavy limestone blocks were stacked, presumably meant to be placed on top of the hatch when it was closed, to make it impossible to push open from beneath. Which implied that whoever had been up here last had left out this way, and so had been unable to seal it up properly again behind themselves.

The passage itself looked solid enough, despite its antiquity. He tested it anyway, placing a hand on either side of the hatch then pushing himself up until his elbows locked, holding his weight like that for several seconds before letting himself carefully back down again, feeling for a rung with his foot. He'd have loved to explore further, but he was no archaeologist and it wasn't his place. He contented himself, therefore, with taking photographs, then making his way back down to show the others. 'What now?' he asked, scrolling through his pictures for them. 'Do we go take a proper look, or seal it back up again?'

'Seal it back up again?' snorted Ravi. 'Where's your sense of adventure?'

'What if something goes wrong?' objected Samantha. 'What if that awful Miller boy and his friends turn up while we're up there, and have this place to themselves?'

'Anna and Quentin should go,' said Elias. 'They're the pros. The rest of us can mind the fort. So to speak.'

'They'll have to film it for us,' said Samantha. 'Film it and take photographs. Lots and lots of photographs.'

Ravi gave a grimace. 'Any idea how long this is likely to take?' he asked. 'Only I need to let the wife know I'll be late, or my dinner will get fed to the dogs. And me with it.'

'So go call her,' said Elias.

'Sure,' he said. 'Except I'll never get a signal this deep underground, will I? And I'm way too old to go scrambling up that slab in the rain. So can I nick the ladder for a bit? I'll only be a minute, I promise.'

They stood aside as he dropped down the top half of the ladder. Elias offered to help him carry it back out, but he assured him he could manage. They listened to the pad of his footsteps on the dirt floor outside, the sharper click of his heels as he reached the atrium mosaic. But then their gazes were drawn back up to the hole in the ceiling, wondering what was waiting for them at the far end of the passage. It was Samantha who broke the silence, turning to Anna. 'This morning, before we opened up this place, you told me you'd found something in the hoard that suggested there'd been a building here once. Was there any hint of this on it?'

'No,' said Anna. 'But then there wouldn't have been. It was on the bowl we found – the one Quentin likes to call the hallowed grail – which we think was made a good hundred years before this chamber was even built. Though I suppose we can't be certain of that until we find the missing piece.'

'Is that the one you mentioned yesterday?' asked Samantha.

'Yes. Exactly. The bowl was originally made up of nine main parts. A flat base at the bottom with eight leaves coming off it, each with a landmark on it. Only the leaf that corresponded to this place was missing, worst luck, so we had to work it out another way. But if we can find it, who knows? And it shouldn't be that hard. If it's not still out in the field, it'll likely be with one of your neighbours. In fact, the more I think about it, the more confident I am that that's the answer. Because Vic recognised it the other night, I'm sure of it.'

'We'll put the word out,' said Samantha. 'Won't we, Quentin?'

But Quentin wasn't listening. Or not to her, anyway. He'd turned to the doorway instead, looking uneasy, even alarmed. 'Did you guys hear that?' he asked.

'Hear what?' asked Anna.

'I could have sworn I heard shouting. I'll bet it's those bloody bikers. Wait here.' He left the chamber briefly, slipping his shotgun from his shoulder as he went, only to return maybe ten seconds later, shaking his head and looking foolish. 'Sorry,' he said. 'I guess it was only Ravi getting heated at his wife.'

'If it's even her he's talking to,' murmured Elias.

'How do you mean?' asked Quentin.

Elias didn't answer at once. 'Maybe it's nothing,' he said finally. 'But could it have been Melissa Ward, do you think?'

Quentin frowned. 'It could have been, I guess. I only heard his side of it. Why? Does it matter?'

'It may do, yes.' He bit his knuckle, then looked from Quentin to Samantha. 'Have either of you two ever met Melissa's daughters?'

'Not me,' said Samantha.

'She brought them by the site one morning, on their way to school,' said Quentin. 'But they never even got out of the car. Why?'

'What did they look like?'

'Like schoolgirls,' said Quentin. 'The older was maybe eight or nine, I'd guess. The younger one, six or seven. But I'm hardly an expert.'

'I'm more interested in their ethnicity,' said Elias. 'Did they look Indian at all?'

'Oh,' said Quentin, as he realised where this was heading. 'They did a bit, yes, now that you mention it.'

'What's going on?' asked Samantha. 'What are you both getting at?'

'I think maybe we've got it wrong about who killed Vic and set the fire,' said Elias quietly. 'Maybe it wasn't your lodger, after all.'

'But he admitted it,' protested Samantha.

'Not exactly, no. He implied it, yes – but only when he needed us to believe him capable of murder. What if that was a bluff?'

'Then who?' asked Samantha. She followed his gaze to the doorway and beyond. 'Ravi?' she said, bewildered. 'Surely you can't really think it was Ravi?'

'Why not? We know it was someone who wanted Wynn Grant's parole revoked, right? Someone with a reason to fear him. I wondered for a while about Melissa. She was terrified for her daughters and convinced that Wynn was a real threat to them. That gave her a genuine reason to act. But I just couldn't see her doing it. And the way it's always her parents who do the babysitting for her girls... It got me wondering where their dad is.'

'And you think she and Ravi...?' asked Anna.

Elias nodded. 'You should have seen them kissing goodbye earlier, after he walked her to her car. And what if he is the dad? What if Melissa convinced him that Wynn was a real danger to their daughters. Wouldn't that have given him all the motive in the world? And isn't he the kind of man to take such matters into his own...' But he broke off at the sound of hard heels clacking on the atrium floor. Ravi was on his way back. He gave a grimace then hurried across the chamber to join Quentin in the doorway. 'Your gun,' he said quietly.

'What?'

'He's too big for me. Give me the gun and some shells. Quick.'

'It's okay. I can handle it.'

'Don't be absurd,' said Elias. 'I'm police. I've had firearms training. Have you?'

For a moment, Quentin seemed set to comply. But then, just like that, his expression transformed utterly, from hapless uncertainty to a kind of exasperated rage. 'Nice try,' he said, bringing his shotgun up to aim it at Elias's chest. 'Nice try, but no.'

FORTY-ONE

Ravi arrived back in the chamber with the ladder beneath his arm and a cheerful smile on his face. He dropped both the moment Quentin turned his shotgun on him and motioned for him to join the others, standing against the end wall with their hands up. 'I thought that wasn't loaded,' he said, with impressive composure.

'It is now,' Elias told him.

'You're sure?'

'Pretty sure. He went out while you were on with your wife. Claimed he'd heard shouting. But really it was to buy himself a moment alone. His safety-catch was on when he left. But it was off when he came back in again.'

'That was it?' said Quentin, disgusted. 'That was how you knew?'

'That and how you froze whenever Anna talked about the cauldron's missing leaf. You knew it was only a matter of time before we worked it out.'

'Worked what out?' asked Ravi.

'That it was our friend here who murdered Vic then burned down Sam's house.'

'No!' protested Samantha. 'You're wrong. He'd never.'

'Look at his face,' sighed Elias. 'He's not the man you thought. He's a killer, is what he is. Starting all the way back with Caleb Grant.'

'I never touched that man,' scowled Quentin. 'It was an

accident. He was drunk is all. He fell down those bloody stairs.'

'Maybe so. But you were there when it happened. You could have called for help, but you chose to keep quiet instead. Then you let your so-called friend Wynn spend years in jail for it, when one word from you could have saved him.'

'I don't get it,' wailed Samantha. 'What's going on?'

'It's that missing leaf,' said Elias. 'Anna's right about it having been tugged up to the surface. Only it wasn't found by some random local. It was found by Caleb Grant himself. I mean of course it was. He was the one who'd been ploughing the field, after all. He must have realised straight away that it could be important. He just didn't know *how* important. Luckily for him, though, one of his best mates was a leading expert on the stuff. So he gave him a bell, invited him over.' He turned back to Quentin. 'What happened next? Did you try to bullshit him about what it was? Tell him it was nothing, offer him a fiver for it?'

'No.'

'I'll bet you did. Except he called your bluff, didn't he? Accused you of trying to rip him off. So you got into a fight over it. You smacked him over the head then pushed him down those stairs to make it look like he'd fallen.'

'He fell!' cried Quentin in exasperation. 'How many times do I have to tell you? I told him exactly what it was, how much it was worth and that there was more of it still out there. You could tell by how fresh the seam was, where it had torn away from the base plate. I begged him to show me where he'd found it so that we could dig up the rest, but he was already too drunk. All he wanted was another bottle.'

'You still stole that leaf, didn't you? After he'd fallen down the steps and was lying there. You stole it, and left him to die, and let his brother take the blame.'

'My god,' said Anna. 'No wonder you had your breakdown. No wonder you couldn't get out of bed that day. Which was when Vic saw the leaf, I suppose. While he was doing odd jobs around your house out of kindness, undercharging you on the hours.'

'Exactly,' said Elias. 'He saw the missing piece years ago, then realised where it must have come from when he saw the rest the other night. Our friend here knew it too. He read it on Vic's face, just like you did. He knew if he let him live, even until morning, the whole sordid truth was certain to come out. So he drove back over to Grove Farm in the small hours, he lured Vic out around the back of the house, then he murdered him in cold blood, setting it up to make it look like Wynn Grant did it. But then, yesterday afternoon, he realised that both of us were getting a bit too close to the truth, you by spotting that Vic had recognised the missing leaf, me by working out the significance of the footprints in the sand, so he told that reporter I was on the case and had made some kind of breakthrough, in order to create as wide a suspect pool as he could. Then he drove back over that night to pour a can of petrol through Sam's letterbox and set it blazing, probably hoping that Archie and his mates would get the blame, which they might well have done had Sam's lodger not lost his head. That's why our friend here hit him so hard with that flint, of course. Kill him and the case would be all neatly wrapped up. But still we wouldn't let it go, which is the real reason why he brought the shotgun along tonight. To give himself one last chance at flight if we finally rumbled him. Why else would he have had that overnight bag in the back of his car, if not for doing a runner? Say what else you like about how miserable the past few years must have been for him, living with Caleb's blood on his hands, but at least it gave him time to prepare.'

FORTY-TWO

I am not this kind of man, Quentin assured himself, as he turned his shotgun from Anna to Elias then to Ravi and Sam, before taking it back down the line again. *I am a highly respected historian, archaeologist, author and academic. I am gentle, and thoughtful, and kind. A person of learning, not of violence. I give generously to charity and I willingly and gladly volunteer my time at the library and the museum. That is the kind of man I am. Not this. This is the result of misfortune, not of my essential nature.* Yet he knew he'd never convince these people of that. They'd made up their minds about him. Which in turn made up his own.

Samantha wouldn't stop crying. It made her ugly. He found himself hating her for her crying and her ugliness, hating her for what she was forcing him to do, for the loss of the future together he'd so often dreamed of, for the extra weight it would place upon his soul. But again he had no choice. That was what she'd never understand. None of this was out of choice.

'Put the muzzle beneath your chin,' said Ravi. 'That's all you need to do. Muzzle beneath your chin, finger on the trigger. Then just pull.'

'Shut up.'

'It's going to end that way anyway. You know it is. So why not now, while you still have some self-respect?'

'I said shut up.'

'It'll only take a second. Boom. All over. I'll even do it for you, if you don't have the balls.'

Quentin lifted his shotgun to Ravi's face, his finger on the trigger. 'One more word,' he said.

Silence fell once more. But silence was little better, in truth. It left him alone with his thoughts, and that was not a happy place. Maybe Ravi was right. Maybe he should end it. He'd been dreading this day for many years now, and so – as Elias had suggested – he'd made some modest preparations for it, squirrelling a bit of money away in an anonymous offshore account. He had his passport in his bag for the first leg of his journey, and he knew how to acquire new documents once he was there. But the manhunt would be huge, his chances tiny. And he couldn't bear the thought of prison. He'd seen what it was like every time he'd gone to visit Wynn. The overcrowding, the squalor, the constant state of fear. He wouldn't last a month. But then he imagined putting the muzzle of his shotgun into his mouth, the coldness of the metal on his lips, its hardness against his palate, having to reach way down to pull the trigger. And he knew he couldn't do it. So once more he found himself at a fork in the road. Once more, there was only one viable path.

He turned his shotgun from Ravi to Anna. 'You,' he said. 'Put the ladder back up like it was before.' He edged away from her as she crossed the chamber to where Ravi had dropped it, keeping his gun trained on her all the time, well aware that his biggest danger was Elias and Ravi attacking him together – but also knowing that Elias wouldn't try anything, not while it was Anna who'd pay.

He watched her closely as she extended the ladder once more, rested it back against the end wall. Then he paused for thought, needing to make it as hard as possible for them to get the jump on him. He sent Elias up the ladder first, followed by Samantha and then Ravi, holding Anna back till last so that he could keep the muzzle of his shotgun pressed into the small of her back as he followed her up into the ancient dark space above, to give them no chance of springing an ambush. And, once that had been successfully accomplished, he herded them onwards down the dusty narrow passage in the hope of finding somewhere large enough and open enough for him to finally end this.

FORTY-THREE

The passage was so narrow that they'd have been forced into single file, even had Quentin not insisted on it. And the slab ceiling was so low and rough-hewn that even Anna kept scraping her head against it, while the men ahead of her had to crouch right down. The uncertainty of light didn't help either, for Quentin had the only torch, the powerful one he'd brought from home, and which he tucked beneath his arm in order to keep both hands on his gun, so that it flashed this way and that with every step he took, adding to the general sense of disorientation and nausea – because they were all surely aware by now that they were being herded to their place of slaughter. Yet they were too dazed to do anything about it.

The headroom suddenly improved. Even the men could stand up straight. The passage also kinked sharply to the right. The combination stirred an old memory in Anna, one that she sensed was important, yet which she couldn't quite bring back to mind. Then suddenly she had it. A lecture in her first year at Nottingham University, a guest professor in bright lemon trousers and a jacket of strawberry red velvet talking glowingly of the Greek engineer Eupalinos, and how – way back in the sixth century BCE – he'd been handed the daunting task of boring an aqueduct through Samos's Mount Kastro, to bring clean drinking water to the people living in the island's capital. They'd wanted it done fast, too, so that he'd had to have his crews dig tunnels from both ends simultaneously, hoping to have them meet in the middle, even though they'd started well over a kilometre apart. His survey of the mountain, and his resulting calculations, had proved astonishingly accurate; yet still his two tunnels would have missed one another had he not devised a trick that had later been copied widely throughout the ancient world, kinking the passages forty-five degrees to left and right respectively as they'd drawn close, and making them taller too, massively increasing their chances of running into each other. Surely that was what had happened here too. If so, the two passages were about to meet in the middle, in a sharp left-handed turn that would briefly shield the others from Quentin's shotgun. Her fear melted away in that moment. Her nausea too. She stopped shivering and became unusually clear-headed. She felt – not invulnerable, exactly – but rather acceptant of the risk, prepared to pay the price so long as the others might survive. So long as Elias might survive.

She'd barely come to this conclusion when she saw the junction ahead – a short flight of steps leading up to a sharp left-handed turn, just as she'd surmised. The world seemed to slow on her; to slow and grow remote. She felt light and airy as cotton wool. She had to hold herself back from going too early, waiting until Elias, Samantha and then Ravi had all passed around the corner ahead of her. The moment they were gone, however, she deliberately missed her footing on the second step, stumbling as if by accident to the ground, only to twist around as she went, grabbing the barrel of Quentin's shotgun and turning it to the wall, rendering it momentarily useless.

'Run!' she yelled. 'Run!'

So focused was she on the gun, however, that she forgot about the torch. Quentin seized it from beneath his arm to use it on her like a club, clumping it into the side of her head with such force that it dazed her and knocked her to the floor where she would have been completely at his mercy – except that he'd hit her so hard that he'd broken the torch's bulb, plunging them into total darkness even as he cursed and slapped it in a futile effort to get it working again.

Still groggy from the blow, Anna turned onto her hands and knees to climb the rest of the steps into the second half of the tunnel. She staggered to her feet and lurched away along it deeper into the hillside, only to crash into Elias as he came racing back to help her, knocking them both to the floor. She looked around. Quentin had given up on the big torch and had taken his phone from his pocket instead, turning on its flashlight then tucking it into his waistband, giving himself just about enough light to work by as he took his shotgun in both hands once more, aimed it down the passage. But the torch gave Elias some light too, enough for him to grab Anna by the arm and propel her ahead of him along the passage, covering her with his back as they fled into the blackness.

An explosion of light and noise from behind as Quentin fired his first barrel. Elias cried out in pain and clutched the back of his leg. He was already stumbling to the floor when the second barrel went off, sending him crashing down. At once, Anna stopped and went back for him, even though she could hear Quentin breaking open his shotgun back by the steps, expelling the used shells then reloading it with more from his pocket, only to drop one to the ground in his haste, giving Anna a short window in which to act. She hauled Elias to his feet and helped him out of the shotgun's effective range, an arm around his waist and taking her own phone from her pocket with her free hand, using the soft light from its screen rather than its torch to help them see where they were going without offering Quentin an easy target.

This half of the tunnel was less solidly built than the other. Or perhaps it had simply been subject to greater stresses over the centuries. Whatever the reason, its drystone walls were in significantly worse shape, bellying so far inwards in places that they had to turn sideways to squeeze through. Several of the ceiling slabs had subsided badly, while two had collapsed altogether, falling at an angle across their path, forcing them down onto their hands and knees to make it through the tight crawlspace.

It took a real effort for Anna to heave Elias back to his feet again after the second of these, for he was struggling worse and worse, so that it was anguish for her even to listen to him, the way he was gasping and crying out with each step. She paused momentarily to check his injuries with her torch. Her heart sank at what she saw. The first shell had hit him in a relatively tight cluster just below his left buttock, throwing him forwards enough that the shot from the second shell had struck him in a shallower and more diffuse pattern, spread out across the left hand side of his back. His trousers and shirt and jacket were all shredded. Great quantities of blood had already blotted into them and now it was dripping freely to the ground, leaving dark spatters on the dirt floor. That he needed urgent attention was so self-evident that she considered stopping right there to make her stand, using a stone from one of the walls to attack Quentin as he arrived through the crawlway after them. Except that – thanks to the unhelpful way the slab was angled – he was sure to see her long before she could get at him. He'd see her standing there and blast her legs from beneath her with his shotgun, leaving them both at his mercy.

Onwards they laboured, therefore, praying for a better opportunity. The passage came to an end, opening up into a small chamber several feet square. Except not a chamber, Anna quickly realised, but rather the landing of a spiral staircase that led upwards to their left and downwards to their right. It was built from the familiar drystone walls, only with a vaulted stone ceiling instead of slabs; and though there wasn't much dirt or earth upon its floor, there was enough for her to see the footprints that Ravi and Samantha had left on the upwards spiral, perhaps chosen simply for the advantage of the higher ground.

She looked back along the tunnel. No sign of Quentin yet. He was clearly taking it slowly, fearful of ambush. At least it gave her time to think. The blood that Elias was dripping was sure to give them away, unless she could somehow turn it to their advantage. She stripped off her jacket and blouse, therefore, laid them on the staircase's upwards spiral to catch the spatters as they fell. Then she helped him up and around the corner, until he was out of sight. It was as far as he could make it. He collapsed against the inner wall, smearing the brickwork red. 'You go on,' he croaked, his voice barely a whisper. 'I'll hold him off.'

'Shh,' she said, touching a finger to his lips before getting back to her feet. She grabbed her blouse and tied it as high up his leg as it would go, knotting it into a crude tourniquet. She hurried a few more steps up the staircase then whispered her intention as loudly as she dared, in the hope that Samantha or Ravi would hear. Then she made her way back down again, collecting her jacket as she went and using it to erase the footprints and spread the dust and earth back out as evenly as she could manage, so that it would appear undisturbed.

A violent shudder of cold and fear as she arrived back on the landing prompted her to pull her jacket back on and zip it all the way up to her chin. She risked another glance back down the tunnel and saw that Quentin had started worming his way beneath the second slab. She had maybe thirty seconds. An iron becket on the wall was so corroded by time that it had gained sharp edges. She pressed her left hand hard against it and dragged it down, slicing it open. She waited until the blood was pooling nicely in her palm then lowered it so that it dripped from her fingers in bright red splashes to the dusty floor, giving Quentin a breadcrumb trail to follow. Then she carried on down the staircase, completing a full spiral before stopping to listen for Quentin's arrival on the landing above. She gave her torch a flash to make quite sure that he'd come after her, buying Samantha and Ravi the chance to slip out and away. Even if they took it, though, help wouldn't get here for ages yet, so she carried on down, turning spiral after spiral, dripping blood and scraping her feet to continue the illusion that they'd all come down this way, until she'd reached the foot of the staircase which opened up into a domed chamber with beehive walls and a bucket suspended on a rusted chain above the low stone wall of an ancient well. And a frisson ran through her at the sight, calling to mind as it did another legend about King Arthur – about how he, his men and all his treasure had been buried beneath a hill, with a bell nearby to wake them from their slumber in the hour of the nation's greatest need. For the bucket hung there like a giant clapper, while the chamber's beehive walls made it look like nothing quite so much as the inside of a vast bell.

The scrape of footsteps behind her. She had no time to waste. An open archway in the far wall led to another passage, this one flanked by pairs of ancient rooms, perhaps for keeping stores, or for holding captives, or maybe even as surplus sleeping quarters. In a sense, that's what they still were, for a number of bodies had been laid out upon the floor of each, clearly brought here in the aftermath of some terrible battle – for some were missing limbs, while others had had their skulls crushed or cleaved open, and yet others were stripped to the skin in failed attempts to treat their wounds.

All had been treated with dignity, however, set out in neat rows with their arms down by their sides, to be mummified by time and the sterile conditions, their parchment skin pulled tight over their chins and cheekbones, exposing their teeth and giving them unsettling grins. Their hair and beards were thin and dry, their armour and clothes reduced to rust and rags, yet they were still so human that her torchlight gave them a kind of new life, a zombie army about to rise up around her, one she could have used to fight off Quentin as he arrived at the foot of the staircase behind her.

She hurried onwards, glancing briefly into each of the rooms, looking for a weapon or at least a place to make a stand. But bringing all these men here had clearly been challenge enough without worrying about their swords and shields, and she found nothing. Only when she reached the end chamber did that change, for this had just the one body in it, though clearly a special one, stretched out as he was on a raised bed of limestone slabs, and with a robe of royal red fastened around his throat with a jewelled clasp shaped like an eagle in flight, with a delicate gold coronet around his brow and a torque around his neck, his arms folded piously over his chest so that she could see that there were rings on all his fingers except one. The floor around him was rich with treasures too, with goblets and platters, flagons and bowls, even a bronze cauldron and a spit for turning meat on, as if he were about to hold a feast for all his men. There was a couch for him to rest on, and a low table, and what looked like the materials for a tent or pavilion. The wheels and other parts of a disassembled chariot had been left leaning against the right-hand wall, along with the bridle and reins of a horse. Everywhere she ran her torch, indeed, she lit up something new and wonderful: delicately wrought oil lamps; dessicated leather boots; thick winter furs. A bowl of coins and another of brooches, and what looked to her to be some kind of board game, complete with dice and counters. The chamber was so full, indeed, that Anna had to pick her way carefully through it all to reach the man himself. He looked to be unusually tall and broad for his time, and he was dressed for war beneath his robes, though his chain-mail armour was grievously torn where someone had driven a lance straight through it, with such violence that it had surely passed out the other side too. A mortal blow indeed.

A large oval shield decorated with a cross lay by his side, part covering a sword and a spear whose long wooden shaft looked to have been treated with tar or some other protective coating, for it showed no sign of rot or woodworm. She picked up the sword first, taking it in both hands; but it was too weighty for her to wield effectively, and so blunted by time that it had lost its cutting edge, and so rusted that it looked liable to shatter into pieces the moment it was used in anger, even assuming she could get close enough to Quentin. Besides, if this was Arthur himself, as it surely was, then this was the great *Caledfwlch* – Excalibur itself. Even in these dire circumstances, the historian in her revolted against such sacrilege. She set it back down and picked up the spear instead, the less storied *Rhongomyniad*. It was lighter than she'd expected, and seemed sturdy enough. She tested the air with a jab or two, holding it long enough for the blood from the cut in her left hand to stick to its shaft, making her wince as she tore it open again when adjusting her grip for better balance.

It would do. It would have to.

She turned off her torch and returned quietly to the doorway, standing just inside it, hoping that Quentin's first sight of this place – his first sight of the man he'd sought for so much of his life, lying there right before him, surrounded by all these treasures – would distract him for the split second she was going to need. His throat would be the softest target, but it was the smallest too, easy for her to miss in the darkness, easy for him to sway back and elude. His stomach, then. She practised it in her mind, giving her first strike everything she had in order to drive the blunted iron tip through his clothes and skin, skewering it deep into his gut before going down onto her knee for a second thrust, up beneath his ribcage to his heart. She steeled herself for it, ridding herself of squeamishness or pity by reminding herself that it wasn't just her own life at stake. She was fighting for the others too.

Outside, she could hear Quentin moving slowly from chamber to chamber, checking that each was clear. At last, his flashlight arrived outside. He was here. She took and held a long breath. She pulled back her spear and tensed her muscles, ready to strike. But this was the last of the chambers, so that Quentin would surely be expecting her in here. Not just her, indeed. All four of them. He'd be expecting them to make some kind of stand. It would be the men he'd be most fearful of, of course, seeking to take them out with his first two shells, which might just buy her the extra fraction of a second she was going to need.

A burst of light through the doorway. A flicker of movement. Quentin was familiarising himself with the layout, the better to plan his assault. Darkness returned. She could hear his breathing. Seconds passed, each one an age. She let out her own breath, took and held another. His torch came on suddenly again, only down low this time, slithering along the floor as he kicked it into the chamber. Then he stepped fully into view, shotgun already at his shoulder, sweeping the barrel across the chamber as he searched for threat.

Anna didn't hesitate. She ducked down low and charged, thrusting her spear at his gut with all her might, exactly as she'd planned, catching him perfectly just beneath the ribs. But the wooden shaft had deceived her, bowing and splintering upon first contact and then simply snapping in two. Quentin cried out and stumbled backwards, but in shock rather than from injury. He realised he was unharmed, and that Anna was here alone. He raised his gun back to his shoulder, so that she thought he was going to shoot her right there and then. But he stopped himself on realising he needed her alive for a little while yet, to find out where the others were.

He took his shotgun in both hands, pile-driving its butt down at Anna's forehead. She tried to duck away but it still caught her a glancing blow, sending her staggering backwards, tripping over her own feet and tumbling to the floor. She scrambled away from him across it, pushing aside the goblets and the platters, feeling with her hands for anything she might use to fight back or defend herself. But there was nothing. He clearly knew it too, for, with an almost leisurely air, he retrieved his phone from the floor and tucked it back into his waistband. Then he came after her once more, covering her with his shotgun the whole time, waiting until she'd reached the far wall and could go no further. 'The others,' he said. 'Where are they?'

'Go to hell,' she said.

He raised his gun to his shoulder, aiming it so directly at her face that she could see down the hollow tubes of both barrels. 'Last chance,' he said. 'Where are they?'

'Where do you think, you idiot?' she snapped. 'They went the other way up the staircase. Now they're off for help.'

'Try again. They'd have left footprints.'

'I swept them away, you arse.'

'And the blood?'

She held up her hand to show him the cut she'd scored in her palm, scabbing a little now around the edges, yet still bleeding freely enough for him to see it trickling down her wrist to stain her cuff. 'See?' she said. 'You're done for. It's over.'

Uncertainty clouded his face. He frowned in an effort to remember. When he realised her story wasn't just possible but likely, his face twisted in hatred and rage. He must have known, then, that he was doomed, that he no longer had any kind of path out of this. He still had choices, though. He could choose surrender, or mercy, or one last doomed shot at flight. But no. He opted for vengeance instead. He opted for violence. He lowered his gun briefly as he took another step forwards, placing one foot on either side of her so that he loomed above her, breathing heavily from some perverse arousal, offering her an unwanted glimpse into his true nature. He pressed his shotgun back into his shoulder to brace himself against the recoil, then he moved his index finger back from the trigger guard onto the—

Out of the darkness he swept, rushing up behind Quentin before he'd even realised he was there. He wrapped one of his meaty huge arms around Quentin's chest then grabbed his shotgun with his free hand, wresting the twin barrels up and away from Anna. She couldn't see his face in the darkness, but the size of his silhouette meant that it could only be Ravi, using his massive strength to force up the shotgun until its muzzle was pressed into the underside of Quentin's chin, even as Quentin wailed and flapped in helpless terror at what he knew was coming next.

'I did promise I'd do it for you,' murmured Ravi into his ear, so softly that Anna couldn't even be sure of what she'd heard.

And then he pulled the trigger.

EPILOGUE

They couldn't have asked for a finer afternoon for it, the sky an almost perfect blue and yet not too hot. The forecasters had been promising it for days, but Ravi wasn't the kind to take chances, not for an occasion as grand as this, so he'd had a huge marquee erected in the Manor's back garden, and numerous small tables set up with starched white linen cloths for the day's invited and uninvited guests, and a pair of long buffet tables laden with generous quantities of food and drink. And it was in there that he delivered a brisk and witty speech, donating the Badbury Bowl and the rest of the hoard to the nation, along with the twin estates of Grove Farm and Hillview Manor, in order that they could be properly excavated before being turned into one of Britain's most spectacular heritage sites.

'So we like him now, do we?' murmured Anna to Samantha, as they applauded him off the dais – for he'd paid her top dollar for the Manor and all its grounds, simply to then pass them on to Historic England.

'We do, we do,' smiled Samantha, who'd been in buoyant spirits since the sale, especially as a settlement with her insurers had now also been agreed, enabling her to pay off all her debts and set herself up nicely for the future too.

Wynn Grant was in an equally festive mood. He looked years younger, and not only because he'd somehow managed a shave, a haircut and a decent suit. His name had been cleared at last, his conviction certain to be expunged, and he no longer had to worry about his parole being revoked. He'd be due sizeable settlements, what was more, both for having been deprived of his inheritance and for all those years of wrongful imprisonment – though it would take a fair while yet to sort out who'd be footing those bills, whether the government, Quentin's estate or perhaps even Orlando Wren – or Peter Moorcock, or whatever his real name was – still in hospital recovering from Quentin's assault. Yet it was clear that it was the vindication that meant most to him. No longer being believed responsible for his brother's death. No longer a pariah. Or not for that, anyway.

'Orange juice?' Elias asked him sceptically, when he wandered over to thank him and Anna for their part in it all.

'My new leaf,' he told them proudly.

Elias took his glass from him, gave it a sniff. 'Some new leaf,' he said.

'Well,' said Wynn, with a shrug. 'Mixers. It's a start.'

◆ ◆ ◆

Ravi was in fine spirits too, standing in the corner of the marquee with a benevolent smile on his face that somehow managed to survive the stream of locals, historians and archaeologists who approached him under the guise of commending him for his generosity, only to turn the conversation to their own pet projects, and the modest funding they were so very badly in need of. Anna waited until he'd disposed of the last of these then went to add her own thanks for his generosity. He waved them aside. 'It's all a bit more smoke and mirrors than people think. Plenty of tax breaks for my accountants to make use of, and a ton of good PR into the bargain. Anyway, it's only money at the end of the day. I have all I'll ever need, and then some. It's finding worthwhile things to spend it on that's the challenge.'

She looked out through the open side of the marquee towards the paddock. 'You've found one here, I think.'

'Yes. I believe I have.' He fell silent a few moments, then leaned a little way towards her so that he could drop his voice down to a murmur. 'You heard me that day, didn't you?' he said. 'My last words to that arsehole.'

'Yes.'

'You didn't tell the police?'

'He'd have killed me. You saved my life.'

'Only after you saved mine first. Sam's too. I've never seen anything half so brave as what you did in there. I'll never forget it, believe me. If you should ever need anything... I mean it. Anything at all.'

Pam, Dave and Anish were here from the museum to conduct the archaeological side of the day. Anna and Ravi watched as they briefed the gathered reporters and their crews on what they were and were not allowed to do, then led them out of the marquee through the paddock to the cinder-block building that Ravi had had erected to secure the mausoleum staircase. They'd get to visit and film the first few tomb chambers today, but that was it. Arthur and his entourage would remain out of bounds to the media and the wider public for a fair while longer yet.

A rare cloud passed in front of the sun. It grew gloomy for a few moments, but only with the effect of making everything seem that much brighter once it cleared again. Someone put on music, forcing the happy chatter at the tables to grow louder to be heard above it. Staff emptied the last of their bottles into held-out glasses, while the few guests who were somehow still hungry prowled the buffet tables to snaffle what was left. A few couples even took to the floor, braving the children as they played chase around the marquee, shrieking with delight. Ravi and Anna watched it all in contented silence until finally he leaned back in towards her a little way, the better to lower his voice once more. 'It's soft of me to say it, I know,' he told her. 'But I love this country, I truly do.'

◆ ◆ ◆

The police had found the cauldron's missing leaf in Quentin's cellar – locked in a safe he'd had installed a few weeks after Caleb Grant's death. He'd straightened it out himself, and had cleaned it lovingly, polishing the gemstones until they'd gleamed like a Hatton Gardens shop window. Little wonder he'd tried so hard to put his consortium together. Little wonder, either, that – after that effort had failed – he'd taken other steps to find the rest of the cauldron himself. Because they'd found a second large-scale map of Grove Farm down there too, even more densely marked up with GPR data, making it clear that he'd been holding back some of the juicier prospects in order to visit the fields by night and dig them up himself. They'd even found some scraps of armour, rusted weaponry and the other spoils of his various forays – but nothing to compare to the treasure he'd truly sought.

◆ ◆ ◆

And Elias. The wounds he'd taken from Quentin's shotgun were mending well, for while they'd caused significant blood-loss and done extensive damage to his muscles, tendons and other soft tissues, they'd missed his spine and other vital organs. The paramedics had got to him in time too, thanks to the speed with which Samantha had raced to summon help. They'd stabilised him on the spot, then had swept him off to the Great Western Hospital to pluck out the shot and sew up his damaged blood vessels. They'd taken a split thickness graft from his right thigh to apply beneath his left buttock, and had stitched up the more diffuse puckering across his back. It had all gone as well as could be hoped, his medical team confident of his full recovery, save for some unavoidable scarring and perhaps a slight limp – for which he'd only have himself to blame, one of them had added sourly, for discharging himself while his graft still needed careful attention and regular fresh dressings.

It was impossible for Elias to do this himself, the wounds being so awkwardly situated, so – over his half-hearted protests – Anna had moved back into his cottage. His improvement since then had been remarkable. He could walk further every day, and manage more physio. He could sit down without undue discomfort, as long as he could stretch out his left leg in front of him. He'd even started driving short distances again. But Ingatestone to Badbury was hardly a short distance, so Anna had taken the wheel today instead, with Elias in the passenger seat beside her, pushed back as far as it would go.

Sixteen days she'd spent at his cottage now. Tomorrow would be seventeen, just like last time. He was fit enough to look after himself, assuming nothing went too badly wrong. He could cook and shop and drive himself into the local surgery for his dressings to be changed. He was already back at work, if only at his home computer, and he was growing increasingly impatient to return to his London office. She had her own life to get back to too. Her viva was coming up fast. She needed to prepare. That didn't just mean long hours in the library, it meant a full dress rehearsal with her supervisor Terry and a friend of his who was coming down specially from Durham to York next Tuesday, both to quiz her with the kind of questions her examiners were likely to ask, and to prepare her mentally for the experience itself. And so Elias had been insisting for the past few days that she leave in the morning, once they'd fulfilled their duty here. And she'd agreed.

The prospect of her imminent departure had inevitably brought an end-of-holiday feel into the cottage. Elias had grown noticeably grumpier, while she herself had filled with a leaden dismay. The terrible tug-of-war from last time had started up again inside her, her pride and independence of spirit battling against the simple pleasure of living under the same roof as Elias, changing his bandages, doing his shopping, cooking his meals and driving him to his appointments. It was astonishing to her how much satisfaction it gave her to tend to him in this way, repaying him in some small measure for everything he'd done for her. Not that satisfaction was the right word, she knew full well.

The right word was happiness.

And why shouldn't she be happy, after all? Why should independence matter so much to her? She hadn't dreamed of independence as a teen. As a teen, alongside her career ambitions, she'd dreamed of falling in love, of getting married, of having a family of her own. That had changed as she'd grown older, sure, but not *because* she'd grown older. It had changed because of the night when a man had coshed her over her head while she'd been returning home from her evening shift in the pub. It had changed because that man had gagged and bound her before stuffing her into the boot of his car to drive her off somewhere quiet to rape and then murder her. It had changed because the trauma of that experience had left her unable to trust any man fully enough to let herself fall in love.

She looked across the marquee at Elias, sitting as she'd left him, his bad leg stretched out ahead, only now twisted awkwardly to the side so that the children wouldn't trip over it as they played their game of tag. She suffered another of those sweet little pinches of the heart as she did so – not just of affection, but of longing too. Of hunger. Of desire. And all she'd have to do, she knew, was give him even the slightest encouragement. Because he'd made his own position clear multiple times now, most recently on the night of the fire, after he'd berated her for coming to save him. '*Yeah,*' he'd said, when she'd pointed out that he'd have done the same for her, '*but there's a reason for that.*' As close to a declaration of love as he'd ever get, unless she said something first. And she knew in that moment that she didn't want to return to York. She wanted to stay on in Ingatestone. She wanted it to be her home. And it wasn't even so much that she knew it either. It was that she finally accepted it.

She wandered off into an empty corner of the marquee then turned to face the canvas. This was in part to cut out the hubbub behind her, but mostly so that Elias wouldn't be able to read her lips or even her expression, which he had a knack of doing with uncanny accuracy. She placed the call and spoke for a good five minutes. Only when she was done did she turn back around again, to find Elias watching her, as she'd known he would be. She allowed herself a slight smile as she made her way between the tables to sit back down beside him. 'So who was that you were on with, then?' he asked.

'Terry,' she said. 'My supervisor.'

'Oh,' he said, the gloom back in his voice. 'Giving him your ETA for tomorrow?'

'In a sense.'

'In a sense?'

'I told him you'd had a slight setback. I told him that unfortunately I wouldn't be able to make it tomorrow, as I'd planned. I told him I'd be staying on here for another week at least. More likely a fortnight. I told him sorry, but that – for reasons I was sure he'd understand – you came first with me; and that if I have to go into my viva without a proper rehearsal, so be it.'

Elias turned to gaze at her, a look of uncertain hope upon his face. 'You lied to him?' he said.

'I did,' she said. And a feeling of pure wellbeing settled upon her as she reached out for his hand. 'But there's a reason for that.'

AUTHOR'S NOTE

Writing a book about the "real" King Arthur was a particularly daunting challenge, what with so little being known for sure about the man, and how surrounded he is by such vast quantities of folklore, mysticism and romance. Yet my Warne & Elias series is essentially about exploring the great mysteries in British history, and it would be perverse to ignore Arthur in that.

For those curious about the "truth" behind this version of the story, Liddington Hill near Badbury has indeed been proposed as the site of the Battle of Badon Hill. On the other hand, so too have many other sites. Ambrosius Aurelianus is surely the most likely real-life model for Arthur, though Riothamus has something going for him too. And perhaps they were indeed one and the same person, as I suggest, though the dating is a little tricky. Cadbury Castle is by far the best candidate for Camelot – if Camelot ever existed; and there is some reason to think that Avebury and Amesbury were indeed named for Ambrosius, who has multiple links to the West Country.

The unhappy truth, though, is that we simply don't know enough to be confident of anything. As I say in the book, historians have come to deplore the term Dark Ages for its negative connotations – but, honestly, post-Roman Britain is about as dark as an age can get.

ABOUT THE AUTHOR

Will Adams

Will Adams pursued multiple careers over the years before deciding to concentrate on his lifelong dream of writing fiction. His books have been translated into over twenty languages and have appeared on bestseller lists around the world.